NINE BETTS LANE

When Florence Preston first moved to the house in Betts Lane in 1900, she did not feel there was anything amiss until she became pregnant. This pregnancy was to be the start of a lifetime of unexplained happenings and bad luck. Florence's first child was stillborn. She then received a warning from a gypsy on her doorstep, to leave the house as soon as she could. However, circumstances always prevented her from leaving. Florence felt this sinister house was holding her back, laughing at her. Would she ever be able to leave? Or would the house eventually claim her life?

EILEEN DE LISLE

NINE
BETTS LANE

Complete and Unabridged

ULVERSCROFT
Leicester

First published in Great Britain in 2000 by
Beagle Publications
Southampton

First Large Print Edition
published 2001
by arrangement with
Beagle Publications
Southampton

Although fictional this book is based on true events.
Some names have been retained, other characters and
names are fictitious.

British Library CIP Data

de Lisle, Eileen
    Nine Betts Lane.—Large print ed.—
    Ulverscroft large print series: general fiction
    1. Large type books
    I. Title
    823.9'2 [F]

    ISBN 0–7089–4470–1

Published by
F. A. Thorpe (Publishing)
Anstey, Leicestershire

Set by Words & Graphics Ltd.
Anstey, Leicestershire
Printed and bound in Great Britain by
T. J. International Ltd., Padstow, Cornwall

This book is printed on acid-free paper

I dedicate this book to my family, who were inspirational in the writing of the book, and to the three Johns. John Tennent, who gave me my first chance in writing, as his P.R. John Bateman, who always encouraged me to write a book, and John Barrie-Smith who kept the computer going throughout, and was always on hand at very short notice to deal with each emergency as it arose.

1

The sun was hot on Florence's back as she bent to tend her vegetable patch in the garden of her terraced Victorian house in Betts Lane. The sky was blue and cloudless on that late August afternoon in 1900. She paused for a moment from her gardening to mop the sweat from her brow, and as she did so she glanced back at the house. Fear struck at her heart and she began to tremble uncontrollably. The house was shrouded in a terrible black mist. The windows looked almost as if they had black blinds at each one, instead of the pretty chintz curtains she had sewn so lovingly when they moved in. She just stood there, a mixture of emotions flooding through her. Was she going mad? Like the previous owner of the house, who was carted off to the asylum a babbling wreck. Poor Matilda, the local children called her batty Matty. After several minutes the black mist disappeared and the house was as before. The grey slated roof glinted in the sunlight, but the house still had a sinister look about it that had not been noticed by Florence before.

As the heavily pregnant Florence made her way back up the garden path to the house she still felt an icy chill about her which she could not explain, as the temperature was still well into the eighties. On entering the house she set about preparing the evening meal. Her husband Fred would be home within the hour, hungry as ever, looking forward to a good solid meal after his hard day's graft as a painter, decorator and handyman, and any job he could lay hands on to help feed them both and pay the rent.

All the while she was preparing the meal she felt an uneasiness, as if she was being watched, and at one point she felt someone had touched her on the shoulder. She began to shake, fear gripping her once more, to the point where she felt she was going to pass out. Suddenly she was brought back to reality by a loud banging at the front door. It was Amelia her sister.

'Just called round for a chat. Why Flo, you look that poorly like you've seen a ghost or something, so white and shaking all over. Shall I fetch Dr. Fisher?'

'No, no I'll be fine, it's just the heat got to me. Doing too much in the garden.'

'Now you sit yourself down and I'll finish

preparing the evening meal for you both. Mother sent me round to see if I could give you a hand with anything. Lord knows what would have happened had I not arrived when I did.' Florence agreed wholeheartedly with this.

★ ★ ★

'You're very quiet this evening lass, anything wrong?'

'No I'm just a bit tired, the pregnancy is getting to me a bit. I'll be glad when the baby is here.'

'Aye, I'll second that. I wish sometimes we could be back in Yorkshire among the Dales where I roamed as a boy. Good country fresh air.'

'Fred you know I couldn't leave Mother and all my sisters, I would miss them most dreadfully. Since Father died we have all become so close. You promised when we wed that you would always let me live close to my family. Especially since you have no family left in Yorkshire.'

'Aye you are right Flo, and I'm not one to break a promise. I'll tell thee what, how about if we organize a big picnic on the Common with Mother and all your sisters. That should put the roses back in thy cheeks.'

'Oh Fred that would be wonderful. How about if we go Saturday? I can bake all day tomorrow, then we can set off early Saturday morning.'

★ ★ ★

The next day dawned bright and sunny. After Fred had gone to work Flo quite cheerfully set about the task of baking Fred's favourite fruit cake. Quite suddenly and for no apparent reason she was suddenly gripped with a terrible sense of foreboding, as if some terrible disaster was about to overtake her. In spite of the bright sunlight outside, the house had taken on the dark depressive gloom she had sensed the day before, and she thought she could hear a baby crying. In the distance at first, then it seemed to be getting closer until the crying was inside the house. Fear and searing pain seized her at the same time and she realised she had gone into labour a month early. She rushed to the front door hoping a passing stranger could summon help but no one was in sight. She slumped back in an armchair and prayed. 'Please God, let the baby be alright, please God don't take my baby.'

Alas her prayers were in vain. The baby was stillborn, a little boy.

★　★　★

For several months Flo was in a deep depression. All the while she could not get out of her mind that the tragedy that had befallen her had happened before in the house, to some other poor woman whom she had never met.

★　★　★

Christmas came and did nothing to lighten her spirits. Uncle John, her mother's brother and a local butcher, presented her with a turkey to be cooked for all the family on Christmas Day. Uncle John was a bachelor but had set his sights on Christine, a young widow four doors away from where he lived. He felt he had made some progress in the relationship and hoped to pop the question very soon.

Christmas Day was bright and very cold with a hint of snow in the air. The whole family arrived at 12 noon. Uncle John, Mother, sisters Amelia, (nicknamed Ame), Mary and Rose. Florence at 22 years was the eldest of Beatrice's four daughters, Ame was 19, Mary 16 and Rose, the baby of the family at 14, was much loved and very spoilt by her sisters.

The family ate a hearty lunch and thanked God to have such good food and health on this Christmas Day. After lunch was cleared away the family sat around the Christmas tree, exchanged presents and sang carols. Suddenly everyone stopped singing. They all heard the front door open and close, and footsteps down the long passage to the sitting room at the back of the house. Silence fell as everyone waited expectantly for the door to open. Nothing happened. Fred was on his feet in an instant and flung open the door. The hall was dark and quiet, and felt quite chill. The only light at the end of the hall was from the gas lamp outside the house which shone an eerie pale light through the glass in the front door. Fred could see well enough that there was no one there. He snatched an oil lamp from the sitting room and did a thorough search of the house, checking the bedrooms, scullery, front room, till there was nowhere else to search. He returned to the sitting room and guests then reassured them all that there was no intruder.

'It must have been a creaking of the floor boards, as they cooled down after the heat of the cooking, and the heavy tread of all the visitors through the day.'

Florence was not convinced. She sat silently thinking. They all heard the footsteps and the front door open and shut, but are too nervous to say anything. Well at least I'm not going mad or imagining things. There is definitely something uncanny in this house.

★   ★   ★

Spring seemed to arrive early this year, Florence mused as she was in her garden looking at all the spring bulbs sprouting from the earth. There had been no further incidents since Christmas Day. Life began to feel good again. She was pregnant, and Uncle John had popped the question and was marrying Christine in the summer. Yes, life was indeed good again. Perhaps all that nonsense last year was my imagination to do with the bad pregnancy. They say some women can actually go mad when pregnant. I'm glad I didn't get to that stage.

★   ★   ★

Spring quickly turned to Summer, July was soon upon the family, and the great day of the wedding fast approaching. Amelia, Mary and Rose were all bridesmaids. Amelia was the prettiest of the three girls, and soon caught the eye of one of the guests, a young soldier Tom Burrows. He was the son of an old army pal of Uncle John. When it came time for Christine to throw her bouquet over her shoulder before leaving for their honeymoon in Cornwall, it was Amelia who caught it. 'Oh well done Ame,' squealed the sisters, 'your turn next.'

★ ★ ★

Florence and Fred returned to their neat little home feeling happy and tired, and were soon sound asleep in their bed. The grandfather clock in the hall had just struck three when Florence was suddenly awoken with a terrible jolt. She sat up in bed and looked around, her eyes gradually beginning to focus in the darkness. Everything seemed normal, what on earth could have woken me? Feeling very uneasy she settled down and tried to sleep, but sleep eluded her. All the time she felt that she was being watched, and even felt a heavy sensation on the bed as if someone was sitting there, pressing down heavily on the bed-clothes. This is no good, I must try and pull myself together, I'll fetch a glass of water from downstairs. She could not move, she could not scream, though fully awake. It was as if she was paralysed. She prayed silently to

8

herself. Oh please God help me! What is happening in this house? She was instantly released from the paralysis that held her. The room became instantly brighter although still night, was dimly lit by the street lamp outside their window. Only minutes before the room had been in complete darkness, as if the lamp was out and there was a thick black curtain at the window. Everything now was as before. Fred had slept through the whole incident totally unaware of the blackness and the fear that had enveloped her. This slightly annoyed Flo, to think she had suffered this horrible experience all alone, but Fred was a good hard working man and would do anything for her. So she decided not to burden him with her fears, not just yet anyway.

★   ★   ★

The following morning Florence could still not get out of her mind the events of the night before. A plan began to form in her mind. The house wants to take my baby again, but I won't let it this time. I'll go and stay with Mother and the baby will be born there. She's only a block away. I'm sure she won't mind. Later in the day when Florence visited her mother, she asked if it would be alright if she had the baby in her mother's

9

house. Making the excuse that as she was born there, and all her sisters, she would like her baby to be born there as well. Not giving the true reason. She was sure her mother would not understand. Beatrice was both delighted and flattered that her daughter wanted to come home to have her baby. Poor love, she needs her mother at a time like this, she thought. Her mind drifted back to happier days when her dear Josh was alive and the joy each of her girls brought to the house as they were born. Each one strong, healthy and pretty. I feel that Flo's baby will be alright this time. I just know it. This house has always been a happy one with lots of love and laughter. The only sad time was when my dear Josh passed away so young with a lung disease. He always had a weak chest poor man, and little Rose only 5 years old at the time. I have tried to keep his memory alive with the large picture of him that hangs on the wall, and to talk of him constantly as if he were still with us. I do feel he's still here in this house with us all, watching over us, and I know he'll be as pleased as me that our Flo is coming home to have her baby.

★   ★   ★

Beatrice was brought back to the present by Flo's voice saying, 'I must go now Mother and tell Fred the good news. I haven't discussed it with him yet, though I'm sure he won't mind.' I hope, thought Florence secretly. I can't let him know the real reason. Nobody understands that awful house, only me. I hope that one day we'll be free of it for good. We must try to save hard, and who knows one day we may have a little place of our own.

After Flo's departure Beatrice sank into her favourite armchair. I have an hour before the girls are home. I'll just rest awhile. Beatrice hated the fact that she was beginning to feel her age a tiny bit more than she cared to admit. Her thoughts soon drifted back to Florence as a little girl. She was so sweet with her golden hair and ringlets, completely different from her other two sisters. She was shy in some ways but she had a terrific inner strength about her. She kept her thoughts to herself and tried hard not to show her true feelings. She has some indefinable qualities we all seem to lack. I remember the time when our dear old collie dog Nipper nearly died of distemper. Nine years old at the time and crying her eyes out. Then she suddenly stopped as if she was talking to someone, and said 'It's alright Mother, Nipper is going to

11

live. If I keep stroking him and loving him, he'll be alright' and he was, much to everyone's amazement. Strange child, special child, almost as if she had some sort of healing power.

Florence was mentally preparing herself to tell Fred she wanted to have their baby at her mother's home and not theirs, when the door burst open and in rushed Fred, flushed and excited.

'Flo, Flo, I have the most wonderful news. I could hardly wait to tell thee. You know my boss, Mr. Griffin, not only my boss but also our landlord.'

'Yes, go on tell me before you explode.' Florence could not possibly think what could cause such excitement. She was not ready for the shock that was to come.

'Well as you know Mr. Griffin is an old man and has no family as such to leave his building company to, and all the property he owns in the area. I think he has a second nephew living in Africa, I think it's a cousin's son. He barely stays in touch, just a card once a year.' Florence wished he would get to the point so she could get her bit of news over with.

Fred took her in his arms. 'Florence, you're going to be so pleased. I was called to the office today. I thought it was just about work but it wasn't. Mr. Griffin said he is giving us this house as a present. Now, immediately, not when he dies. He wants to see us enjoy his house while he's still alive. So no more rent as from this week. The only conditions are that I remain in the house, and his employment during his lifetime. It's great news isn't it?'

Florence felt a knot of fear in her stomach and a crushing sensation in her chest, she could not breathe. She felt the house was laughing at her and saying you can't escape me. Mr. Griffin was only seventy years old and strong as an ox. He could live for another twenty years at least.

2

Christopher Frederick Preston screamed his way into the world on 19th September 1901 at 2 o'clock in the afternoon. A healthy 7lb golden haired baby. The birth went well. Flo and Fred were bursting with pride. Flo stayed on at her mother's house for another 2 weeks after the birth and returned to the marital home in early October.

★   ★   ★

Autumn was gradually turning into Winter. A distinct chill could be felt in the air. The day was quite cold and Florence thought the house was even colder, in spite of the roaring fire Fred had in the grate. It was a welcoming sight, the table laid for tea, with bread, and jam and home made cakes Flo guessed had been made by her mother. She sunk down in a comfy chair and cuddling baby Christopher, made a silent vow. This house will not harm our baby son. I will protect him with my life, he will grow up to be strong and handsome just like his Daddy. I will put a crucifix by his crib and pray to God to

14

protect my baby against the evil that lurks in this house. So strange that nobody else senses it.

★　★　★

A loud banging at the front door interrupted her thoughts. Still holding the baby, she walked down the long dark hall to answer it. On the doorstep stood a weather beaten Gypsy woman of about 50 years of age, clutching a basket full of silks and laces, interspersed with a few twigs of heather.

'Buy some lucky heather or laces from a poor Gypsy woman luv?'

'I've no money to spare for such things.'

'Go on luv, cross a gypsy's palm with silver for good luck and I'll tell ye your fortune, and the little baby boy's too.'

'How do you know he's a boy?' The baby was dressed all in white and wrapped in a shawl which had been lovingly crocheted by her mother over several months.

'Ah Rosa knows lots of things my pretty. Your boy will grow up to be a fine man and marry a girl from over the water. He will have a brother too. You have known sadness, the loss of another baby, a boy, but you're a strong girl and you've the gift that is given only to a few of us. Whatever life has in store for you, you'll cope with. I don't like this house and will not tarry any longer on your doorstep. I bid ye good day fair lady.'

'Please wait, I could spare you a penny.'

'No, keep your money. Save it so one day you may leave this house. Already I stayed too long in such a bad place. Goodbye pretty lady, I'll not call again.'

Florence closed the door and shivered slightly. Well at least I'm not alone in thinking this place has something bad about it. The Gypsy couldn't wait to get away.

★ ★ ★

Two years almost to the day of Uncle John's wedding, Amelia and Tom Burrows announced their engagement. The wedding was to be a year later in the Spring. Amelia always wanted to be a Spring bride.

★ ★ ★

Harry Rolleston called for his usual Friday evening meal with Fred and Flo. He had been a good friend to Fred for many years since he had arrived south from Yorkshire and helped Fred secure the job with Mr. Griffin. Harry being a bachelor had always appreciated good home cooking and what started out as just a few meals on a Friday night had now turned into a regular occurrence. With Fred and Harry ending the evening with a few jars of ale in the local public house, The Elm Tree. Harry had always loved the sea. He had been born and bred in Southampton, coming from a long line of seafaring folk. Before joining Mr. Griffin's building company he had been a shipwright and longed to return to that sort of work again.

★   ★   ★

After the meal was over Harry had some news to impart.

'What do you think I heard today, Fred? There are two great ocean liners to be built in Scotland and Newcastle, and will be almost eight hundred feet long. Can you imagine that? I want to be part of it all. The wonderful sense of pride and achievement at having worked on one of the world's greatest liners. I've heard tell it's hoped they will recapture the 'Blue Riband'. So at the end of the month I'll be heading north for the John Brown Shipyard on Clydebank. I'll give Mr. Griffin a month's notice, being such a kindly man, and then I'll be off to Scotland. When the ship is completed I hope to get the chance to sail on her as an ordinary seaman. What do you say

Fred? Do you think I'm mad?' Fred was stunned into silence for a moment or two. Knowing the sense of loss of a good friend. At that moment he did not know how great the loss was going to be.

'Ney lad thee must follow thy heart and do what really makes thee happy. Who knows, you might meet a nice Scots lass to wed, who will keep thee under control.' Florence also felt a sense of foreboding and loss and tried hard to hide her feelings by making light of it all.

'As long as you stay in touch with us, Harry. We shall expect a letter at least once a week, then it will be like we're all still having our Friday night get togethers. Now off with the pair of you for your ale. Amelia will be here soon to discuss the design of her wedding dress Mother is to make for her. You won't want to listen to a lot of women's talk on weddings.' The men wholeheartedly agreed and were soon heading for the front door. As it closed behind them and Flo was alone, the sense of sadness and loss was overwhelming, she felt tears pricking her eyes. She must pull herself together and not be so irrational. After all Harry was only going to Scotland, not the ends of the earth, and he will be back to see us again sometime. A bang on the door heralded Amelia's arrival, full of chatter and excitement as usual. Then the pair settled down to an evening of wedding plans.

★ ★ ★

The whole of the next twelve months the house was filled with women's prattle, pieces of material, pins, cottons. The sewing machine was never put away. Dresses being fitted then refitted. Christopher now aged 3 was considered old enough by the family to be a page boy, of which he felt quite proud. Mary and Rose were bridesmaids again. Mary now eighteen, hoping she too would meet a suitor at the wedding, as Amelia had done previously at Uncle John's wedding. Perhaps Tom will invite some nice eligible bachelors from his regiment. Oh I do hope so, she mused. Mary had little time to meet any nice young men. She worked long hours at the haberdashery shop, and her boss Mr. Cunningham was both stingy with her wages and time. Days off were few and far between. Most of the customers who came to the shop were old ladies, and if any men came in they were accompanied by their wives. I am eighteen and not a suitor in sight, I do hope I won't end up an old maid. Her day dreaming was soon brought to a halt by Mr.

Cunningham's sharp words.

'Stop the day dreaming my girl and get those shelves dusted down while we have no customers in the shop. Idle hands make work for the devil.' Silly old fool, thought Mary.

★ ★ ★

Rose was in service at the big house nearby, to a wealthy family the Leyton-Barries. Much of her time was spent playing nursemaid to baby Raith. Edwina Leyton-Barrie did not have a maternal instinct in her body. How she conceived and gave birth to such a lovely little baby was beyond Rose's comprehension. She spent most of her time titivating herself in front of the mirror. Anthony, her husband, was several years her senior and spent most of the time away in London on business, or at shooting parties in the country. Edwina accompanied him to a few but soon became extremely bored with the whole affair. She spent most of her time buying hats and having even more clothes made by her dressmaker. She had so many clothes that one day the rail in her dressing room collapsed under the weight, sending all her precious clothes to the floor in a big heap, much to the amusement of Rose and all the other servants. The rest of her time was spent socialising with her own social set and playing lady of the manor, ordering the servants around. When she was out for the day Rose would sneak up to her bedroom with Daisy the scullery maid and try on all her fancy clothes and hats.

'Oh Rose you are a caution. What if the Mistress came back and caught you? You would be in serious trouble, and lose your position.' Rose just laughed off her fears.

'She won't be back for ages yet. Once she's with her own kind she'll be gone all day.'

★   ★   ★

Fred was rather overwhelmed by a house full of females all the time and secretly longed for the wedding to be over. He sorely missed Harry and the male companionship. Especially the Friday nights they'd spent together for many years. At first Harry was as good as his word and wrote every week, but gradually the letters had dwindled down to once a month, but he at least stayed in touch.

★   ★   ★

It was a Saturday morning when the latest letter arrived from Harry. Full of news and excitement. He had met a Scots lassie named

Isabel with whom he was currently stepping out, just as Fred had predicted. The rest of the letter contained lots of information about the big liner. Flo was disappointed, she wanted to hear more about Isabel and if it was serious, but the last paragraph of the letter caught her attention.

'Listen to this luv! The liner is to be launched next year by Mary Lady Iverclyde on 6th June 1906 and will be watched by thousands of people. Harry is wondering if we could save up and be there at this momentous occasion. What do you think Flo, shall we try to be there?' Florence was stunned into silence. The date 6/6/6, the number of the beast. It's a bad omen, I do hope Harry doesn't sail in her. Fred was staring at her awaiting an answer.

'Why Flo, you have gone quite pale. Whatever is the matter?'

'Oh nothing, I'm alright. I was just thinking if we could afford it. Having just had Amelia's wedding and all the expense that caused, what with the price of the material for little Christopher's outfit, and the present and all. Still we have a year to save up for the fare to Scotland, and now we don't have to pay any rent to Mr. Griffin. Perhaps we'll be able to make it after all. I shall continue with my little sewing jobs for the grand ladies in the area. I have a job at the moment to sew a navy ribbon on a hat and no money to buy navy cotton. I only have white so I thought of a clever idea. I will dip the white cotton in navy ink. I know how much it means to you to see Harry again, and I can't wait to meet Isabel.'

★   ★   ★

The next year flew by. Fred and Florence scrimped and scraped, and managed to save enough for the train fare to Scotland. Harry and Isabel were at the station waiting to greet them as they alighted from the train. Flo was struck by the sheer beauty of Isabel. She had long black hair tied up in ringlets and a pretty little hat perched on her head. There was much hand shaking, kissing and hugging of one another. Everyone was so pleased to be together. They made a truly handsome couple, thought Flo.

★   ★   ★

The next day the ship was launched. Flo was in awe of the sheer size of this magnificent vessel. She had seen nothing like it in her whole life.

'Harry it's so enormous, it just takes my

breath away looking at her.'

'Yes, they say if you stood the Lusitania on its stern next to St. Paul's Cathedral, it would only come half way up her hull.'

The moment had come. Lady Iverclyde took to the platform and the crowd went quiet as she performed her duty and duly named the liner 'Lusitania', to tumultuous applause and cheers from all the workers and onlookers of the day. Caught up in the gaiety and excitement of the day, Flo began to feel that her previous fears were foolish. Nothing could happen to such a magnificent ship.

★　★　★

A year later the Lusitania set sail from Liverpool on her maiden voyage, bound for New York with Harry Rolleston aboard. Having achieved his ambition to be part of the crew on this beautiful ship. A month later in October 1907, the Lusitania won back the 'Blue Riband' from Germany. Harry was beside himself with pride and joy. He felt life had been good to him, and privileged that he had been allowed to achieve all his ambitions. Some men go all through their lives being miserable and never seem to achieve anything. I'm so lucky. I have my beautiful Isabel waiting for me back in Scotland. I must propose to her the minute we dock back home, before someone else snaps her up.' Harry's thoughts were interrupted by one of the other seamen.

'There you are lad. I've been looking all over for you. What are you doing hiding down here in your bunk?'

'Right Jim, I'll be right with you. I was just thinking.'

'You've no time for day dreaming lad. We set sail again within the hour.'

★ ★ ★

Flo had some surprising news for Fred as they sat down for their evening meal.

'Fred I have something really wonderful to tell you. I can hardly believe it myself. I'm expecting again. I thought I couldn't have any more. It has been so long since Christopher's birth but Doctor Fisher confirmed it today, so I'm not mistaken.'

Fred was overjoyed at the news, as Flo guessed he would be and she could not wait to tell Beatrice and her sisters the wonderful news. On arrival at her mother's house the next day Flo was in for a few surprises herself. Amelia was sitting at the table sipping tea and looking radiant.

'Mother, I'm expecting again. Isn't it wonderful news?'

Ame jumped to her feet squealing, 'Snap, so am I.'

'I'm sure it's a boy again, I think yours is too Ame. They could grow up and play together, not only cousins but friends for life.'

'Florence, what nonsense you talk some-times. How could you possibly know if you or Amelia are carrying boys or girls?'

'I just know Mother, I know.'

Amidst the chatter and excitement, the door was suddenly flung open and Rose stood there, white as a sheet and shaking from head to toe. Beatrice was on her feet in an instant.

'Why Rose, whatever is the matter, you look awful? What are you doing home from work? Did they send you home because you're ill?'

'No Mother, I've been dismissed.'

'Whatever for, love?'

'Telling lies Mother, but I'm not. It's all true.'

'What is it love, you can tell us, we're your family and love you dearly. I'll go and see Mistress Leyton-Barrie and tell her there has been some terrible mistake, none of my girls ever tell lies. I have brought them up to tell the truth at all times, no matter what the

26

consequences are. I'll ask for your job back, I'm sure she'll listen to me.'

Rose had collapsed into uncontrollable sobbing, then screaming at her mother.

'I'm pregnant Mother, pregnant! Do you hear me, and the Master is the father. He denied it all. The Mistress said I was a naughty wilful, wicked girl, and must leave their employment immediately, without references, and she would see that I never worked in service again for any other family. Oh Mother, what am I to do?'

Amelia and Florence looked at one another in stunned silence.

Beatrice was the first to speak.

'Now Rose, dry those tears and pull yourself together. If we were rich we could sue Mr. Anthony Leyton-Barrie for what he's done to you, but alas we are not and no one would believe us. It would be our word against his. If there was a way I could make him face up to his responsibilities I would but sadly there is not. We must try to manage alone.'

'But Mother,' wailed Rose, 'we have no money. How can we manage?'

Beatrice raised her hand gesturing for silence.

'Enough said Rose! We'll manage somehow. I did not think when I got up this morning I would be a Grandmother three times over by the end of the day. My darling little grandson Christopher has been alone these past seven years and suddenly he will have three little playmates within the year.'

★ ★ ★

That evening Flo told Fred the news about Amelia and Rose, but Rose was uppermost in both their minds.

'Aye it's a bad business, lass. There is one law for the rich and another for the poor. You'll get nought out of Master Anthony Leyton-Barrie. I've heard tell he's a right womaniser, he thinks his money can buy anything. Whatever possessed Rose to take up with him? She must have known it would all end in tears.'

'Being the youngest, I suppose we all spoilt her. Perhaps it is our fault. Letting her have her own way all the time, doing exactly as she pleased. I felt so sorry for her, not knowing the joy of growing up with a father. She missed the fun and laughter, and games he used to play with us all. I don't suppose she remembers much about him. Only being 5 years old when he passed away.'

'Ney lass, you can't blame yourselves. She knew what she was doing alright. She made her bed and now she must lie in it. What did your mother have to say? It must have been a terrible shock for her.'

'It was. She was as white as Rose and I could see her hands trembling but she was magnificent, so calm and composed. She even made a joke and said 'It would be nice to have a bit of aristocratic blood in the family. It would improve the Ford line no end.' Rose was screaming and hysterical, and all I wanted to do was slap her face hard. Bringing all that shame and worry on poor Mother. She just totally spoilt mine and Amelia's news. Mother was so happy before Rose burst in spoiling things as usual. I don't know what Mary will say when she gets home from work and finds out all her sisters are pregnant. All she ever wanted was to settle down and have a family.'

'Not much chance of that, lass. I don't mean to be cruel but she's so plain and shy compared to the rest of you. Always in a day dream. I fear she may be left on the shelf poor lass.'

'I think that is enough said about my family for one day. Let us change the subject please. This morning before I went to Mother's, I was cleaning the back bedroom when suddenly there was the most dreadful smell.'

'What sort of smell?'

'Like something had died and was rotting. It was the most foul smell I've ever encountered. There must be a dead cat or bird trapped somewhere. You will have to take the floorboards up at the weekend, look up the chimney, or search in the roof space.'

'Has the smell gone now?'

'Yes, I threw open all the windows and let the fresh air in.'

Fred did as he was told and searched everywhere but could find no trace of a dead animal or bird anywhere. Strange he thought, it must be her pregnancy. She gets these funny notions when she's pregnant. I remember last time, she thought the house was haunted. I'll just humour her till it's all over and she produces another champion son or daughter just like Christopher.

3

Bridget Collins waited nervously in their neat little house looking out on the harbour, at Queenstown for her husband Willy's return from Cork city. He had gone to the city to seek some work. She did not know how she was going to tell him she was expecting their third child. They already had two daughters, Margaret three and Annie just one year. He will go stark raving mad when he finds out. She braced herself as she heard his key in the front door.

'Any luck Willy?'

'No and before ye say any more I'm not going with cap in hand to your family to ask for work on the farm. I'll look after me own family meself. I was thinking of going back to sea again, if nothing turns up here. You're looking very pale, are ye not feeling well Bridget?'

'I've something to tell ye Willy. I'm carrying again.' She blurted it out before her nerve failed. Knowing what the response would be.

'Jesus woman have I not got enough on me plate without another mouth to feed?'

'Don't shout at me Willy Collins, it takes

31

two to make a baby. I didn't conceive it all alone. It's not the Immaculate Conception you know.'

'Don't blaspheme woman. I hope you remember what you just said, when you confess your sins to Father O'Malley next time you go to confession. Another thought crossed me mind when I was wandering the streets of Cork today. How would you like to go to America and start a new life? My cousins would put us up till we got settled, and I got work. It would be a grand start for us all. What do ye say Bridget?'

'It all sounds fine to me, but how are we going to get the fare together for five of us, pray?'

'I've already thought of that. What say ye if I go on ahead, find work, set up a home for us all, and send for you and the children when I'm settled?'

'Well I suppose so.' Jesus, Mary and Joseph what will the man think of next? He has these high faluting ideas. Saints preserve us! Best agree with him for now.

★ ★ ★

True to his word Willy Collins joined a ship and worked his passage to New York as a stoker. On arriving there he soon found work being the grafter that he was, people were glad to employ such a handy man. He could repair anything put in front of him. He had the patience of a saint when working with his hands, but no patience at all with people. Frequently his Irish temper would flare up and he would get into fights, usually after he had a few tots of whisky. While in New York he stayed with his cousin Tommy O'Shea and wife Molly. He spent most evenings at his hobby putting ships inside bottles, or the whole family would gather around the piano singing Irish songs and reminisce about the old country. Tommy would get maudlin when he had too much to drink and end up crying on Willy's shoulder, ending up with the pair collapsing on the floor the worse for wear. Molly would throw a blanket over the pair and go on to bed tutting to herself and thinking, there is no way I'm going to try and get those two strapping men to bed. They can stay there till morning for all I care.

★   ★   ★

Next morning Willy was up bright and early for his job at the bakery. Drink never stopped him getting up and going to work. He seemed completely unaffected by the night before. Tommy was the exact opposite. He was like a bear with a sore head.

'Will ye get me something for me poor head woman, I'm dying here in agony.'

'Serves you right, you shouldn't drink so much, then you won't feel so bad in the morning.'

'Tis not the drink woman, it's me poor health that I'm cursed with from time to time.'

'Huh! A likely story. Anyway the postman is coming up the front steps with a letter. I'm going to answer the door. A letter for you Willy from Eire.'

'It's from Bridget. She's had a little girl and wants to call her Ellee. They're both fine. Mrs. Finnegan next door assisted with the birth. Ah tis great news on this fine April morning. She wants to know if I'll be home for the baptism at St. Colman's. I think I've enough saved to go home and bring them all back with me to start our new life together in this great country.'

Willy made for the front door grabbing a piece of toast on the way out. He was whistling softly to himself and thinking of his family of females back home as he stepped into the road. He did not see the cab come hurtling around the corner. He looked up too late. He tried to jump back but it was useless. The cab struck him a glancing blow and he was flung back onto the pavement. He felt the impact and then blackness. Molly heard the screech of brakes and screaming from a woman passer by. She was out in the street in a flash. Praying it wasn't Willy but in her heart of hearts she knew it was. A crowd had gathered around and someone called 'get a doctor quick, he's still alive.'

Molly knelt down and cradled his head in her lap, tears streaming down her face. Someone covered him with a coat. She was numb with shock. How was she going to let Bridget know in Ireland.

Perhaps the New York Police would get in touch with the Irish Garda. The ambulance arrived and Molly went with it to the local hospital. The wait was interminable before a doctor came to speak with her.

'I'm Doctor Lever. Are you next of kin?'

'I am a cousin and we're the only family he has in the States. Tell me Doctor, is he going to be alright?'

'Yes he'll live, he was very lucky. He has broken legs, ribs and injuries to his back. He should make a good recovery but it will mean many weeks in hospital. Has he any insurance to cover the cost?'

'No but he has a lot of money he saved to bring his family over from Ireland.'

Many months passed and Willy made a

35

good recovery. He was anxious to get back to Bridget and the girls. He was penniless. The high cost of the medical bills his accident had incurred only left enough money for his fare back to Eire. He felt devastated, a failure, he had let his family down. Most of all he found it hard to accept he had let Bridget down and not fulfilled his promise of a new life, in a new country across the sea. America! A land of promise and opportunities. He knew now this was never to be.

★ ★ ★

Once back in the bosom of his family, Willy soon settled down to a normal life again. Snatching work where he could to support his family. Bridget never blamed him for using all the money he had saved on medical bills for his accident. She just thanked God he was returned to her safe and sound and never mentioned the money again. Soon after his return from the States, Bridget found herself pregnant again with their fourth child. The birth went well and another daughter was born to the family. Bridie had a mass of black hair and was the image of Willy. Fay Finnegan had been present once more at the birth, and commented.

'No mistaking who her father is. She's the

spitting image of ye Willy.'

'You think the good Lord would send me a son Fay. What am I going to do with a household full of women. Lord save me when they all grow up.'

Secretly Willy was overjoyed that he had created another human being in his own image and likeness. Ellee was a beautiful little girl with golden hair, just like Bridget. Margaret and Annie had brown hair and was a mixture of both of them, but Bridie was special and he knew there would always be a special bond between them. He was not a man to show his true feelings and covered his emotions by pretending he wanted a son.

★ ★ ★

A year had passed and there was still no significant change on the work front. When hurrying home from his odd jobs one lunchtime Willy had an idea, but was not too sure how Bridget would accept his plans. Feeling she would not be in favour of them.

'Bridget, I've heard today the 'Titanic' has left the Belfast shipyard for Southampton, bound for her maiden voyage to New York. She'll be calling in at Queenstown and I thought I could get work aboard as a stoker. What do ye think? It would be an honour to serve on such a magnificent ship. There has never been another like her. They say she's unsinkable.'

Bridget was not at all happy. She had heard all the boasts about how the ship was unsinkable. She was not at all sure, she felt very uneasy about this monster of a ship. She felt a shiver go through her at the mention of its name. She was not at all happy for her Willy to sail on her. Bridget waited anxiously for Willy to return from the harbour office, where he hoped to sign on for work aboard the Titanic. She gazed out of the window across the harbour and prayed to God he would be unsuccessful.

God had answered her prayers. He was unsuccessful, all crew had been taken on at Southampton. He arrived back at the house a half an hour later, a sad dejected figure. Feeling he had missed a really good opportunity, not only for himself but his family.

God does not seem to be with me. First the New York accident and now this disappointment. How am I supposed to support me ever growing family. Bridget did not seem to worry at all over money, she'd just say 'Trust in the Lord he will provide.' More likely her rich family, with their farms, butcher shops and pub. I'll not touch a penny of their

38

money as long as I have breath in my body. They never liked me. I'll show them, I'll be successful one day. I hope Bridie is the last of our children. This wish was not granted either. Bridget announced she was pregnant again. Willy felt even more depressed.

★   ★   ★

Then the day dawned when the terrible news arrived. The Titanic had hit an iceberg and sunk, with a great loss of life, 1500 souls were not saved and perished in the cold dark waters of the North Atlantic, that fateful April night in 1912. On hearing the news Bridget sank to the floor in prayer and gave thanks to God for sparing her husband, and saving her children from becoming fatherless. She also prayed for the poor families who had lost loved ones on board this mighty ship. Willy was stunned into silence when hearing the news. How could such a tragedy have happened? He felt had he been on board, knowing his luck his fate would have been sealed and he would not have survived.

★   ★   ★

The following year little Jack William was born. Fine and healthy with thick black hair just like his sister Bridie, resembling his father. Although Bridget was strong and healthy she began showing signs of strain at having had five children so close together. She was pale and seemed very tired all the time, but never complained. Life would be so much easier if Willy would only make it up with her family and let them help out from time to time. He was a proud man and would not take charity from anyone, especially her family. He had never known the closeness of family life until he married. His mother died giving birth to him and his father being a sea captain, left his only son to be brought up by a local family named Dunn. The Dunns had a large family of their own and although his father was well off and sent regular money home for his upbringing, it never seemed to be lavished on Willy. He always seemed to be in second hand me down clothes and had holes in his boots. Boots that had been worn many times by the older children in the family. The family were known locally as the fighting Dunns.

The father and older sons in the family were permanently drunk and looking for fights. Many in the village feared the Dunns and avoided them like the plague when they were the worse for drink. Little Willy would cower in the corner with fear when the front door burst open and the violence erupted. The shouting, swearing, smashing of furniture, and Brian Dunn taking off his buckled leather belt to beat the younger children.

It was a wonder to Bridget that he survived to grow up at all. She wondered how different it would have been if his Spanish mother had lived, or he had been sent to Spain to be brought up with her family.

★   ★   ★

Captain John Collins had left money with the Dunns for Willy to be educated privately, so he would have a good career. The money was spent on drink and replacing the smashed furniture after the drunken binges. By the time John Collins was lost at sea, all the money had been spent and not a trace of his father's possessions were left for Willy to remember him by. Any little family heirlooms left with the Dunns were sold and the money pocketed by them. Poor little Willy was the talk of the village, how he had been cheated out of his inheritance by the Dunns. Maggie, the eldest of the Collins children, was the most troublesome. She was jealous of her sisters and seemed to resent the new baby brother everyone doted on.

'That one has a terrible temper on her,

Willy. It must be the Spanish blood in her. Today I sent her out with money to buy a loaf at the shop. When she saw Ellee outside playing chalkie gods with the boys next door, she told her to go. When Ellee refused she threw the money down in the road and jumped on the boys' chalkie gods and smashed them to smithereens. Peter Finnegan rushed out when he heard the boys wailing. He had a job to keep his hands off her. He said, if he had her he would have drowned her at birth in the harbour.

'He dare lay a finger on any of me children and I'll lay him out flat so I will. Of course the bad temper couldn't have come from any of your side of the family, like your brother Con and his wild ways. Only the good things were inherited from your family,' quipped Willy sarcastically.

Bridget ignored the sarcasm.

'A strange thing happened to Ellee on the way back from the shop. She was passing St. Colman's when she heard the organ playing. As it was tea time and nearly dark she knew there wouldn't be a service on at this time of the day so she peeped inside the door. The church was in darkness, except for a man suspended in mid air playing an organ surrounded by a bright light. She was terrified and ran out of the church screaming.

She collided head on with Mrs. Doyle, who told her she had just seen the ghost of St. Colman's and not to be frightened. She was really shook up and shaking all over. She said the man had gold buttons on his coat. I think she has the gift of second sight and that is something she has inherited from my family. I know you don't believe in my tea leaf reading, but I do have the gift and so does me mother. Now little Ellee seems to have it too. I always thought she was different from the others with her loving quiet ways.'

'What rubbish you talk sometimes Biddy, I don't believe in all that nonsense. I think it is against our religion to believe in it, and you shouldn't encourage Ellee or any of the other children to believe in it either.'

'They say the ghost only appears when there is going to be a death. I hope — ' Before she could finish, Willy had exploded.

'Stop and stop now woman, I won't hear another word on the subject. Ellee was just upset over Maggie and Pete Finnegan losing his temper like that. It played on her mind and she probably imagined it all.'

Before Bridget could answer him there was a loud banging on the front door. It was Billy her younger brother. 'Can you come quickly our Bridget me ma's so upset. Uncle Mikey is dead. He was on duty on his horse last night

43

during the terrible storm, when he was struck by lightning. Ma's in a terrible state, he died instantly. His horse was badly injured and they had to shoot it. She needs you Biddy will ye come?'

'I'll come this instant Billy,' she snatched up her coat and only paused briefly to give Willy a withering I told you so look.

The door slammed and Willy was left alone with his thoughts. All he could think of was Ellee and the ghost. No there can't be anything in it. It was just a coincidence. I'll give Jesse Doyle a piece of my mind when next I see her. Frightening everybody with her superstitious tales.

4

Beatrice was sitting in the garden of number 9 Betts Lane, her grandsons playing at her feet and pondering how strange it was to have all grandsons, when she herself had all daughters. She felt she had the best of both worlds. The neighbours had long since stopped gossiping about Rose's illegitimate son James, now aged 5 years. No one could understand why she had not been harder on Rose for bringing such shame to the family, but she too had a secret which was never shared with anyone. She was also born from aristocracy. Her mother had been a servant in a big house just like Rose, and got herself pregnant by the master's son, who also disclaimed any responsibility. It was like history repeating itself. Rose had turned out wild and wilful just like her aristocratic grandfather.

Now Florence and Amelia were a different kettle of fish. She could not have wished for more perfect daughters. They were respectful, caring and loving dutiful daughters, and devoted to each other. Amelia had even managed to rent the house next door to Flo, number eleven, from Mr. Griffin when the elderly lady that lived there had passed on.

Flo was pleased by this as Tom spent so much time away in India with his regiment that she and little Albert spent long periods alone, just counting the days to his next leave. There was talk at one time of her joining him in India but she decided against it. She wanted little Albert educated in England and growing up with his cousins. He had become very attached to Flo's younger son Lewis and spent more time in Flo's garden than his own.

'Grandma I can hear a baby crying in Aunty Flo's house. Who has come to visit?'

'No one is there Albert. You must have imagined you heard it.'

'No, no I didn't I can still hear it now. You can too, can't you Lewis?'

'I'm not sure I think I did.'

'Well I can't, you're just making it up,' retorted James.

'No I'm not,' Albert immediately burst into tears at being doubted.

'Now boys hush, dry those tears Albert. I expect you were right, it's probably the lady a few doors up having a visit from her daughter and baby grandchild.'

'But the crying came from Aunty Flo's house.'

'No more buts, that is an end to the matter.'

Before Beatrice could say any more, Flo and Ame were running down the garden path shouting and waving their arms.

'Mother, Mother, we are at war. Britain has just declared war on Germany. The whole Lane is out talking about it. Did you not hear the commotion?'

* * *

Most of the men and boys in the Lane were out of work so the war was a wonderful chance to prove themselves as men. Then there would be regular army pay to support their families.

They couldn't wait to join Kitchener's army and were worried it would be all over before they had their chance of glory. The popular belief was 'all over before Christmas.'

* * *

Fred was very quiet and thoughtful and did not say a lot about the war. Flo knew deep down inside he was wrestling with his conscience whether to volunteer or not, to fight for King and country. She prayed he would not. Most of the men in the Lane had now gone to war and he seemed the only man left. This played heavily on his mind and he did not wish to be thought a coward. On the other hand he seemed to realise the perils of war which others did not. He knew it was not all glory and many would not return. He did not wish to inflict hardship on Flo if he did not return. Leaving her a widow, to bring up his two small sons alone with no man as a bread winner. He would leave his decision for a bit longer. Perhaps it will all be over by Christmas as predicted. Then there would be no point joining up for just a few months. Christmas came and went and the war was nowhere near over, it seemed to be gaining momentum.

★   ★   ★

Harry Rolleston was about to make his two hundred and second crossing aboard the Lusitania from Pier 54 at New York. He had just finished a letter to Fred and Flo and thought he would post it before the ship set sail. In the letter he told them about the ship's mascot, a 4 year old black cat called 'Dowie'. It had deserted the ship in the middle of the night. This put many of the stokers in a frenzy saying it was a bad omen. Harry thought it hilarious how superstitious some sailors were. He thought the cat had probably found a better home and was fed up with sea life, as many of them were. He ended his letter by promising to come and visit them as soon as the ship docked at Liverpool.

He would be on the next available train to Southampton. It had been far too long since they last met and with this infernal war going on, no one knew what was just around the corner. Alas Harry was never to fulfil his promise. Six days later at a few minutes past two on a warm May afternoon in 1915, the Lusitania was hit by a German torpedo 11 miles off the Kinsale lighthouse. A local family who had been picnicking on the cliff were shocked to see this gigantic ship hit on the starboard side. There was a thunderous crack and seconds later another larger explosion staggered the ship. A huge column of water and debris erupted out of the sea, and within 18 minutes from the first explosion the Lusitania had sunk. Harry Rolleston was not among the 764 survivors. He was not on duty at the time of the explosion and was taking a nap in his bunk, situated on the starboard side of the ship.

★　★　★

Six year old Ellee Collins ran screaming indoors to her mother.

'Mother come quickly and see. There is apples and pieces of wood, and bodies floating in the harbour. The men are taking the bodies to the town hall. A man lifted me up to the window so I could see the bodies laid out. Mother there are children and babies there as well and they are all dead. There are people wrapped in blankets and crying. Everyone is crying.'

Bridget was shocked to think anyone could lift her daughter up to the town hall window and show her such a terrible sight. If I could find out who that was, I'd give him a piece of my mind.

'Where is Maggie? She should be looking after you.'

'She's still watching all the bodies being brought ashore. I think Pop was there too, helping.'

When Willy returned later that evening, he looked tired, drawn and very shocked at what he had just witnessed.

'I cannot understand what a German sub was doing so close to our shores and why it torpedoed a civilian ship.'

Bridget made no reply. She couldn't understand it either. All she could think of was the poor families of the lost souls. In the days that followed this terrible disaster, Willy paid his own personal tribute to the Lusitania. He made a replica of the Lusitania and put it inside a bottle, it even had all the apples bobbing about in the sea around the ship. This was his hobby and it always calmed his nerves in times of stress.

★　★　★

Fred took the death of his dear friend Harry badly. Everywhere he walked for months afterwards, he kept seeing recruiting posters saying 'Avenge the Lusitania'. This was the final straw, the deciding factor. Fred had made his mind up to enlist. He would give those darn Germans what for. He would fight and kill as many as he could for Harry. Any time his vengeance weakened he would just think of Harry and the great friendship that had been lost and could never be rekindled ever again. Now to break the news to Flo, who half expected something like this would happen. She had seen the sorrow etched on Fred's face for months. She did not remonstrate with him, although she felt sick inside and did not want him to go. She understood he had to do this last gesture for Harry and so in 1916 Fred enlisted and joined the 'Hampshires' on the Western

Front. That night she prayed to God that her man would be delivered back to her safely.

It was the first time in their marriage that they had ever been parted and she could not envisage never being with him again, holding him in her arms, being close. Experiencing the love he had for her. She cried long into the night and finally fell asleep a few hours before dawn. When she awoke she felt a sort of peace and had the feeling Fred would be alright. Had God answered her prayers? Would Fred's life be spared? Or was she being foolish, just wishful thinking? She decided to go next door to Amelia and wondered if she felt the same with Tom away in India, or was it different for a regular soldier's wife?

'Flo you look awful. Didn't you get any sleep last night?'

'I'm alright now. I feel better after the good cry I had. Look at us, we are a right pair of grass widows. I don't know how you cope with Tom being away so much.'

'You get used to it, but I must admit it gets very lonely at times. I'll tell you what we'll do from time to time to keep our spirits up. We'll go to town, and look at the huge map outside the 'Southern Daily Echo' offices, it keeps everyone abreast of the events in Europe.'

Fred soon settled down to army life. Many found the harsh discipline of army life hard to handle. Hard graft never worried Fred, but he was appalled by the terrible conditions of the trenches. The mud, filth, degradation, the food shortages. So this was Kitchener's wonderful army. He realised the bullshit people had been fed of Glory and Victory over the enemy. How could men have been so gullible to believe in all that stuff. There were some boys as young as 13 years old, who volunteered and lied about their age and were here fighting. Nowt but children. What were the recruiting officers thinking of! They must have realised how young these boys were. The oldest soldier to volunteer was Henry Webber 68 years old. Fred thought he shouldn't be there either, but he admired his fighting spirit and bravery. Other men of his age would never have volunteered. He settled down to write a last letter to Florence before the battle of the Somme which was to take place the next day at 7.30 am Saturday 1st July 1916. He decided not to mention the terrible conditions they were all living in. It would only add to her anguish. Instead he told her about a new friend he had made, private Jimmy Cox. They had kept their spirits up by singing songs each evening in the dug outs and talking about their families and what they would be doing after the war was over. There was a lot of gossip all along the front and was passed from one soldier to another. He told her about the observation balloon shaped like a huge sausage the Germans flew above the valley south of La Boisselle. The soldiers christened it 'Sausage Valley' and the other valley became 'Mash'.

He knew she would laugh when she heard the name the Germans had given the Scots regiments in their kilts, 'Ladies from Hell.'

★ ★ ★

The tension in the trenches grew as 7.30 approached. Some men were visibly shaking with fear as the minutes ticked away.

'Well Jimmy lad this looks like this is it. Over the top we go me lad, to whatever fate awaits us.' The men shook hands and wished each other good luck.

The whistle blew and the men bravely went over the top. Some of the men from one of the other regiments kicked a football over the top as the whistle blew and so the bloody battle of the Somme had begun. The carnage was terrible, men had been torn limb from limb. There were bodies everywhere, men screaming out in pain for help, parts of their bodies missing, dying in dreadful agony. They could not be reached until nightfall, when the medical orderlies went out to retrieve the sick and dying. The 1st Hampshires were hit badly with a loss of 26 officers and 559 men. Fred and Jimmy had been lucky this time. They had both returned to the trenches unscathed but they knew the terrible sights they had witnessed that day would remain with them for the rest of their lives. If they survived this bloody war.

★   ★   ★

Florence was gradually getting used to life without Fred. The fear of losing him was being replaced by another fear. A fear of the house and being alone in it. With the onset of Winter and the dark evenings the house seemed even more sinister.

While the boys were at school one day and Florence was alone upstairs cleaning the bedrooms, she heard footsteps coming along the hall and up the stairs. She froze in horror knowing none of her family were about. Amelia had gone shopping with their Mother, and all the boys were at school. The floor boards outside the bedroom door creaked, and as she looked towards the door, which was partially opened — she saw a man standing there leering at her. He had black hair, a stubbly chin, and looked dirty and unwashed. He wore an open necked shirt, a plaid waistcoat, and dark trousers. Florence just stood there and screamed and screamed with terror. The man disappeared in an instant. Florence sank onto the bed and sobbed uncontrollably. Who was he, what does he want from me? When she could cry no more, she sat up and pulled herself together. She must not let Chris and Lewis see her in such a state. They will be in from school shortly and she didn't want them frightened by any of this. Neither of them seemed aware of anything unusual about the house, thank God. Only Amelia's little Albert seemed aware. When these happenings are at their worse, the child seems very uneasy in the house. The worse times are November and December and when I am in the garden around August time. I can hear a baby crying in the house. Such a pitiful, mournful cry, I have never heard a baby sound like that before, and yet when I enter the house all is quiet again, just this heavy feeling of depression and sadness. Like something really terrible has happened here. The house is really old and many people have lived here in the past. How can I find out what has gone before and what could I do about it, if I did know? Perhaps if I see the man again I could ask what's troubling him and how could I help? That is, if I can stay calm and overcome my fear of the unknown. The previous occupant of the house, Matilda Whitcombe, went completely mad while living here and ended up in a lunatic asylum. Well that's not going to happen to me.

I'm sure all the happenings in this house must have pushed her over the top, especially if she was a little bit unstable, and living alone like she did. The terrible shock she had suffered years before. To have her man back from fighting in the Crimean War, only to come home one day and find him hanging from the cherry tree in the garden. Poor, poor woman!

★　★　★

She heard the click of the front gate next door and knew Amelia was back from shopping. At the same time the three boys came yelling and screaming up the garden path.

'Mum, Mum, where are you? Can James and Albert stay to tea tonight? Please Mum,' pleaded Lewis.

'Yes but we must wait for Christopher to

get home first. In the meantime you can all sit down and be quiet. Little children should be seen and not heard. You can all look at some story books while I have a quick word with Aunt Amelia.'

Beatrice was just leaving as Flo went next door.

'Mother we have James indoors for tea. Can you tell Rose please, in case she's wondering where he's got to?'

With Beatrice safely out of the way, Flo settled down to recount the afternoon happenings to Amelia.

'What do you think Ame? Please tell me I'm not mad. You do believe me don't you?'

'Well' . . . There was a long pause. 'I think you are probably a bit overwrought. Missing Fred like you do. I know how close you two are. I think you probably sat down on the bed and fell asleep and dreamt it all. Dreams can be so realistic, you can persuade yourself that the things in the dream did really happen.'

'Oh Ame, I thought at least you would understand.'

'I do Flo, oh I do. You can always tell me anything you know you can and it will always be just our secret.'

'I must get back to the boys now. God knows what mischief they will be getting up to.'

Flo went back home feeling desolate, totally alone. Is there no one I can talk to that would understand. I had better keep my mouth shut from now on, or everyone will think I'm mad as well, just like Matty.

★   ★   ★

Things settled back to normal again. There were no more sightings of the dark haired man and Florence began to relax again. She thought she would ask her mother and sisters around for Sunday tea. After tea Florence announced she had something to show them all. She had managed to get hold of some cheap material, and had run up a summer dress on her sewing machine.

'I'll just pop upstairs and put it on. I'm sure you'll all love it. It has such a pretty floral design and the material was so cheap. I picked it up at a stall in the market.'

Florence was standing at the top of the stairs, smoothing out a few creases in her dress, when suddenly she felt an almighty shove and she was falling, all the way down the stairs. She landed in a heap at the bottom of the stairs. Beatrice and her sisters were there in an instant.

'Flo are you alright? Whatever happened? Did you trip? Did you bang your head?

Thank God you're not badly injured.'

'No Mother, I didn't trip. I was pushed and I banged my back all the way down. I'll have a nice set of bruises tomorrow.'

'What do you mean pushed girl? There is only us here. Who pushed you?' She turned to the others. 'I think she must have banged her head and is concussed.'

At that point Florence gave up any further explanation. I knew the instant before I fell, I sensed someone was there beside me. I was definitely pushed, but none of them will ever believe me.

So what is the point of trying to convince them that this house is definitely haunted.

★   ★   ★

A few weeks later Florence was sitting in the chair, resting her back. She was still feeling after effects from the fall down the stairs. When suddenly a loud banging at the front door made her jump. She hurried down the hall to answer it, her heart beating fast. She was not expecting any callers. Who could it be? She opened the front door, then froze in horror. A telegram boy stood on the step.

'Telegram for Mrs. Preston.'

'Yes that's me. Thank you.'

She closed the door and leaned against the wall her hands trembling, she opened the envelope. The words seemed to leap off the page at her, 'Missing presumed killed.' Oh no, no, not her Fred, darling Freddie. He can't be. I don't believe it. I won't believe it. He's coming home to us, I know he will, he will. He wouldn't leave us all alone, his boys without their Daddy.

★ ★ ★

The neighbours began to gossip about the way she took the news of Fred's death.

'That Florrie Preston is walking around like her man is coming home. What makes her think she is so special? Why can't she accept bad news like the rest of us had to?'

'Do you suppose she's gone a bit funny in the head? Like the previous occupant of that house, Matty. She used to say it was haunted, much to everyone's amusement, poor Matty. Perhaps it was a bit unkind of us all to laugh at her.'

'I don't know, I'm sure. All I know is, she will have a sad awakening when the war is over and her man doesn't come home.'

Mrs. Butler was interrupted, when the corner shop door opened and in walked

Florence. The shop fell silent.

'Good morning Mrs. Butler and Mrs. Jones, having a good gossip are we? At someone else's expense. Now I wonder who it is today. Could it be me by any chance?'

'Well!' said Mrs. Butler scarlet faced. She quickly left the shop with Mrs. Jones close on her heels.

Both Florence and Mr. Blackman burst out laughing.

'You soon put those two old biddies in their place. Good for you Flo. That's what they have needed for a long time.'

Mr. Blackman grew serious.

'Don't build your hopes up too much luv on getting your Freddie back. I'd hate to see them dashed when the war is over.'

'Until they find a body, I'll go on hoping.'

'They may never find a body my dear.' He gently patted her hand. He did not want to go into too much graphic detail about men blown to bits and no remains found. He did not wish to distress her further. He had always had a soft spot for Florence. She was his kind of woman, strong, could take care of herself and would always stand up and fight for her family and what was right. Yet she had a kind gentleness about her that was pleasing to all who met her. Fred Preston was certainly a very lucky man, marrying such a good catch. I do hope Florrie is right and her man does turn up safe and sound. She seems so sure he will be back. I do hope she is not deluding herself.

5

'Willy is that you?'

'And who else do ye think it is woman? Your fancy man perhaps?'

'Stop playing the goat, Willy. Billy has just come down from the farm to tell me our Katey had just given birth to twins. I'm just going up there to give Mother a hand.'

'Why can't Dermot Flynn look after his wife and new babies?'

'Because husbands are no good at that sort of thing. Anyway, where were ye when all our children were being born? No one saw hide or hair of ye till it was long over. Now out of me way man, I want to get going. The sooner I'm gone, the quicker I'm back. You're only grumbling because you have to get yer own tea and the children's. It won't hurt ye for once.'

Bridget gave him a quick peck on the cheek and was gone.

Willy was left moaning under his breath. Damn her family. They only have to call and she goes running every time.

★ ★ ★

64

Bridget returned a few hours later, cheeks rosy and hair blowing in the wind as she climbed the hill to their home.

Willy was waiting for her on the doorstep. She looked so radiant and happy, he could no longer be angry with her. She looked so beautiful. He thought how lucky he was to have her and their five healthy children. He felt a tiny pang of conscience, about how he had spoken to her earlier.

'How was your sister and the babies? Are they all strong and well, and as good looking as our little beauties?'

'Oh Willy they are two beautiful little girls. She's going to call them Josephine and Bernadette. They'll be baptised at St. Colman's in a few weeks time, as we all were.'

Willy swallowed his pride and attended the Baptism, and the tea that followed at the farm, for the sake of family peace.

Although he had a soft spot for Katey, who was very like his Bridget, he could not stand her brothers, Con, Mikey, Kevin and Billy. The feeling was mutual. He stood in one corner of the room, drink in hand looking sullen and sulky, glaring across at the brothers and Dermot in the other corner of the room. They were discussing the Easter uprising in Dublin two years previous.

'The war in Europe is over, but our

troubles are only just beginning. What do ye think Con?'

'I think you're right Mikey. I feel it in me bones. Big troubles are coming. Sure as day follows night.'

And you'll be in the middle of it, thought Willy rather sarcastically. He had long suspected that Con was a member of the Irish Republican Brotherhood. Con looked up and caught the sneer on Willy's face.

'I've often wondered Willy. Are ye any relation to the big fella Michael Collins? Him being a Cork man as well, but then I tought, no ye couldn't be. You're far too short.'

Willy was across the room in an instant. Fists clenched he took a swing at Con, and sent him and the table of drinks flying. Con was on his feet in seconds, raining blows on Willy. Both were giving as good as they got. The women were screaming for the fight to be stopped. Mikey grabbed Con, and Dermot, Willy and between them, with the help of the other men they managed to stop the fighting. Bridget was furious that Willy had risen to the bait and with her brother for starting the fight in the first place.

'I think we'd better leave. Come along children. Where's Ellee?' She's in the bedroom with the twins, chorused the children.

'Ellee come along it's time to go.'

'Aren't they beautiful Mother. I want lots of babies just like them when I grow up, but I want to be a nun as well. Do nuns have babies? I haven't seen any at the convent.'

'No darlin', they don't. You'll have to choose if you want to be a nun or a mother with a husband and family, but there is plenty of time to think about that when you grow up.'

'But why don't nuns have babies?' Ellee persisted.

'Because they don't have husbands. They have taken a vow of chastity and they will devote their life to Christ. They are virgins.'

'Mary was a virgin and she had baby Jesus.'

Bridget had no answer to that, so she asked. 'Why do you want to be a nun anyway?'

'Because they do beautiful knitting. The nuns at school are teaching me to knit gloves on three needles.'

'Ellee you don't have to become a nun to do beautiful knitting. You can still do your knitting and have a family as well. You'll be able to knit lovely baby clothes for your children.'

Bridget was finding it very difficult to contain her laughter.

'Now hurry up and put your coat and scarf

on. Daddy is waiting downstairs with your sisters and brother, we have to leave now. It's getting very dark. I must ask Uncle Kevin to fetch us a lantrin from the barn as the lane is very muddy and we don't want all our best clothes spoilt, do we now?'

'Can I come and see the twins again soon Mother, please . . . ?'

'Yes, now down the stairs with ye quick march.'

★ ★ ★

Two months had passed since the baptism of the twins and Bridget had not set foot on the farm since. She did not trust herself, not to have a blazing row with Con over the goading of Willy and being the cause of the fight. Bridget loved her family dearly and wanted to heal the rift between Willy and them. It was not so much the female side of the family causing trouble. It was her brothers, they never thought Willy good enough for their sister, having been brought up by the fighting Dunns. Ellee had been pestering the life out of her to see the twins again.

So when the children got home from school she decided to take them all up to the farm before Willy got home from work.

★ ★ ★

As they were entering the farm yard, Mikey rushed out waving his arms frantically.

'Biddy I'm so glad to see ye. Ma is beside herself with worry. It's our Katey and the twins. They're desperately ill with the Spanish flu. I tink they're going to die.'

Mikey could contain himself no longer and burst into tears.

Bridget was touched to see her big tough brother crying for their sister and baby nieces.

'I'll be there directly Mikey. Now calm yerself. We don't want the others seeing you like this, especially Katey.'

'No wait. You can't take the children in there, they might catch it. I don't want to lose any more of me family. I'll get our Billy to take them home and wait with them till your Willy gets in. Father O'Malley is with them now, administering the Last Rites.'

Bridget was just in time to say goodbye to her beloved sister. One of the twins had already died and the other soon followed.

Katey lasted an hour after the death of her babies. She was so ill herself, she was not even aware they had died. They still lay in her arms one each side wrapped in their beautiful little shawls, knitted so lovingly by Mary their doting grandmother.

*　*　*

No expense was spared for the funeral. A special white extra wide coffin was made, so Katey could be buried with her twins, as they had died, one laid each side in her arms. Ellee got her wish and was allowed to see the twins in the coffin, one last time before they were all laid to rest. The wake was a much quieter affair than the baptism two months before. There was no fighting or high jinks. The whole family seemed to have the stuffing knocked out of them. Con and Willy acknowledged each other with a brief nod. The rift between them had still not healed. The funeral Mass had been a sad but beautiful occasion.

The choir sang 'Ave Maria' and there was not a dry eye in the church, which was packed to capacity. Being a well known family in the area, people came from miles around to pay their last respects. The wake was held in the family pub and was a very subdued affair, unusual for Irish wakes.

*　*　*

The children found it very hard to sleep that night. It was the first time they had been to a funeral. They did not attend Great Uncle Mikey's, when he was struck by lightning while on duty in the Guards. He was their mother's uncle and usually dropped in to see her long after they were all tucked up in bed. His shift work never seemed to coincide with them being around. They were either at school or in bed when he called and Bridget never knew which shift he was on, to take the children to see him.

'Pop will ye read us a story? We can't sleep,' called Bridie.

'I'll tell ye what. I'll teach ye some more of the Irish language and you can tell me what the nuns have been teaching you at school about Eire. Who knows how Cork got its name? Have they not told ye? Well Cork got its name from one of the islands in the river Lee. Corcaigh, meaning marshy place.'

'Why do some people call where we live Cobh and Queenstown as well? Why has it got two names?' asked Jack.

'Well, Cobh was the original Irish name, and one day Queen Victoria, the Queen of England came to visit here. She liked the place and the people so much it was decided to call it Queenstown. Now one quick story then off to sleep with ye all.'

'I know a secret Pop. Do ye want to hear it?'

'What is it Maggie? Go on tell us then, I know ye are bursting to let us in on yer secret.'

'Well I don't know if I should or not.' Maggie was enjoying catching everyone's attention, knowing everyone was dying to know what the secret was.

'Well . . . '

'Maggie for Jesus sake are ye going to tell us or not. If not, then shut up.'

Maggie sensed her father was losing patience with her. So with great satisfaction she spat her secret out. Knowing full well it could cause a lot of trouble and at last she could get her revenge on Pete Finnegan. She had not forgotten the telling off she had received from both Pete and her father over the chalky gods incident.

'Yesterday at dinner time, when I went to call for me friend Sadie who lives next door to Kathleen Devlin, I was in her back garden waiting for her to come out, when I saw Pete Finnegan kissing Kathleen and then they started taking their clothes off.'

On hearing this Willy nearly choked himself and spluttered, 'That's enough of your stories Maggie. You'd better stop now before you cause a lot of trouble.'

'It's not a story I did see him.'

'How could ye child?'

'I just happened to look up at the bedroom window next door and there they were standing near to the window. I could see everything. They didn't shut the curtains.'

'Now Maggie, I don't want ye to repeat what ye saw to anyone at all.' Looking around at the other children, 'the same goes for all of ye. Do ye understand?'

The children nodded in agreement. Only Maggie protested.

'But why Pop? Everyone knows in the Street. Sadie said he is always around there when her husband Seamus is away.'

Willy nearly exploded. 'Because I say so. I'm warning ye Maggie. There will be big trouble if ye disobey me.'

Later when Willy went downstairs and related to Bridget what Maggie had just told him, she was shocked to the core.

'Poor Fay. She's such a good woman. She helped me so much when I was having all me babies. How could he do such a thing to her? Some men are like beasts of the field.'

'I tink it best if we say nothing for the moment. Although Maggie says everyone knows about it down her street. When Seamus comes back from sea, if he finds out he'll kill him. He's such a big powerful man. I swear murder will be done.'

* * *

Maggie was revelling in her new found knowledge and the hold she felt she had over Pete Finnegan. He won't get me in trouble quite so quickly again. She made a point of getting up extra early the next morning so she could greet him before he went to work.

'Good morning Mr. Finnegan.'

Pete scowled at her. He could not hide the dislike he had for this child. The others were good kids but this one was different. In the past he had teased Bridget, asking if she was really hers. Being so wilful compared to the others, but lately she was getting beyond a joke. The older she was the worse she was getting.

'What's a matter with ye, saying good morning?'

'Nothing. I was just wondering if I'll be seeing you around at Kathleen Devlin's today?'

Pete was white with rage. That little bitch has discovered me affair with Kathleen. I'll swing for her one of these days, sure I will and it will be worth it. Before he could reply, Bridget was calling her in.

'Maggie what are you doing out there. Come in and have yer breakfast this instant.'

'Just coming Mother.' She gave Pete a triumphant smile as she shut the front door.

Willy and Bridget were totally unaware on the taunting, being carried out by Maggie on Pete Finnegan, but both agreed he looked quite pale and strained of late.

'Ah that will be his guilty conscience to be sure,' remarked Bridget when Willy commented on how ill he looked lately.

Even Fay noticed how strained he looked. 'Are ye alright Pete? You're not going down with the Spanish flu, God forbid.'

'I'm alright woman, stop yer mythering on for God's sake.'

'I'm only worried about ye Pete. This Spanish flu is so bad it is taking thousands of people. Look what happened to poor Katey and her little babies. Bridget is still in a state of shock. I don't think she'll ever get over it, or not for a long time at least.'

Pete made no reply and walked out to the back garden to get some peace, and to think what his next move should be. When a child's voice came from the other side of the fence.

'Hello Mr. Finnegan.' Maggie's head appeared, with a sly smile on her face.

Christ it's her again. Pete made no reply. He walked back in doors.

'I'm off to the pub Fay, perhaps I'll get some peace there,' he mumbled to himself.

★ ★ ★

He sat in the corner alone with his pint, mulling over his situation. I wonder who that little bitch has told? She's obviously seen me comings and goings. I wonder if she's told Bridget and Willy? Bridget has been rather cool towards me of late but I put that down to the bereavement she has just suffered. Perhaps I'll have a word with Willy, man to man, he'll understand and might be able to keep her under control before she wrecks me marriage and me life. Dan Kelly did warn me I was playing with fire, getting mixed up with Kathy Devlin. As far as I know he's the only one who knows anything about us. He'll not say anything about it, being me best mate an all. Christ if Seamus ever finds out, I'm a dead man. Him and his brother Batt would beat me to a pulp. Dan keeps nagging me to get out while I'm still in one piece, but I can't. I can't give the woman up, she's so beautiful, she drives me crazy. Fay is a good woman but so bloody damn boring, fussing around all the time with her saintly do gooder ways. His thoughts were interrupted by the saloon bar door being flung open. In walked

Willy followed by a group of local men. The bar was beginning to fill with the evening regulars. Pete signalled to Willy to come and join him at his table.

★ ★ ★

'Willy I need your help, I'm desperate.'

After Pete had explained the situation with Maggie, Willy was red with anger and could hardly contain himself. Pete had to stop him from rushing home and giving her a good hiding.

'That will only make her worse and she'll be sure to let Fay know, not to mention Seamus.'

'I'll sort her out Pete me boy. I'll think of something to stop her filling other people's mouths with gossip. Now have a whisky on me and we'll enjoy the rest of the evening together. After all I couldn't have yer death on me conscience now could I.'

Willy gave a hearty laugh but Pete just shivered. He could not even joke about the situation. Fear was beginning to get a grip on him and the more he drank through the evening, the bigger the image of Seamus Devlin hovering over him became unbearable.

Till he finally passed out, the worse for

77

drink. Willy and some of the other local boys had to carry him home. Apologising to Fay when she opened the door.

'How come Willy Collins none of the rest of ye are in the same state as him? I'll give him what for in the morning, see if I will.'

'Well ye see Fay, he had a head start on the rest of us. We didn't get to the pub till later in the evening. Paddy behind the bar said he started drinking quite early on.'

'I'd say he was drowning his sorrows,' laughed Sean.

Willy glared at him, to hold his tongue.

'Sure what sorrows has he got? None, it's just an excuse not to practise self control, he has never known when to stop.'

This caused a lot of sniggers from the men which only added to Fay's fury.

'It's something you could all do with, a bit of self control. Thanks for bringing him home. I bid ye all goodnight.'

⋆　⋆　⋆

The next morning good as his word, Willy sorted the Maggie problem out. She was threatened with no more trips to the farm and being allowed to ride Uncle Con's horses. If she dared to speak one more word on the subject, either to Pete or anyone else.

'But Pop' she protested. 'I only said . . . '

'I know what ye said and next time ye open your mouth on the subject you'll feel the back of me hand.'

The next morning Willy tried to reassure Pete that Maggie was well and truly under control, but to no avail. He was a ghastly white colour and shaking like a leaf.

'Steady up Pete or you'll give the game away.'

'I know, Fay is already insisting I see the Doc. I just don't know what to do.'

'Tell her it's just the drink, promise her you'll go to confession next week and try to be a better man. That should please her and keep her quiet for a while. Till everything settles down again.'

'The stupid woman thinks I've got the Spanish flu, she's obsessed with it since your sister-in-law died of it. Between her and Seamus, sure I'd stand a better chance with the flu.'

Fay appeared at the door, 'I'm just off to St. Colman's to say a little prayer for yer health Pete. Now keep an eye on the boys, I'll not be gone longer than an hour or so.'

Pete nodded and looked at Willy, exasperated.

6

Florence awoke bright and early, feeling unusually cheerful for a Monday morning. She could not understand it. She had nothing to feel cheerful about living in this depressive dismal house with no husband. She heard the click of the letter box, as the postman pushed some letters through. As she passed the bottom of the stairs in the hall, on the way to the front door, she called up to the boys.

'Chris, Lewis hurry up or you'll both be late.'

Chris had started his first job with the Post Office and was very proud. Lewis had just celebrated his 10th birthday and had wished his Dad had been there to help celebrate it.

★   ★   ★

She bent to retrieve the letters, the first one she opened was from the war office. She could not believe her eyes. Fred had been found in a French hospital, suffering from amnesia, due to the effects of German gas and was shortly to be shipped home.

'I knew it, I knew it, I knew he wouldn't

leave us, he would come back.' Florence danced around the room with sheer happiness.

'What is it Mum? Why are you so happy? You knew what?' asked Lewis looking quite bewildered by this sudden outburst of joy.

'It's Daddy, he's alive and coming home to us soon. Isn't it marvellous. I must pop next door and tell Aunty Amelia the good news.'

All thoughts of getting her sons off to work and school, gone from her mind. The neighbours were all quite surprised. They had all long since accepted Fred would not be coming home and poor Florrie was deluding herself and one day she would have a sad awakening. Florence was going to organize a party for Fred's homecoming but then decided against it. Knowing the private sort of man he was. He would just want to be quiet with his immediate family around him and she did not know how badly he had suffered. There was never a word of it in any of his letters before he went missing. She had heard the horror stories from the men who had already returned home and knew Fred must have suffered a similar fate.

★ ★ ★

On his return, Flo knew she was right not to organize a big party. She was shocked at the sight of him. He was so pale and very thin. His flesh seemed to be hanging on his bones. He was quiet and subdued, he just hugged the three of them and could not speak for a long time. When he did, he spoke to the boys first.

'If there is ever another World War, I'll put thy legs under a horse and cart, before I let thee go to war and suffer as I did.'

Florence burst into tears, knowing he had suffered greatly, she would not ask any questions now. There would be plenty of time for that later. The main thing was she had her man home and she hoped there would not be any long term effects from the gas.

★   ★   ★

Fred began to settle down to civilian life again, and seemed to be getting his strength back. Flo tried to build him up by cooking his favourite meals. The thing he said he missed most was her suet puddings, especially 'spotted dick'. While he was in the trenches, he and Jimmy Cox used to dream of home cooking and being back safe and sound in the bosom of their families.

It was the only thing that kept them going.

Jimmy was also returned to his family, more or less in one piece. He had part of his index finger on his right hand blown off. After all they had been through together the two men vowed to remain friends for the rest of their lives. After a few weeks Jimmy got in touch and invited Fred and family over to tea one Sunday, to meet his wife Doris, two pretty daughters and small son.

* * *

During the tea party little was spoken of their terrible ordeal, except to mention how lucky Fred was to have survived the German gas called Phosgene. Clouds of the gas could travel quite a distance killing everything in its wake, birds, rats, not to mention the human toll. It even corroded metal. Fred must have been on the tail end of its path of destruction, to have survived. During their last battle, Fred and Jimmy got separated, each thinking the other had been killed. Jimmy was taken to a different hospital than Fred, with his hand injury.

It wasn't till much later, when Fred recovered his memory that they met up. Both were overjoyed the other was safe and sound.

'Enough of this war talk, let's look to the future and the land fit for heroes that Lloyd

George had promised.'

'Aye I'll drink to that,' and Fred raised his glass and winked at Jimmy.

★ ★ ★

The next one to receive good news was Amelia. Tom was coming home. He had been in a battle at some place in India called Amritsar, and would be home within a few weeks. Amelia was elated as she related the news to Florence and Fred. Florence hugged her younger sister.

'I'm so glad Ame. You'll have your man back too. Perhaps please God we can now live peacefully for the rest of our lives.'

★ ★ ★

When Tom Burrows arrived home, even Flo was shocked by his appearance. She thought that Fred had looked bad enough, so pale and thin, when he had returned from war, but Tom looked totally different. He had been well fed, so he did not look thin and under nourished, as Fred and the other men in the Lane had. The difference being, Tom had a terrible stare in his eyes and he did not speak. The only words he kept muttering over and over again were 'terrible, terrible, so much blood, all the blood, innocent people' and then he would scream out in terror. The nightmares were worse at night. He would wake up screaming in a cold sweat and then end up sobbing. Amelia did her best to comfort him and try to coax him back to normality, but all to no avail.

★   ★   ★

Eventually she called in Doctor Fisher and pleaded for help with Tom, who was making no progress whatsoever.

'What did the army doctors tell you about Tom's condition Mrs. Burrows?'

'They said Tom had been discharged as being medically unfit for future service with the Regiment, he was suffering from nerves probably due to battle fatigue.'

'Mrs. Burrows your husband is suffering a nervous breakdown, due to some terrible thing he has witnessed.'

'But Tom is a regular soldier, or was. He was used to doing battle with the enemy. Will he ever recover? Will I ever get my Tom back? Tell me Doctor please . . . ?' Amelia pleaded.

'It is impossible to say. Sometimes people make a good recovery and some never do. The one thing I can tell you, he must have witnessed something really catastrophic to have this effect on him. Perhaps time will heal and gradually this thing that upsets him so much may fade from his mind. Time is a great healer and with the passing of time memories dull and become less real. All you can do for the moment is carry on with the tender loving care and pray to God your husband will be returned to good health.'

★   ★   ★

Fred was now feeling much stronger and had returned to work for Mr. Griffin, who was delighted to have him back. He had kept an eye on Flo, while Fred was away. From time to time he had sent his housekeeper down to the house with a basket of fruit and some gifts of clothing for the boys. He was careful not to do it too often, as Flo was a proud woman and did not take too kindly to charity. He always slipped a little note in saying, 'To my adopted family, whom I love very much. Please accept these small gifts and make an old man very happy. Yours Louis Griffin.'

Florence always accepted the gifts and made a point of calling on the old man with the boys to thank him. It would seem churlish to refuse his kindness. She did try to scold him, in a kindly way, over his generosity to them.

'You have done more than enough for us Mr. Griffin, by giving us our home, without spending more of your money on us.'

'I have no one else to spend it on my dear. You are the nearest thing I have to a family.'

*   *   *

Tom had now been home over 3 months. It was Summer, the sun was shining and everyone was happy. It was their first Summer in 4 years without war and the dread it brought. People felt good to be alive, but still there was no improvement in Tom. Amelia had persuaded him to sit in a chair in the garden and enjoy the sunshine. He would just sit there staring into space. It could have been pouring with rain for all he knew or cared. Fred and Florence were also puzzled at what could have caused Tom's mental state.

'I don't understand it Flo. There has been nothing in the papers about this place Amritsar in India, where Tom came back from. So what could have upset him so much? Unless there was some sort of block on the newspapers reporting it.'

By October news of the massacre at Amritsar began to filter through and at last Tom was beginning to talk about his bad experience there. One evening he took hold of Amelia's hand and begged her to listen to him.

'I could not speak of what happened before now. It was so terrible, but I feel I must talk so people will know and understand what really happened. You must be brave my dear, for what I am going to tell and describe to you is so horrific, it may upset you terribly.'

'If it helps you to get better by talking about it, then I will be brave and strong and listen to every word you say. I will not flinch or shy away from what you are telling me, no matter how terrible it is. I'm just so pleased to have you back with us again. I would have paid any price for your safe return.'

'My garrison was stationed 50 miles away at Jullundur. Sir Michael O'Dwyer had summoned reinforcements for the local garrison. We arrived by train. Brigadier General Reginald Dyer came with us to take up the Amritsar Military Command. It was Sunday 13th April, a day I will never forget for the rest of my life. This was the day of an important Sikh festival called 'Baisakhi Day'. People had travelled from miles around to celebrate this important festival. The weary travellers rested at Jallianwala Bagh. That is a piece of waste ground, which was surrounded by high walls. The only access was through a narrow alleyway. The order was given to about 50 of us, to fire at the crowd. No warning was given to these unarmed civilians, panic ensued. There was no escape for the poor devils. I saw the utter disbelief and shock and look of fear on their faces. One poor chap was trying to run away when he was shot in the back. His white clothing was soaked bright red with his blood. A dark haired lady stood over him screaming and lamenting. Her screams were terrible. I can still hear them now. They did not last long, for she was shot too. There was blood everywhere. It was like one big red river, running with innocent people's blood and I was part of that.'

★   ★   ★

At that point Tom broke down and sobbed uncontrollably. Amelia was so touched by his genuine remorse. She had never seen her big strong handsome Tom cry before. She tried to comfort him as best she could, but she felt inadequate. What could she say, what could she do? It was so terrible, in her whole life she had never heard anything so terrible. He would never be the same again, she knew that now. The devil may care, full of fun Tom, that had first wooed her at Uncle John's wedding. He was so handsome and dashing in his uniform. A uniform he would now be ashamed to wear. That Tom was gone from her forever.

'Tom don't upset yourself any further. Please that's enough for today. You can tell me the rest another day.'

'No I must finish. There were bodies everywhere. I think there must have been as many people mown down as lost their lives on the Titanic. I tried very hard not to kill anyone, by deliberately trying to miss them, but I'm sure I did. In the panic people were darting everywhere. They just dropped like flies. Then the order was given to 'Stop, about turn and withdraw'. We marched rifles at the slope, back down the alleyway. Leaving a terrible carnage behind us. I don't even know if anyone managed to survive. I feel so ashamed to be British.

This was the British army I was once so proud to serve. When I first joined the army as a regular soldier, I knew I would have to fight and kill for the country I loved so much. This was acceptable to me, in a fair fight, soldier to soldier. I did not know I would ever have to kill unarmed civilians. I come from a family with a long history of military men and I too wanted to carry on the family tradition and was very proud to do so but now I'm so pleased to be away from army life, and am glad to have been discharged. If Albert ever has any thoughts of joining up, I will do all in my power to stop him.' Tom by now was exhausted and soon fell asleep. While he was asleep Amelia took the opportunity to run around to Doctor Fisher's house to explain what had just occurred with Tom. Doctor Fisher said, this was a good sign, that Tom was now talking again and by bringing out in the open what had been troubling him. It showed he was now on his way to a good recovery. He gave her something to help Tom sleep that night, just in case he could not get to sleep after his afternoon exhaustive sleep.

'He may sleep for many hours, but leave him be. He needs the rest so don't worry.'

Fred had been right. A press censorship had been imposed. The massacre had taken place on 13th April 1919 and it was October before London knew. Official death toll was put at 379, but Indian sources claimed 500 to 1,000 as the true figure. The Hunter Committee was set up to establish facts and apportion blame, and Reginald Dyer was asked to resign.

★ ★ ★

Gradually Tom began to recover and thought that he must soon find a job to support his family, especially now as Amelia was pregnant. Amelia was over the moon finding herself pregnant.

She and Tom had just started living as husband and wife again and she fell pregnant immediately. Uncle John had offered Tom a job in his butcher's shop. One of his assistants had been killed in the war and he was rather short handed. Tom had to decline his kind offer, although it would have been a Godsend.

He could not stand the sight of blood any more, even animal blood. To see all those carcasses of hanging animals made him want to puke.

★　★　★

Flo told Fred the good news about Amelia's pregnancy. They were so pleased Tom was improving and getting back to his old self again.

'Have you noticed how old Tom is looking lately? He has a sad look about him all the time. He's lost that boyish cheeky grin he always had. It seems like his youth has gone from him too early. He's still a relatively young man, yet at times he looks really old.'

'Aye it's a bad business, war.'

Florence looked at Fred and suddenly felt

sorry for him. He had suffered too through this terrible world war and had been awarded medals. He had received the General Service Medal and Victory Medals. Florence flung her arms around his neck and kissed him.

'I love you so much Fred. I can never tell you how much. You have suffered greatly as well. Everyone seems to have forgotten you and what you went through for your country. As soon as Tom came home, the whole family centred their attention on him and seemed to forget about you.'

'Never mind lass. I've got you and my two fine lads, I'll not ask for more and I came home in one piece. Tom is to be pitied though. I fought a fair battle against other soldiers who were at war with us, not waging war on innocent civilians as Tom had to. He deserves all the sympathy he can get.'

★　★　★

The following year Amelia gave birth to a little girl. They named her Alice, Jane. Fred and Florence were happy to have been asked to be her Godparents. Her brother Albert was now 11 years old and was very pleased about the new addition to the family.

He was still very sensitive and did not like being in Flo's house for very long. If he was left alone in a room for any length of time, he would immediately go to where there were other people in the house. If he sensed a presence in the house, or a change in temperature, he would immediately glance across at Flo. He knew that, she knew as he did, that all was not well in the house. Flo never discussed it with any of the children for fear of frightening them and Albert had learned a long time ago not to mention ghosts and things to his cousins, for fear of ridicule, especially from James. Flo was very fond of Albert.

He was her favourite out of their two nephews. She found James a bit too cocky and sure of himself and was a right little know all, even at the age of eleven. Probably takes after his arrogant father Leyton-Barrie, who thinks he can do just as he likes, trampling all over people.

'You're very quiet lass. Anything wrong?'

'No I was just thinking about our Rose. She's getting a bit of a name for herself, always out and about with men. Some of them married, I've heard tell. She is the exact opposite to Mary, so quiet and timid. She would dearly wish to find a husband and settle down. There does not seem much chance of that with nearly a whole generation of young men killed in the war. There doesn't seem anyone suitable about. She would make a wonderful wife for some man, so caring and loving.'

'Unfortunately a lot of men would prefer Rose, who has spirit and is rather headstrong and full of life. Poor Mary is a bit plain and dull. No doubt about it, you and Amelia are the lookers in your family.'

'What are you after Fred Preston?'

'A nice cup of tea and a piece of your home made fruit cake.'

7

'Bridget have ye heard the terrible news?'

'What news Willy? Calm down, and tell me what ails ye.'

'The Lord Mayor of Cork, Tomas MacCurtain has been shot down and killed. The assassins were heard to speak with an English accent. That means it was either the Auxies or the scum of the earth Black and Tans. Things are sure as hell getting worse. I knew they would. The minute Lloyd George sent over the Black and Tans I knew there would be trouble. No self respecting Irish man is going to take this lying down.'

'Oh God not more reprisals! They'll do no good at all and we'll be the ones who have to bear the brunt of it. The innocent people will be the ones to suffer.'

'I was going to have a farewell drink with Desmond O'Leary tonight. He's had enough and is moving to Southampton. He has family already over there. They are happy and well settled and have been asking him to join them for ages. So he's decided to go before things get any worse here. Are ye alright Biddy? You look very pale, are ye sickening for something? If ye don't want me to go I won't. I'll be after telling him yer sick. Annie can pop down to his house with a note.'

'No I'm just tired. You go I'll be alright. I didn't get much sleep last night. That's all. I'll have an early night.'

'Can we sleep in yer big bed till Pop comes back from Desmond's, Mother? You could read us all a story,' pleaded Jack.

'Now leave yer Ma alone children. I'll read ye a story, but first we'll have our lesson in Gaelic. Now who can count to ten for me?'

'I can count to three Pop.'

'Can ye Jack. Go on let's hear it then.'

'A haon, a dho, a tri. Did I get it right Pop?'

'Yes Jackie me boy, ye certainly did. Well done.'

'Huh that's not very clever. I can count to ten.' Jack looked upset and had tears in his eyes at Maggie's sharp words.

'Alright Miss Clever Knickers, answer me this then. What does Sinn Fein mean?'

'That's not fair. Jack's question was much easier than mine.'

'Maggie you're 14 years old. Jack is only seven. His question was just as hard as yours. Sinn Fein means 'We ourselves'.'

'Willy I don't want ye teaching the children anything political. These are hard times we are living in and the least they know about the troubles the better. I mean it now, do you hear me.'

Willy was about to protest but seeing how ill Bridget looked, thought it would keep for another day. She had been looking ill a lot lately. Willy felt a slight pang of unease. I'm sure everything is not well with her. I must try and get her to a Doctor, and soon. He thought he would change the subject.

'Jesus, that Maggie is so jealous of her brother and sisters. I swear to God she was born with jealousy in her soul. Jealousy is worse than galloping consumption. Twas Mrs. Dunn's favourite saying when her brood were fighting over some possession or other.'

'Was there ever a time then, when the family were not fighting? I think they are still fighting to this day.'

They both laughed and gave each other a hug, and Willy set off down the hill to Desmond's house. He lived at the bottom end of Harbour View.

⋆ ⋆ ⋆

Bridget washed the dishes and tidied up before she decided to settle down for the night. The children were bouncing about on their double bed and the noise was getting unbearable. As she had to go upstairs and sort out the children, she thought she might as well stay there herself. Willy won't be back for hours yet. Once he gets talking to Desmond, it could be the early hours of the morning before he is back.

'Now quiet children. The boys next door were asleep long since. I thought you were all coming tru me ceiling, the way ye were all jumping off our bed like that.'

'Can we stay in yer bed a little bit longer Mother, please?'

'Ten more minutes Bridie, that's all.'

Bridget undressed and got into bed and within a few minutes was sound asleep. The children gradually one by one fell asleep.

They were all woken suddenly by shouting, yelling and the front door being pounded and eventually kicked in. Bridget suddenly sat up in bed and looked at the clock. My God it's midnight and Willy is still not back. There was a thunder of heavy boots on the stairs. The children began to cry and shake with fear.

'Hush children. Don't cry, don't say anything and don't look up at the soldiers. Keep yer heads down and be quiet now.'

The children clung to Bridget and had their arms around each other. The bedroom door was flung open and into the room rushed a posse of Black and Tans.

'We're searching for IRA. You had better not be hiding any.'

'There is no one here, save me and the children.'

After a further search of the house, they left. Bridget began to shake with delayed shock.

'Don't be upset Mother. They are gone now.'

'I'm not upset Ellee, just a little cold.'

She could still hear the yelling and shouting next door at the Finnegans and wondered if Pete was with Willy saying farewell to Desmond, and if Fay was alone with the boys as she had been with her children. She hoped Pete was not there either. Knowing his temper he would not be able to keep his mouth shut and may be taken out and shot, or accused of being IRA and marched off somewhere to be interrogated and killed later. As luck would have it, most of the men were all still in the pub wishing Desmond 'Bon Voyage'. The only male occupant of the whole road, was the elderly deaf man a few doors away. Bridget thanked the Lord all the men folk were safely out of the way while the military searches were taking place.

A few weeks later Bridget was returning

from shopping when she thought she heard some shots being fired in the distance. She looked around and could not see anything so she continued her journey home. She was just approaching the steps between the houses which led up to Harbour View, and dreading the long climb up them. These days she was always exhausted when she reached the top. She must be getting old or something. As she reached the bottom of the steps she saw a large crowd had gathered half way up and Jesse Doyle was rushing back down the steps in a state of great agitation.

'Jesse what's happened? Why are all those people there?'

'It's the deaf man. He's been shot down dead by the Black and Tans. He was climbing the steps to get home when they called out, ordering him to halt. He didn't stop. They called out again 'Halt or we'll shoot'. Still he continued slowly up the steps. One of the women in the cliff houses rushed out and pleaded with them, not to shoot him as he was stone deaf. They just ignored her and shot him anyway.'

'Did they not hear her call out to them, Jesse?'

'Of course they did. They just wanted an excuse to shoot a poor defenceless old man.'

Bridget continued up the steps trying to

choke back the tears. The poor old man. He was always kind to the children, always a smile and a wave as they went off to school, they were all fond of him too. I don't know how I'm going to tell them what has happened to him. As she reached the crowd, she gasped in horror. On the ground lay the poor old man in a crumpled heap. Blood was seeping from his terrible wounds. There was a bloody hand print on the wall. He must have reached out and tried to grasp the wall before he fell to the ground and died. How could anyone be so cruel to a poor old man who never did anyone any harm. Bridget's blood began to boil, anger and hate began to fill her heart. A hate she never knew she was capable of before. For the first time in her life she began to wish she was away from her beloved Ireland, that she was somewhere safe with her family. Where they could roam safely, without being in fear of their lives. She had never had any wish to leave her homeland before. She loved everything about it. The countryside, the beautiful scenery. Her lovely little home that looked out on the harbour. She had been happy there. Willy was the wanderer in the family. He would live anywhere, provided he could earn a living to support his family. She had put his wanderlust down to his father being a sea captain and him not having a very happy and stable upbringing as a child.

* * *

Bridget had decided to tell the children that the old deaf man was coming back from the shops and was on the very steep steps up to their road when he died. He was now in heaven with all the other members of his family that had gone before him.

She asked them all not to use the steps for a while, but to walk down the road when going and coming home from school.

She hoped that the blood would all be cleaned away before the children would see it and be upset by it. But the people living within the vicinity of the cliff and steps had other ideas.

They had a meeting and decided to leave the blood there for all to see, as a constant reminder of what the Black and Tans were capable of.

* * *

Willy was as shocked as Bridget when he heard.

'They're not content with marauding tru our homes in the middle of the night. They are now killing our neighbours off. I tell ye Bridget no-one is safe anymore. They are nothing but a bunch of evil murderers. Several of the men in the pub were talking last night and are going to join the IRA.'

'I hope ye weren't one of them Willy?'

'No Bridget I wasn't and neither was Pete next door. But young Sean Lynch is one of them. I had suspected he was a member for a long time. He was trying to put pressure on Pete to join the cause and said it would be a pity if Seamus Devlin found out about him and Kathleen. He was very drunk at the time. I hope it was only the drink talking for Pete's sake.'

'What did Pete say to that?'

'Nothing, he went very white, drank up and left the pub.'

★   ★   ★

The next day all the children arrived home from school together, led by a triumphant Maggie. Ellee, Bridie and Jack were all crying and Annie was badly shaken.

Maggie could hardly wait to tell Bridget what she had found out at school.

'All the girls at school said the deaf man was murdered by the Black and Tans and all his blood was on the wall and steps. So we all went around and had a look after school. They were right. There was blood everywhere.'

'Maggie, Maggie, what have ye done? I specifically told ye to keep away from the steps. Ye deliberately disobeyed me and have upset your sisters and brother. Look at the state they are all in. The little ones will have nightmares tonight, I shouldn't wonder. Now get up to your room this instant and I'll tell your father when he gets home. He'll think of a suitable punishment for yer disobedience. Next time you go to confession, don't forget to confess to the Priest yer disobedience and upset ye have caused yer family today.'

Maggie began to protest. 'But all the girls at school,' before she could finish Bridget screamed and pointed a finger towards the stairs.

'Go and go now before I totally lose control.'

★   ★   ★

A few weeks had passed since the old deaf man's murder and things seemed to have quietened down, for the moment at least. Ellee was returning from school one lunchtime with her best friend Sarah. They chatted for a while at the top of the cliff and made arrangements to walk back to school together after dinner.

Ellee had to run an errand for Bridget and was a little late meeting Sarah at the top of the cliff. As she approached the meeting place, she could see Sarah was not waiting for her. She thought she must have got fed up and went on to school without her. There was a commotion going on in the yard of one of the houses at the foot of the cliff. A boy from her school rushed up the steps and said 'Sarah Courtney fell down the cliff and she's dead.'

Ellee stood for a long time, not moving, numb with shock, till one of the neighbours gently took her hand and led her down the steps and into the house. She was taken to a room where she saw Sarah laid out. She could not recognize Sarah, her head was completely swathed in bandages, she only knew it was her from the clothes she had been wearing that day.

Paddy Murphy decided it was time to take Ellee home and guided her gently to the door.

'I'll take ye home Ellee, you'll not be going back to school this afternoon.' Ellee still could not speak, she was in a state of utter shock.

* ⋆ ⋆

Bridget tried to comfort her as best she could but words failed her. She knew how much Sarah meant to her, she was her best friend. A few days later Mrs. Courtney sent one of the boys up to the house with a few trinkets for Ellee which had belonged to Sarah. She said Sarah would have wanted Ellee to have them. Bridget was deeply touched by her kindness, in thinking of Ellee in this very sad period of deep family mourning.

⋆ ⋆ ⋆

'Here's a letter from England with the post. It must be from Desmond.' Willy opened the letter eagerly. 'Sure he seems very happy in Southampton. He said to come on over. He tinks we would be able to find work over there, especially for Maggie and Annie. There are lots of positions for young girls in service.'

'Sure I'm not going into service and being someone's servant. I hate housework and cooking.'

'You'll do as yer told me girl.'

Bridget called out from the kitchen. 'Now stop it you two. I can't stand the arguing this early in the morning. It gives me a headache.

We'll discuss going to Southampton another time.'

'Do you mean it Bridget? You have never before even considered leaving dear old Cobh.'

'I've been doing a lot of tinking lately, tings are getting much worse. I cannot see an end to the troubles for a long time. A new start may be just the ting we all need, but not just yet. I don't want to rush into anything, I have to gradually get used to the idea.'

★   ★   ★

Later that afternoon Bridget thought she would pop down to the shops, to get a few things she had run out of, when she met Fay on her way back.

'Who do you tink I just saw coming from the harbour Bridget? Seamus Devlin! He's back in port and he was heading for his house at great speed with a look as black as thunder on his face. I've never seen that man move so fast. You would tink the divil himself was after him. Do ye tink he's trying to catch Kathleen out with a man? He must have been told something.'

Bridget thought, God I hope Pete is not in there, remembering what Willy had said about Sean Lynch's threat. Poor Fay, she hasn't any idea.

* * *

As luck would have it Kathleen was sitting having a cup of tea with Marie O'Connell, another loose young woman. Also deceiving her poor gullible husband Martin. She would tell him she was baby sitting for the neighbours to earn a little cash to help the family income in these hard times, but any cash she received was not from baby sitting. He would stay home looking after their three children while she was out cavorting around with Kathleen, in pubs and people's houses. Anywhere they could find some fun and entertainment. When he smelt the drink on her breath, she said the grateful people she was sitting for insisted she had some spirits to keep her warm through the long evening till their return. And she didn't like to hurt their feelings by refusing. Martin said to go easy on the drink as sometimes she'd stagger home very drunk. She promised she would and laughed to herself, how easy he was to deceive.

* * *

The door burst open and Seamus stood there. Red faced and puffing from exertion, from his climb up the hill. Although Kathleen was shocked to see him standing there, she did not know his ship was due in yet. She managed to put on a big smile and seemed pleased to see him.

'Hello darlin'. What a lovely surprise. I didn't know you were due home yet. Why didn't you write me and sure I could have had a lovely meal cooked for ye?'

'Don't darlin' me. What's this I hear about you and another man? I received an anonymous letter while away at sea, saying you were carrying on with another man. When I find out who he is I'll break him in two, sure I will.'

Kathleen was shaken by this, and managed to put on a good act of a wronged woman with the help of Marie.

'Jesus who would write such a letter about me? There is an evil tongue at work here. A very evil tongue indeed, to want to come between a happily married woman and her man. It must be jealousy, pure and simple jealousy.'

'Seamus, Kathleen has been with me most evenings. Baby sitting to earn a little cash for me family. She comes along to keep me company. It gets a bit lonely sat on yer own, staring at the four walls, in someone else's house. Ask my Martin he'll tell ye, what I say is true and may God forgive the sinner of these terrible lies.'

'I intend to. Is he home from work yet?'

'No, but he'll be home within the hour. I'd best be off now to prepare his evening meal. Goodbye Seamus. You and Kathleen have a lovely evening together now.'

Once outside Marie thought, I must find Pete to stop him making his usual teatime stop off on the way home. God that Seamus would break him in two. I don't know how Kathleen ever came to marry such a brute. Before she could get to Pete, Sean Lynch had got there first.

'Have you heard the news Pete? Seamus Devlin is home, and on the war path so I hear. Looking for the man who's carrying on with his Kathleen.'

'Ye bastard, you've told him.'

'Steady on Pete. He doesn't know who it is yet, only that there is someone. It would be a great pity sure it would, if he were to be given the name of that person.'

'You wouldn't do that to me Sean. I've never done you any harm. Why are you doing this to me?'

'Now calm down Pete, there is an easy solution to your little dilemma. Come along to the meeting of the cause tonight and he'll never find out.'

'What! . . . Join the IRA, I could be killed.'

'Well as I see it Pete me boy, ye are going to be killed anyway. Either by your Fay, when she finds out, or more likely by Seamus and Batt Devlin. It would be a terrible ting, if tomorrow we wake up to hear the sad news of yer body floating in the harbour, all battered and tortured. No, yer best bet would be to join the IRA, you'll be safest with us, and ye will be fighting for yer country. A very noble thing to be doing. Shall I tell the others to expect ye tonight then?'

'You leave me no choice.'

'Good man. I'll call round for ye about seven then. We'll tell your Fay, we are after going for a drink down the pub with a few of the boys.'

Pete began to walk slowly home, saying over and over again to himself, Jesus what have I done, what have I done? As Willy came sprinting up the hill behind him, he caught sight of the dejected figure of Pete walking slowly ahead of him, head down and shoulders hunched over. Even from a distance he could see something was seriously wrong. Pete usually had a confident air in his stride and always seemed in control and cock sure of himself, but this was something different. A Pete that Willy had never known before, a sad dejected looking figure, someone to be pitied.

'Pete stop. What's the matter, you look dreadful? What's happened? Did Seamus catch up with you? I've heard he's back in port.'

'No not yet, but if I don't join the IRA they will hand me over to him and Batt. So I had no choice, I've agreed to join.'

'Ye did what! Pete ye eejit! Do ye know what you're getting yourself into?'

Pete was ashen. He just kept shaking his head, and saying 'I had no choice, no choice.'

'Well I hope Kathleen Devlin is worth risking your life for.'

The conversation ended between the two as they reached their respective front doors.

8

Tom Burrows sat in the neat little kitchen of number eleven, relaxing, reading the newspaper and enjoying a cup of tea with his dear beautiful wife Amelia. Alice was asleep in her pram and Albert was at school. He was making a fast recovery from his breakdown and began to feel that life was worth living again. He still could not find work he was suited to after spending years in the Regiment. While he continued to search for a decent job, he decided to do odd gardening jobs for some of the rich old ladies in the area. As it was lunchtime he thought he would pop back home and spend an hour with Amelia before his afternoon gardening job. He was still as much in love with her as the first day they had met. He knew then it was love at first sight and wanted to spend the rest of his life with her. Still so beautiful, always kind and loving. He was a lucky man indeed, to have someone so special in his life.

Perhaps it was a blessing in disguise to come out of the Regiment the way he had. Now he could spend every day with her for the rest of his life. They say every cloud has a silver lining, Tom mused to himself.

★ ★ ★

He turned the page of the newspaper and an article caught his eye.

'Amelia listen to this. 350 of the Connaught Rangers stationed in Jullundur in the Punjab, that's where I was stationed — laid down arms and refused to soldier for England any longer, as a protest at the news from Eire. 62 were court martialled, 1 executed and others sentenced to terms of penal servitude for periods of 2 – 20 years.' He suddenly looked saddened.

'It was a pity we didn't do the same at Amritsar, those poor devils would be alive today.'

'Tom don't go upsetting yourself all over again. We can't turn the clock back. We must try to go on with our lives as best we can.'

'I know you're right Amelia, but it is not that easy to forget. It will stay with me till the end of my days. I still have nightmares you know.'

'I know, I know my dearest love.' Amelia put her arms around him and held him tightly. Not saying a word, just loving him.

No words were necessary between them.

115

Her love for him was as great as his was for her. As Amelia moved her head slightly, she caught sight of the clock on the mantelpiece.

'Speaking of clocks Tom, look at the time it's gone two o'clock. You'll be getting the sack for being late for your afternoon job, and which old lady is it this afternoon pray?'

Tom laughed, 'It's Mr. Griffin's garden actually. So don't go getting jealous of all my old ladies.'

He gave her a quick peck on the cheek and was out the door in an instant.

★   ★   ★

Amelia was smiling to herself as she started to clear away the dishes. He's right. I do get jealous when he's out of my sight. Despite all he has been through, he's still a very handsome man. Her thoughts were interrupted by the opening and closing of Florence's front door and then the sound of heavy footsteps walking down the hall. That's funny, they are all out next door. I know Flo has gone to spend the afternoon with Mother, she left more than an hour ago. Anyway it sounded like a man's footsteps. Perhaps Fred had come back for something. I'd better go and check. Amelia felt decidedly uneasy. She went out to the back garden and

116

through the gap in the hedge and up the path to the back door. Everything seemed to be in order. The back door was securely fastened. She looked through the scullery and parlour windows, she could see nothing amiss. Everything is silent as a grave she thought, and shivered slightly, although it was a hot afternoon. She decided to check the front of the house. She looked through the letter box down the long dark hall and then the front room window. Everything appeared in order. She must have imagined she heard someone. She went back indoors feeling very uneasy.

★   ★   ★

When Flo returned a few hours later, Amelia related what she had heard. Flo just shrugged it off and said, 'It must have been the ghost.'

'Flo, how can you joke about something like this. It really frightened me. I thought it might have been a burglar.'

'I have lived with that ghost all these years and no one will believe me. So I've decided to ignore him, then perhaps he might go away and leave us all in peace, but I must agree with you. It can be quite frightening at times.'

'Flo you said he. How do you know the ghost is a man?'

'Because I've seen him.'

'When, where? You didn't tell me.'

'It was the time when Fred was away at the Western Front. I was woken up one morning by a movement at the bedroom door. When I looked up, I saw a man peering at me. He was horrible, he had black hair, was dirty and unshaven and was wearing a plaid waistcoat. He was a real down and out, almost like a tramp. I was paralysed with shock. I couldn't even scream. I could only manage a gasp and then he disappeared. I rushed into the boys' room. They were alright both sound asleep. I decided not to tell anyone. The neighbours were already saying I was going mad, thinking Fred would be back from the war after I received the telegram saying he was missing, presumed killed.'

'No one was saying that Flo, were they?'

'Oh yes they were. I walked into the corner shop one day and Mrs. Jones and Mrs. Butler were deep in conversation about us. Neither heard me open the door. They were saying Florrie Preston had gone mad, thinking her husband would be coming back, and as for that stuck up sister of hers with her husband in the Regiment . . . So I gave them both a piece of my mind and they left the shop very red faced, much to Mr. Blackman's amusement.'

'Well really.' Amelia was quite indignant.

'And I thought they were so nice. Always saying good morning and asking after Tom.'

'Dear Amelia, sometimes you are so innocent. You must learn never to trust everyone. They are not what they all pretend to be. Mrs. Butler has more faces than the town hall clock and she likes nothing more than a good gossip.'

Amelia began to laugh, Flo could always cheer her up, make her laugh when she was down. She had a wonderful sense of humour.

'Seriously Flo, I'm worried about you in that house, especially when you are alone. Does Fred or the boys ever sense anything strange?'

'No never. Perhaps that is a blessing in disguise. I think the less they know, the less they will be troubled by the ghost.'

'But Fred heard the footsteps that Christmas years ago. We all did.'

'Do you remember how he explained it away? Floorboards cooling down after the heat of the cooking and the heavy tramp of people all day. He always says, 'There is a logical explanation for everything,' which I don't agree with, but I have given up arguing over it long ago.'

'Are you not frightened by it all?'

'I used to be, but I'm still here after all these years. If he wanted to harm me he would have done it long ago, but sometimes it does get a bit unnerving. Now let's change the subject. I'm fed up talking about him.'

'A little bit of news from Mother. Rose is currently walking out with a sailor named Bill Edmonds. He spends a lot of time away at sea. So Rose can continue the life style she has become accustomed to. Out drinking every night, playing the field. Mother is quite distressed by her behaviour. She does exactly as she likes, with not a thought for others. The whole neighbourhood is talking about her. Poor Mother, she always did worry about what the neighbours thought.'

'I can just hear Mrs. Butler talking. 'Poor Beatrice, what she has to put up with, those daughters of hers. There's Florrie quite mad, thinks she knows everything, and Amelia, stuck up little madam with her husband once being in the Regiment. That Rose, well I wouldn't give her house room, nothing but a cheap little whore. Then Mary, an unclaimed treasure. She's so plain I'm afraid she's doomed. Doomed I'd say, to remain an old maid on the shelf forever. Still she is harmless enough I suppose, not like the other three, way above themselves.'

Amelia collapsed in the chair, laughing uncontrollably, she paused for a moment to catch her breath, then began laughing all over again.

'Flo you're such a good mimic. That sounded just like Mrs. Butler. But she's wrong you know about our Mary.'

'What do you mean? Don't tell me she has met someone at long last.'

'Not exactly. Ernest Cunningham has proposed to her and she's seriously thinking about accepting his offer.'

'What marry her boss! He's years older than her and a tight old skinflint at that. He's looking for a nurse maid to look after him now he's getting old. I don't think she should accept. He's nothing but a slave driver. I don't know how she has put up with him all these years.'

'But Flo, this may be the only chance she ever gets and after all she will be well provided for if anything happens to him.'

'Nothing will happen to him. He'll live to a hundred, the old buzzard. I bet he's still here long after Mary. He'll have driven her into the ground with hard work.'

★   ★   ★

In spite of Florence's warning, about what she was letting herself in for and trying to persuade her that marriage to Ernest

Cunningham would be no bed of roses, Mary was adamant she was going to marry him and that was that. The marriage was planned for the late Autumn. It was a small affair, which did not surprise Florence one bit. Too tight to give our sister a decent wedding, the old Scrooge thought Flo venomously. The only people at the wedding were Mary's immediate family and one niece from his side. He did not want a church wedding but this was the one thing Beatrice insisted on and eventually got her way. Mary looked radiant in a gold brocade suit, the family had never seen Mary look so attractive, she just glowed with happiness. Uncle John gave her away and Ernest's niece Angela Cunningham, was the only bridesmaid. After the ceremony a small reception was held in the church hall and then the happy couple left for a honeymoon in Cornwall.

The honeymoon was soon over for poor Mary. They were no sooner home and back working in the shop together, when another more crueller side of Ernest emerged. He was even more demanding of her than when she was employed by him. She seemed to be forever at his beck and call, more like a servant than a wife. She dreaded the evenings when his business associates would call.

He seemed to get great pleasure from

ridiculing her in front of his friends. Mary longed for the evening to be over so she could creep away to bed and often cried herself to sleep.

Within a month of marriage Mary realised the terrible mistake she had made. Florence had been right all along, she had never liked him from the first day she set eyes on him. When I first went to work for him I knew he could be a hard man but I did not know the depths of his cruelty.

★   ★   ★

Soon the terrible beatings began. Usually after a drinking bout with his friends. One evening she was sat by the fire, it was her birthday and Ernest had not even acknowledged the fact. During the day all the family came round to the shop with presents for her. When they asked what Ernest had given her, she lied and said that she would have his present that evening. He was away on business in London and would be bringing her back something nice from the big city. The real truth was a different matter. He arrived home from London roaring drunk and saw her sat by the fire with the presents on her lap from her family. A cardigan lovingly made by Beatrice, a book from

Florence. A beautiful frilly blouse made by Amelia and a bottle of perfume from Rose.

'What's all this rubbish then?'

'It's not rubbish Ernest, it's my birthday and they are all presents from my family,' replied Mary timidly.

'Your family, your family,' mocked Ernest cruelly. 'I'm fed up with hearing about your family' and with a sudden swoop he scooped up all the presents and flung the lot on the fire. The perfume had dropped from his hand and broken in the grate. The air was filled with the most beautiful aroma of the perfume. Only half an hour before she vowed to put it away and only use it on very special occasions. Rose had asked one of her sailor friends to bring back the perfume from America. It was very expensive and Mary had been delighted. She lunged forward to try and retrieve the presents from the fire but it was too late, the flames had greedily devoured the lot. Each item was so badly burnt that even if she could have retrieved them they would have been useless. All she could do was watch the remainder of the items burn away to ash. Tears streaming down her face, she knelt down to pick up the remains of the perfume bottle. It contained a small amount in the base of the bottle.

Perhaps she could save these last few drops of the perfume. Suddenly she felt blows raining down on her head and she was being viciously kicked in the ribs. She thought she was going to die and then mercifully she fainted.

She did not know how long she had lain there, but when she came to she was cold and stiff. There was no sign of Ernest, having kicked her half senseless he retired to bed. She was black and blue from the beating. Dry blood was crusted around her mouth from a nose bleed and some of her teeth had been knocked out. She looked a terrible sight in the hall mirror. The pain from her ribs was excruciating and she was in agony when she breathed. She realised she probably had broken ribs.

★   ★   ★

When Ernest eventually appeared, he eyed the pitiful sight before him. 'I best call Dr. Fisher and let him see the terrible state you're in after falling down the stairs.'

Mary opened her mouth to protest, she caught the meaningful look in his eye, daring her to speak or go against him. She knew with a sinking heart there would be plenty more where that came from, with or without drink.

She knew he was capable of cruelty beyond her imagination.

★ ★ ★

When Dr. Fisher arrived he was appalled at the state Mary was in.

'My wife is such a stupid clumsy little thing Doctor. Fancy her falling down the stairs like that. She fell from the top to the bottom you know. I thank God it was not more serious. I keep telling her to stop rushing around, there is plenty of time, but will she listen no.'

'Is that right Mary? Is that how all this happened?' Fisher had his suspicions about her injuries but could not prove it.

Mary meekly nodded her head in agreement with her husband. After bandaging her ribs and confirming several were broken, he left the Cunningham's residence troubled and not knowing what to do for the best. I don't know what her mother and sisters will think when they find out. They are a strong lot, I hope they can sort him out. Falling down stairs indeed. He must think I was born yesterday. She took a beating from him more like. She's absolutely terrified of him. The bastard. I never liked the man but I wouldn't have had him down as a wife beater. It just goes to show you never can tell about people.

'Flo I was just going shopping. I thought we could go together and drop in on Mary and see what present Ernest brought her back from London.'

'Good idea Ame, I'll just get my coat and basket.'

As they both approached the shop they could see Mary through the window. She had her back to the window so she did not see them coming. She did not have a chance to escape into the back room, as she had planned if any of her family should come into the shop that day. The door was suddenly flung open and in marched Florence and Amelia, talking and laughing loudly.

'Did you have a lovely 36th birthday and what did?' Amelia did not finish the sentence. The words died on her lips, so shocked were they both at the sight that met their eyes. A swollen eyed battered looking Mary. Her face was covered in bruises.

'My God Mary whatever has happened to you?' Amelia waited almost frightened of the answer she was going to get.

Florence stood staring at Ernest, knowing but hardly believing he had some hand in all of this. Her stare was so penetrating it unnerved him slightly for a moment. Then he gained his composure and answered.

'Your silly little sister fell down the stairs. I keep telling her to be more careful. She's getting very clumsy and accident prone of late.'

'How dare you call our sister silly. The only silly thing she ever did in her life was to marry you,' stormed Florence. 'And what's more if I find out you had any part in this . . . ' Florence hesitated, 'so called accident, you will pay and pay dearly. I will personally take it upon myself to see that you do. I shall leave no stone unturned till I get to the bottom of this.'

Florence left the shop, slamming the door loudly with Amelia close on her heels. Once outside the anger subsided and the tears began to flow.

★ ★ ★

Inside the shop a shaken, angry Ernest advanced on Mary, fist clenched. He came to within an inch of her face. Mary backed away, frightened there would be a repetition of the night before.

'If any of your family interfere with me or my business, they will be the ones sorry not me. I think you had better take a trip around to your sisters tonight. Explain how you fell down the stairs and how she was mistaken in thinking I had anything to do with it. And you had better make it convincing my girl, or next time it will be worse. I may even chop you up and feed your remains to the swans on the Cemetery Lake. When your sisters are strolling on the Common, dressed in their Sunday best, they won't have a clue that pieces of you are so close to them in the lake.' Ernest gave a cruel laugh.

★ ★ ★

At that moment Mary truly believed every word Ernest had said. She honestly believed he was capable of murder. She felt such terror, she thought she was going to die on the spot with fear. How was she going to convince her family. Flo was no fool. She had guessed what really had happened. She must put on an act like she had never done before. Her very life depended on it. She had to convince them that all was well. When Flo got a bee in her bonnet about something, she was like a dog with a bone and wouldn't let go at all costs. That evening Mary set off for Betts Lane with a sinking heart, knowing her task would not be easy. She had tried to cover the bruises as best she could with powder and rouge but they were still clearly visible.

* ★ *

At the end of the evening Florence and Fred were still not convinced. Flo could sense the fear in Mary and thought best not to say any more for the moment as it would only make things worse for her. She would be watching him like a hawk from now on. She had to do something, but what? The Police would not interfere between husband and wife, in some quarters it was quite commonplace for a man to beat his wife. Doctor Fisher would be no help either. He had taken the oath of confidentiality between doctor and patient so he would be unable to disclose anything about her condition. What can I do? I must do something but what? Relating the whole sad story to Rose the next day, Florence was horrified by her response.

'Would you like one of my sailor friends to take care of him Flo? He could have an accident. He could fall off the Town Quay and be found floating in the docks one morning.'

'Rose where do you get such ideas from? That's murder and is as bad as he is. I think you really have been associating with a bad lot lately.'

Rose looked sulkily at Flo, 'Well have you any better ideas?'

'I must sit down and give this whole situation some serious thought. I'm sure I will think of something.'

'You were right all along Flo, you said she shouldn't have accepted his proposal.'

'That's no consolation to me now. Perhaps a bit of friendly persuasion might change his ways. I've got an idea. Something I heard about him a long time ago. I'll tell you about it later, if it works.' Florence grabbed her coat and was on her way around to Cunningham's shop.

★   ★   ★

Flo flung open the shop door and as she stood there framed in the doorway, the first person she caught sight of was Mary. She thought what a sad pathetic sight she looked, dejected and hunched over the counter. She guessed she must still be in a lot of pain.

'Ernest I want a word with you now, in your back room if you please.'

Ernest's face reddened as his anger began to take hold. No woman had ever spoken to him like that before. The audacity of the woman, who does she think she is? She could do with a good hiding as well. That would take her down a peg or two.

Flo smiled sweetly at Mary.

'Mary dear, you'll look after the shop, while I discuss something with Ernest in private.'

Mary nodded, by now her face was ashen. Wondering what repercussions Flo's outburst would have on her. Would she pay dearly, perhaps even with her life? Flo turned and gave Ernest a long hard look. Then marched straight through to the back room. She sat down at the table. Took off her hat and gloves and made herself comfortable. Ernest could hardly contain his anger. He looked liked he was about to explode any minute.

'I'll come straight to the point Ernest, we'll put all our cards on the table. Right then! I know that you beat my sister.'

Flo raised her hand, 'No don't interrupt me until I finish. First of all Mary did not tell me you had beaten her. She is totally loyal to you and will not hear a word against you. Heaven knows why. I'm no fool. I could see those injuries were from a beating not falling down stairs. You can't pull the wool over my eyes.'

'How dare you come into my home and accuse me of injuring my wife.'

'Just stop the pretence and listen to me.'

Florence would not be intimidated by him, or anyone else for that matter.

'Some years ago you took a trip on the ill fated Titanic?'

'Yes what if I did? I don't see ... ' Florence interrupted him.

'Hear me out please. Everyone said it was a miracle you were saved and thanked the Lord. I know different. A friend of ours was also on the Titanic. He was crewing one of the lifeboats, the very one that saved you from drowning along with all the other brave men. He said you had gained your place in the lifeboat by dressing up as a woman. Shame on you. Call yourself a man. You're nothing but a coward. If this piece of information ever got out you would be ruined. No one likes a coward. Your shop would be boycotted and your precious business would be right down the drain.'

Florence had never seen Ernest look so shocked and be so silent.

'I thought that would take the wind out of your sails. Now then, if I ever catch you laying another finger on my sister, or being unkind to her in any other way, your long kept secret of eight years will be out. I will take great pleasure in telling everyone what the real you is like, a coward and wife beater, that you are. Certainly not the gentleman and solid good citizen everyone believes you to be. Are we in agreement then?'

Ernest struck speechless could only nod his agreement.

'Good, then that's alright.'

Florence picked up her hat and placed it back on her head, put her gloves on, bag on arm and head held high she walked back out to the shop to have a word with Mary. Florence was pleased to see there were no customers in the shop so she could talk quite freely. Ernest did not follow her. He was still in the back room digesting what he had just heard and trying to gain his composure.

'Now Mary, I've had a little talk with Ernest. I know what happened the other night and he has promised me nothing like that will ever happen again and if it does, you are to tell me immediately. Do you hear?'

'Yes Flo, but what did you say to him?'

'Never mind for now. I will tell you sometime perhaps. We will see how things go from now on. I'm sure you'll find everything will be much better and Ernest will start to treat you more like a wife than a servant.'

9

Willy decided to tell Bridget about Pete joining the IRA. He knew he could trust her completely and it would go no further than their own four walls.

'But Willy, I don't understand why he didn't just confess to Fay. I'm sure she would forgive him. He's a lot of tings but never a violent man.'

'Because he was threatened with 'Bas gan Sagart'.'

'Oh God no! 'Death without Priest'.'

'Fay would forgive a lot of tings, but one ting she never would tolerate is one of her family dying without having received 'The Last Sacrament'. I tink she would be around to the Devlin's and personally take Seamus and Batt apart bit by bit.'

'Willy it's not a joking matter. Pete could be killed fighting for the cause. Saints preserve us, what are we all going to do?'

★   ★   ★

During December Pete was called upon to take part in his first raid. He was part of an

135

ambush party which successfully attacked an Auxiliary patrol with grenades and revolvers at Ballyleen, yards from the military barracks. They killed an Auxiliary and wounded several others. News of the attack spread terror through the city of Cork.

★ ★ ★

Willy had seen Pete before the raid, white and shaking in fear of his life. He would not disclose what was about to take place but he asked Willy to look after Fay and the boys, should he not return.

★ ★ ★

The Auxiliaries took revenge. They stopped trams in Patrick Street, forced passengers to alight and be searched, hands above their heads. Several men were beaten up, including a Priest who had refused to say 'To hell with the Pope'. Then the Auxiliaries and the Black and Tans set fire to two houses near Ballyleen and prevented attempts to extinguish the flames.

They began crowding the streets, shooting into the air and yelling. Flames reddened the skies above the city as the central shopping district was looted and destroyed by bombs and arson.

A group of drunken Black and Tans were singing and dancing through the streets with a bevy of Irish girls, while the Auxies were treating the ladies of the town to looted drinks in back parlours.

A triumphant Pete returned from his first raid, a different man to the one who had left Harbour View hours before. He greeted Willy with the same cocky self assurance he always had in the past, before he was threatened with exposure. Pete bragged to Willy about the success of the evening's events.

'Jesus man, Ballyleen. Biddy has relatives up there. I hope to God they are all safe and sound. You look like you actually enjoyed it.'

'I did me boy and I'm looking forward to me next mission.'

Bridget's cousins in Ballyleen were all safe, as it turned out. A party of Black and Tans raided a farm at two in the morning and killed two sons of the house, who were active volunteers.

★   ★   ★

The aftermath of the damage was estimated at three million pounds. In Patrick Street 21 shops had been completely destroyed. 40 shops burned to the ground. 24 partially damaged and many more looted.

★ ★ ★

Bridget and Willy found it very hard to come to terms with Cork city centre being burnt down and firemen attempting to put out the blaze had their hoses cut. To add insult to injury, the Irish Chief Secretary tried to claim that the citizens of Cork had deliberately burnt down their own city.

'It's a good job Willy, we've no room with our five children, to have Black and Tans billeted in our home, like some poor souls have to. After the burning of Cork city, if we had one billeted here, so help me God, I don't know what I would do to him.'

'Hush Bridget, yer beginning to sound like Pete. He is so full of himself at the moment. I hope he's not heading for a fall.'

'It's a good job I'm not a man. For I might be tempted to join the IRA along with Pete and the others.'

Willy walked away smiling to himself. I reckon she would an all.

★ ★ ★

The Commanding Officer of the Auxies returned to England and a few weeks later shot himself on Wimbledon Common. His company were withdrawn to Dublin and wore burnt corks in their glengarries as a defiant memento of their riotous night out, in Cork on 11th December 1920.

★ ★ ★

With Seamus and Batt Devlin back at sea and safely out of the way, Pete Finnegan felt he could resume his relationship with Kathleen, the love of his life. He had grown in her estimation since joining the IRA and she felt quite proud to be seen on his arm. She was not quite aware how exactly he came to join in the first place, but it did not matter too much to her. She just revelled in playing the part of a gangster's moll and the new found respect she and Pete had gained in some quarters. One evening she was having a drink with Marie, while waiting for Pete and Sean to join them, when into the pub strolled two Black and Tans.

'Look Jimmy, over there. Two beautiful Irish lassies.'

'Not lassies Robbie. You're not back in Scotland now. Over here they are called colleens.'

'Aye Jimmy, I expect you're right. Let's go over and talk to them.' They wandered over to the bar where Kathleen and Marie were standing.

'Good evening. Can we buy you both a drink? We have not seen two such beautiful colleens since we arrived in Ireland. I'm Robbie and this is my friend Jimmy, and what might your names be?'

Kathleen swung around in an instant and quick as a flash she answered, 'pog mo toin'. Declan Quinlan almost choked himself at Kathleen's answer and went into a coughing fit spraying beer all over the bar. Marie patted him on the back, saying he must 'take the drink more slowly'. The two Scots looked at one another and eyed the women suspiciously, wondering if they were having the mickey taken out of them.

'And what does that mean?' asked Jimmy quite sharply. The atmosphere was beginning to change and not for the better.

Declan who had now recovered, regained his composure and answered.

'It means in Gaelic, 'Greetings and welcome'.'

This brought the smiles back to the Scotsmens' faces and a lot of other people in the bar as well. The atmosphere began to lighten again, when the door opened and in walked Pete and Sean.

'Pog mo toin,' called Robbie to the two Irish men.

Sean's face was like thunder and he was

about to take on the pair of them single handed when he was dragged outside by Declan and Pete. Sean was raging.

'Let go of me. I'm not having any Black and Tans telling me to kiss their ass. I'll kill the pair of them so I will.'

A few minutes later a giggling Kathleen and Marie emerged from the pub.

'Christ Kathleen, what are ye trying to do, get our heads blown off?'

'Ah to be sure Declan, they don't know what it means.'

'They very nearly found out when Sean came through the door. If we hadn't dragged him out when we did, God knows what might have happened.'

★ ★ ★

The next day Pete related the happenings of the evening before to Willy, who found it all very amusing, but warned Pete to be careful as he thought they were all playing with fire. Pete just shrugged off Willy's warning and went back in doors whistling a rebel tune. It was a wonder to Willy, how Pete managed to keep his affair with Kathleen and his terrorist activities from Fay. She seemed totally oblivious to all his goings on. One day me boy, one day, it'll all catch up with ye, thought

Willy as he finished painting the outside of their house.

* * *

It was the first week in April when they all heard the news that Michael Collins' homestead at Woodfield was destroyed by the Essex Regiment under the command of Major Arthur Percival. Neither Michael or his brother Johnny were in the house at the time. There were eight children there, aged 1 – 12 years being looked after by a young housekeeper. The children were only allowed to take their bed clothes. The neighbours were rounded up at bayonet point and forced to throw straw into the house, then pour petrol on it and set it alight. The soldiers said Michael Collins' neighbours had burned down his home.

* * *

This latest incident only served to make Pete more determined that the IRA raids he took part in were completely justified and wondered why more men in the street didn't join the cause.

* * *

On 22nd June 1921, King George V came to Belfast to open the Northern Parliament and make an appeal for peace. On 24th June the IRA mined and derailed a train which was part of the King's escort returning to the South. Four troopers of 10th Royal Hussars were killed and twenty wounded. Eight horses were either killed or so badly injured they had to be destroyed. Pete was in Belfast at the time of this raid, supposedly visiting his sister. He told Fay she had suddenly been taken ill and he had been called to the family home to be at her bedside. Fay swallowed this story completely and said she would say the Rosary for her recovery that night. Even Pete could not believe his luck in what he was getting away with, leading a double life. On the surface he was a respectable family man who attended Mass every Sunday. Only those very close to him, knew of his double existence. Willy wondered if Pete had been on the raid. Pete never mentioned the raid and Willy thought it best not to ask. The less he knew of Pete's activities the better.

★ ★ ★

When Pete returned to the family home and said his sister was much better and well on the road to recovery, Fay said it had been a miracle granted by God. He had heard her prayers and answered them, she would go down to St. Colman's that night and give thanks. As she left the room, Pete just stood there shaking his head in disbelief.

On numerous occasions Pete could not stop boasting to Willy about his missions, and he frequently begged Willy to join him.

Willy was quite emphatic that he would not be joining in with any violence or taking of life, cause or no cause. Pete knew Willy was such a good true friend that he would never reveal to anyone that he was an active member of the IRA, or of him carrying on with Kathleen Devlin.

★   ★   ★

It was late on the night of 26th June 1921, when Bridget and Willy were awoken by a loud banging on their door.

'Jesus Christ, not more Black and Tan raids,' swore Willy as he stumbled out of bed.

'Willy be careful what ye say.'

Willy opened the door to a white faced Pete. He was agitated with tears in his eyes and seemed to be in a bad state of shock.

Willy thought that at last some of his actions had caught up with him and wondered what he could have done to end up in such a bad state.

'What is it man? Come in. Has some of your antics caught up with ye at last?'

'Willy shut up and listen to me. Where is Bridget? I have some really bad news for ye.'

'I'm here Pete. What is it?'

Pete looked at Bridget and thought how beautiful she looked, even having just been awoken from a sleep, she stood there looking serene and calm. He was about to change all that with the news he was about to impart. The calmness would be turned to immediate sorrow. He could stand the thought of it no longer and collapsed in the chair, sobbing uncontrollably. Willy got him a whisky, from his bottle he had been saving for special occasions.

'Here drink this and tell us what is so bad to get ye in this state.'

Pete gulped down the whisky and asked for another. Then gradually, as the warmth from the alcohol began to take effect.

He felt slightly relaxed and began to feel more in control of himself. He was ready to begin.

'Bridget I'm so very sorry. Your cousin up at Dillons Cross, Billy Horgan, has been murdered by the Black and Tans.'

Bridget was stunned. She could not speak or move for a while.

'But how, why? He was not a member of the IRA. He was only 20 years old. I don't understand. Please tell me it's not so.'

'You had better tell us what happened Pete,' Willy said as he cradled Bridget in his arms. 'Were you there?'

'No I wasn't, I swear to God. I only heard about it on me way back from Kathleen's.' There was a long pause before Pete began again. 'Two Black and Tans had wandered a bit too far from their barracks and ended up in the village pub. There were quite a few IRA members in the bar at the time. They plied them with drinks and pretended friendship. When it was time for them to leave, they were so drunk they didn't know which way to go to get back to their barracks. A few IRA offered to show them a short cut through the woods. One was executed but the other managed to escape.' Willy noted how Pete said executed and not murdered.

'When he got back to his barracks and the others heard, immediately a lorry load of Black and Tans arrived demanding to know the name of the person who had killed one of their soldiers. They got hold of one of the locals and tortured him until he gave them the name of Billy Horgan.'

'But Billy wasn't,' protested Bridget. Before she could finish the sentence, Pete continued,

'I know he wasn't, I know . . . but there is a serving member called Billy Horgan. They just got the wrong one. It was a case of mistaken identity.'

'How did he die?'

'Bridget I don't tink ye need to hear all the details. It will only upset ye further,' Willy warned.

Bridget ignored this piece of advice from her husband.

'Go on Pete, tell me all of it I need to know. Did he suffer much?'

'Yes Bridget he did. Oh God I can't go on.' Pete broke down again.

'Pete you must please,' pleaded Bridget. Willy handed Pete a third whisky which he accepted, grateful for the few minutes pause before he had to continue.

'They dragged him from his bed and took him back to their headquarters in the lorry. On the way he was beaten and stabbed with their bayonets several times. Some say he was then shot but others have said he was already dead when he arrived, due to the loss of blood from all the stab wounds.'

Bridget was frozen to the spot with the horror of what she had just heard. She could not move, speak or cry. She was in total shock. Willy thought, I wish to God I got me family out of here years ago, to the States as I

147

planned. If only I hadn't had that accident and lost all the money on medical bills. I could have spared Bridget hearing this first hand. Hearing it in a letter would not have seemed half so bad. Perhaps when we have got through all this, I'll get us all over to Southampton. Desmond seems happy enough and settled there.

★　★　★

The whole family took the death of young Billy badly. He was buried in Cork cemetery. The inscription on his stone read 'William Horgan. Murdered by British Crown Soldiers on 26th June 1921, aged 20 years.'

★　★　★

By October the withdrawals of the Black and Tans, and Auxiliaries had begun. On 6th December 1921 the Anglo Irish Treaty was signed. De Valera rejected the treaty and plunged the country into civil war. The following August, Michael Collins was shot in his home county of Bealnablath, County Cork. He was ambushed by anti-treaty IRA.

★　★　★

Since Billy's murder, Pete had simmered down a lot. He began to realise that war was not quite so glamorous as it had at first seemed. It struck home to him the real suffering of the families on both sides of the conflict that had lost loved ones.

I suppose even the Black and Tans, and Auxies have families somewhere who would mourn their loss. Now our leader Michael Collins has gone as well, shot down in cold blood. There doesn't seem a lot of point going on. Michael Collins had been his hero. He modelled himself on his image. He began to imagine what life would be like for Fay and the boys if anything happened to him. He had been lucky up to now, he had got away with murder . . . literally, he began to smile to himself. Perhaps it was time to call it a day, with Kathleen as well. They had had a good run and it was time he returned to respectability.

★ ★ ★

Willy was delighted with the news, when Pete disclosed his plans to him. Although he thought Pete a fool, he liked him a lot and considered him a true friend.

I don't know how Kathleen will take it. I

must tell her tonight, when I meet her for a drink.

Kathleen too was beginning to grow bored with Pete. Since Billy's death, all the fun and life had gone from him. His heart was not in anything anymore. She had been thinking of dumping him and now he had saved her the trouble. She already had his replacement lined up. Another member of the IRA, a young hot head named Terence Moloney, whom she found both handsome and exciting. After Pete had told Kathleen it was all over between them, something he had been dreading doing all evening, he was quite miffed by her response.

'Fine Pete, if that's what ye want.'

She immediately turned to Marie and began giggling. Keeping one eye on the door, hoping the new love of her life would come in.

Pete had been dismissed, he could not believe it. Had he meant nothing to her all this time? He had risked so much to be with her. He didn't want a scene, or to hurt her, but this offhand dismissal of him. He couldn't believe it. Had everyone who tried to warn him off her been right about her all along?

'Kathleen I . . . ,' his voice tailed off, as she turned and gave him an icy stare.

'Yes Pete, did ye want something?'

She did not wait for his answer, as the door swung open and in stepped Terence Moloney, Sean Lynch and Dan Kelly.

'Come Marie, let's go and join some real men and have ourselves an evening of fun.'

Marie followed obediently, as she always did when Kathleen spoke. Kathleen flung her arms around Terence and began kissing him.

'Ah to be sure, tis lovely to see ye again Terence. Come and sit down with me and Marie. I'm sure we'll all have a grand evening together. When the pub closes, perhaps ye would like to come home with me? Maybe I'll have a little something for ye, in gratitude for seeing a girl home safely on a dark night. Ye never know what unsavoury characters are about late at night.' She glanced at Pete as she said it.

A loud roar of laughter went up in the bar at her last remark and all eyes were on Pete, who by now was bright red with embarrassment and anger. Why she is nothing but a cheap little whore, with her loud talk and giggling with that other silly little bitch. How can she have one man in her bed and then go straight on to the next without so much as even a pause. I can't believe it of her. I thought I loved her once. What a fool I've

151

been and now everyone is laughing at me, not just behind me back but to me face.

★　★　★

Dan Kelly was at Pete's side in an instant.

'Pete I'm sorry. She has been after Terence for a few months now. It was a rotten way for ye to find out.'

'It's alright Dan. I came here tonight and told her it was all over. So ye see it doesn't matter.'

'Oh yeh, a likely story,' chipped in Declan who was propping up the bar.

'Do ye expect us to believe that Pete. She has dumped ye good and proper and everyone here knows it,' added the barman Paddy Murphy.

'But it's true, I swear. Oh what's the use.' Pete left the bar slamming the door loudly behind him. How can I ever go in that pub again and hold me head up. Oh Kathleen, Kathleen ye have made a right mug out of me, so ye have.

10

It was another 2 years before Willy managed to get the fare together for his family to move to Southampton. They arrived in the Summer of 1924. Desmond O'Leary was waiting to meet them all when they arrived. He had proved to be a good friend and had stayed in touch with Willy over the years. He even found a big family house for them to rent in St. Andrews Road. It overlooked the park. He seemed to take control of everything. He had a list of jobs that the girls and Willy could apply for.

★   ★   ★

Willy managed to secure work in the docks. Maggie was still adamant about going into service. No way was she being anyone's slave, she would say time and time again. She was an excellent seamstress and applied for a job with a local upholstery company, and was successful, much to everyone's surprise. Annie the quiet, brainy one of the family, found a job in the office of the local grocery store. Ellee now aged 15 years, did not mind going into service as a trainee cook. She happily took up her post with the Leyton-Barries in their big house off The Avenue. Bridie and Jack were still too young to work and soon settled into the local school.

* * *

Bridget began to feel a bit more secure. The first time she had felt like this in years. All her family were settled in work and regular money was coming into the home. What more could she have wished for in their new life. At times she would feel homesick for her family and the way of life she had always known. The peace was short lived, when a letter arrived from Maggie's boss giving warning of her bad behaviour.

Although her work was of an excellent standard, her fiery temper and attitude towards the other workers left a lot to be desired. If her behaviour did not improve she would find herself out of a job, and without a reference. Bridget was worried and upset by the letter but Willy was furious and was waiting for her when she returned from work.

'What is the meaning of this letter? What do ye tink ye are playing at? Whenever there is peace and harmony, ye have to rock the boat.

Come on spit it out. What have ye been doing?'

'Tis not my fault. They are taking the mickey out of me Irish accent and Charlie Higgins keeps pawing me and trying to kiss me. I can't stand him, he's awful looking and he won't leave me alone. So I tru me scissors at him. They just missed him and stuck in the notice board. He went white as a sheet and started shaking. Sure I never had another word out of him all afternoon and he hasn't bothered me since. The crawler must have gone and told the boss Mr. Turner. He's always crawling around him, making out he's such a good worker.'

'Well I suppose that trows a different light on the matter. Do ye want me to go around and have a word with the boss about him?'

'No thanks Pop. I can take care of meself.'

She gave Willy a peck on the cheek and he thought she can an all.

Bridget and Willy heard nothing more from Maggie's boss, Edward Turner. Willy suspected she was probably getting a hard time from this Charlie Higgins and some of the other workers as well.

He knew she was a strong willed tough girl but he didn't like to think of her being hurt or unhappy at work.

Higgins was sulking over Maggie not getting the sack and began to plot how he could get his revenge on her. Most of the other workers actually liked her. She was a good worker but they were all a little weary of her Irish temper which could flare up at any time without warning. One afternoon Charlie stopped at her machine, bent down and whispered in her ear so the others could not hear what was being said.

'I'll get you Maggie Collins, you just wait and see. You could have injured me seriously with those scissors. You'll pay for that. You won't be so cocky anymore. You'll be begging to be my friend by the time I've finished with you.'

Maggie stopped machining and laughed in his face.

'You and whose army? I'm not frightened of you Charlie Higgins or anyone else come to that.'

Everyone stopped working, sensing there was going to be more fireworks. All eyes were on Charlie. He said nothing but his face reddened with anger. She had humiliated him yet again in front of everyone. She really will have to pay for her actions. I'll get some of the boys in our street to teach her a lesson she won't forget, we'll see how tough she is then. Little Miss prim and proper, goes to Church every Sunday with her family. When he got home from work, he thought he would enlist the help of his older brother Roger to get revenge on Maggie. Roger was one of the local bully boys and hung around with a gang from the bottom of the town, who all thought they were so tough. They had planned between them to lay in wait for Maggie as she walked home alone from work. She would be dragged into an alley and roughed up a bit to frighten her then threatened with a knife if she did not obey them.

★　★　★

Maggie never gave Charlie another thought. He was just too silly to bother about. Never for one moment did she take his threat seriously. She had seen far worse than the likes of him in Ireland. That evening as she prepared to leave work she covered her machine and said goodnight to Mr. Turner's secretary Gwen. She was a nice looking lady and had always been kind to Maggie since she started the job. She lived a few roads away from Maggie's family and sometimes when Maggie was walking home she would catch her up and they would walk part of the way together. She was very interested in Ireland and where they had lived. She said her grandfather was Irish, although he had been over here all her life. She had never been to Ireland herself but had always wanted to go and see where he had lived.

★   ★   ★

Maggie was deep in thought as she walked home. She was worried about her mother. She had not looked at all well lately. She always seemed so tired and sometimes there was no colour at all in her face. I really feel Mother should see a doctor, we must all try to persuade her. I am so frightened there is something seriously wrong with her. Maggie's thoughts were suddenly interrupted. A gang of youths in their late teens had suddenly surrounded her and barred her way.

'Excuse me please,' Maggie tried to push pass them.

'Excuse me please,' one tried to mimic her Irish accent, the others all laughed.

'What do ye want? I have no money on me, is that what ye want, money?'

Roger Higgins towered over her, looking menacing.

'We don't want your money. What is this I hear about you upsetting my little brother

158

Charlie?' He pushed her roughly and she fell against some of the gang, who in turn pushed her back. By this time she was beginning to feel a little frightened, although she did not show it. Then one of the gang produced the knife.

'Here you are Roger. Do you want to scar her pretty face or shall I?'

'I will have that pleasure Tom. Here give it to me.'

Maggie tried to make a dash for it but one of the gang tripped her up. She fell badly, tearing her stockings and cutting her knee. She was very frightened by now and thought they were going to kill her, then she heard a familiar voice calling.

'Stop, stop at once what do you think you are doing?' It was Gwen. 'Just a minute I know you don't I?' She recognized Roger immediately. He was furious he had been identified.

'We were just having a bit of fun Miss. No harm was meant by it.'

'A bit of fun indeed. This poor girl is badly shaken and bleeding. You haven't heard the last of this. I may even call the police.'

'No Miss please don't. We weren't going to hurt her, really, it was just a game.'

Gwen took hold of Maggie's arm, glared at

the group and led her away.

'You'll be alright now Maggie and Mr. Turner shall hear about this tomorrow. I think the record is going to be set straight on that sniveller Charlie Higgins. He won't be such a blue eyed boy after Mr. Turner hears what I have to say.'

'I don't want any trouble Gwen. I may lose me job. Mr Turner gave me a final warning and wrote to me parents. He'll tink it is all my fault, not his.'

'No he won't. It will be alright Maggie, don't worry.'

Gwen escorted Maggie to her front door and explained to Willy and Bridget all that had gone on over the last few months. How it wasn't Maggie's fault and she would get it all sorted out the next day. When she had gone Willy commented on what a fine woman Gwen Smith was.

'Now Pop, don't you go making Mother jealous,' teased Maggie.

Bridget stood up to clear away the tea things. Momentarily she felt the sensation of dizziness and the room growing darker.

Her legs crumpled from under her and she found herself on the floor with the family bending over her. She had broken out in a cold sweat and felt very sick and weak. She couldn't move.

Willy took control and was giving the family orders.

'Annie go and fetch the doctor at once. Tell him it is urgent, your mother has collapsed.' Bridget tried to protest but couldn't, she felt far too ill.

'Maggie fetch a pillow and blanket from upstairs. We must make her comfortable down here. I'm going to lift her onto the settee. Ellee fetch a glass of water from the kitchen. Now hurry all of ye.'

When the doctor arrived he immediately called an ambulance. He suspected she'd had a mild heart attack. His diagnosis was correct, confirmed by the hospital. She was to stay in hospital for several weeks, with complete bed rest and no stress. The family visited every day and had to take turns in shifts of two, to sit by her bedside. The matron was an old dragon and would not bend the rules for anyone.

'Rules is rules, two only, no exceptions Mr. Collins. Your wife needs complete rest and I must ask you all to leave the minute you hear the bell go at the end of visiting. Thank you.'

She marched off down the corridor to terrorise some young nurses who were giggling outside a ward.

'My God, what a tyrant. She must give all the patients the will to recover and get out of here as quickly as possible,' Willy commented. The family all laughed, in spite of the growing fear they all had that they might lose a very precious person.

They all adored Bridget and no one could imagine life without her.

* * *

As the weeks passed Bridget began to grow stronger and was beginning to look like her old self again. When Maggie came to visit on her afternoon off she asked about her job and what happened to Charlie Higgins? Maggie explained, Gwen was as good as her word and set the record straight with Mr. Turner. He had given Charlie one last chance, any more sign of trouble and he would be out on his ear so fast his feet wouldn't touch the ground.

'He keeps bringing me presents. Trying to crawl around me since Mr. Turner had him in the office. God he's such a crawler. I told him to keep his presents. I don't want them, I just want to be left alone.'

'Now be careful Maggie. Don't start up any more trouble.'

'No Mother, I won't. I promise.'

* * *

162

Maggie was invited to the wedding of a girl from work. As Bridget was well on the road to recovery, she felt she could attend.

Elizabeth Drayton made a lovely bride. She wore a long white silk gown and carried a bouquet of pink rosebuds that matched the colour of the bridesmaids' dresses worn by her two younger sisters. The best man was the bridegroom's cousin, Ronald Newman.

From the moment Maggie first saw the back of his head in church, she couldn't take her eyes off him. He had lovely black hair and looked very nervous and shy about his duties as best man.

At the reception in the church hall he stumbled over his words when reading the telegrams and cards. His hand was shaking slightly as he proposed a toast to the bride and groom. This made him all the more endearing to Maggie. She hated the big mouth, blow your own trumpet sort of man. This Ronnie was a different kettle of fish altogether. She wondered how she could get to know him, with him being so shy. Her chance came later on in the evening when in walked Charlie Higgins. Elizabeth had invited everyone from work to the evening reception. Maggie felt quite honoured to have been invited to the whole wedding and not just the evening.

★ ★ ★

The music for the evening was supplied by Uncle Cecil at the piano, Uncle Alfred on the accordion, a friend with a mouth organ and Aunty Hilda singing a few songs.

'Take your partners for the first dance,' boomed out Uncle Alfred.

Charlie made a beeline for Maggie. Oh God no, why won't he leave me alone. Maggie had a sudden flash of inspiration.

'May I have this dance Maggie please?' smarmed Charlie.

'I'm so sorry Charlie, I've promised it to me boyfriend Ronnie over there. Look he's looking over for me. So sorry but thank you for asking,' she said rather sarcastically.

She rushed across to Ronnie and dragged him onto the dance floor.

'Come on darlin' this is our dance we promised each other.'

Ronald was totally amazed. Being so shy he had never had much luck with girls, and here was this beautiful dark haired girl he'd seen in church actually wanting to dance with him. He was speechless. Maggie pulled him closer and whispered in his ear.

'Please help me. I'll explain all later. Ye have just saved me from a very boring evening.'

164

Maggie stayed close to Ronnie all evening, never daring to venture far from his side in case she got stuck with Charlie again. Ronnie couldn't help but notice the admiring glances from all the other males at the reception and wondered how he managed to have by his side this beautiful Irish girl. His luck had certainly changed. Then he began to wonder, was she just using him for the evening to ward off the dreaded Charlie. Perhaps he may never see her again after tonight. I'll offer to see her home, then at least I'll know where she lives.

'May I walk you home Maggie?'

'Oh please do. I would be truly grateful.'

When they reached Maggie's front door, Ronald asked if he might see her again. Maggie's heart leapt with joy. She had not felt so happy in a long time. In fact when things were quite bad at work she wished they had never left dear old Queenstown. She never let the others know this for fear of upsetting her parents, especially Pop who was so set on coming to Southampton.

They made arrangements to meet the next day for a Sunday afternoon stroll in the park. She explained she had to attend Mass in the morning with her family, so she could not meet him till after Sunday dinner.

★　★　★

Romance began to blossom between Maggie and Ronnie. She would spend hours in front of the mirror getting herself ready for her dates with Ronald. One wet afternoon she was in front of her bedroom mirror positioning her hat and talking to herself, completely unaware she was being watched from behind the door by Annie, Ellee and Bridie.

She placed her hat to one side saying, 'Mrs. Ronald Newman,' then she moved it to the back of her head saying, 'Mrs. Maggie Newman.' Then she pulled it straight down on her head saying, 'Mrs. Ronnie Newman.'

Bridie could contain herself no longer and shrieked out with laughter. She made a quick getaway with Annie and Ellee close on her heels. Maggie's temper was roused.

'I'll kill the lot of ye when I get hold of ye.'

They were out the back door in an instant, into the pouring rain with Bridget calling after them, 'Put yer coats on ye'll catch yer death.'

They all made a beeline for Willy's shed and hid behind the wood pile till they heard the front door slam and were sure Maggie had left.

'I tink it's safe to come out now. She's gone,' said Annie.

'When are we all going to meet this love of yer life Maggie?' quizzed Willy one tea time. 'We know nothing of him, except you seem pretty smitten.'

'His name is Ronald Newman and he's a baker for a cake shop in Shirley High Street,' replied Maggie rather haughtily. 'I could bring him for Sunday tea if ye like.'

'Yes do that Maggie, we are all dying to meet him,' said Bridget in a kind voice.

Bridie began to giggle chanting, 'Our Maggie has got a fella and she's in love. Ain't love grand.'

'Mother, tell them to stop or I won't bring him home. He's shy and won't come again if he has the mickey taken out of him.'

'Now ye stop at once, all of ye. Ronald will be made welcome and treated with respect and if he's not, I will be very angry indeed. Ye all know what the doctor said. I must not be upset or worried about anything.'

The room fell quiet. Bridget knew they had all taken notice of what she said and there would be no further trouble. For they all loved her dearly and were so scared of losing her. They would all do anything to keep her safe and not cause any upset which might make her ill again.

* * *

Ronald arrived for tea the following Sunday. He was worried sick that Maggie's family wouldn't like him, or would think he was not good enough for their lovely daughter.

'Ah don't ye be worrying yerself Ronnie, they'll all love ye as I do.'

Ronnie blushed bright red to the roots of his hair. She said she loved me. I can't believe it. Maggie saw the look of disbelief on his face at what she had just said. She smiled and gave his hand a little squeeze.

* * *

After tea was over Maggie and Ronnie went out for an evening stroll, Willy commented to Bridget, 'He seems very shy. Not at all the sort for our Maggie. He's the exact opposite to her. I expect she tinks she will be able to get her own way with him. She has always liked that, always been strong and wilful. He seems such a nice bloke. Poor man, I pity him having to put up with our Maggie.'

'Now Willy don't be unkind. I tink he will be good for her. Ye know what they say about the attraction of opposites. She certainly has simmered down a lot, since meeting him.'

'I'd better start saving for the wedding then, shall I?'

★　★　★

Maggie had no such qualms about meeting his mother and sister Elsie, his father had died a long time ago. The only thing she was worried about was her Irish accent. Would they laugh at the way she spoke, as some of her work mates did when she first arrived. She need not have worried, they didn't take any notice of her accent and liked her immediately. Mrs. Newman was quite relieved that at last her Ronnie had found a nice girl to take care of him when she had gone. She had her two children quite late in life. She and Elsie both doted on Ronnie and always fought his battles for him. He was never any good at standing up for himself. In Maggie she saw a strong person who would stand up for him. She was well pleased with the match. If they married she would go to her grave a happy woman, knowing he had someone to care for him as she had all these years.

★　★　★

'Do ye tink yer Mother and sister liked me Ronnie? Did they say anything about me Irish accent?'

'Of course they did and no they wouldn't say anything about your accent. They are not like that.'

'But I wish I could speak nice, like the English do.'

'I love your accent. You must not be ashamed of where you come from or how you speak. Look if it really worries you, I'll teach you to speak like us, if you like.'

'Oh please Ronnie, will ye.'

'Yes I will. The first lesson in English then. Stop saying ye. The English always say you and say think and not tink. You must sound the th. When we go to the pictures to see the films, say film not filum.'

'Oh Ronnie thank you. I'll try to remember, I'll really try.'

★ ★ ★

Ronnie was quite elated. Never in his life had anyone looked up to him or asked for his help. In fact everyone thought they were better than him and were never really interested in anything he had to say. They were all far more interesting and worldly, and had done so much more than him. Some of his friends at work who were the same age as him were already married, others had scores of girlfriends queuing up to go out with them.

But he didn't care, he had Maggie. She was his first and his one and only. He was not interested in hordes of girls. He would be happy to spend the rest of his life with her. The men at work used to tease him about her.

'Better hurry up Ronnie and get her to the altar. Before she changes her mind and one of us takes her off you.'

Ronnie ignored all the jibes.

* * *

The family had noticed Maggie was trying to change her way of talking.

'What ails that one Biddy? Jesus why has she gone all posh on us. Are we not good enough for her anymore?'

'Shush Willy. Don't upset her now. She's trying really hard with her job and trying to speak nicely. Now promise me ye'll say nothing to her.'

'I suppose so. It's better than her fits of temper she has every so often.'

11

Christopher Preston had been courting a girl from the Isle of Wight for some time. Bessie Deane also worked at the G.P.O. She was a very striking girl. Tall, slim with short bobbed black hair. He had been contemplating for some time asking for her hand in marriage. He was just coming up to his 23rd birthday and thought it was time he settled down. Granny Ford had just passed away in her sleep and Florence had been a bit down for a while. A marriage in the family was just what Mum needed to cheer her up. I'll ask Bessie tonight, if she will do me the honour of becoming my wife.

★　★　★

Bessie Deane didn't need asking twice, she jumped at the proposal of becoming Christopher's wife. They had been going out together for four years and she began to feel he was never going to ask her. Over the years Fred and Florence had become quite parsimonious with their money. They both worked hard and through the kindness of Mr. Griffin, giving them their house soon after they were married, they had managed to acquire a couple of other properties cheaply in the Bitterne Park area of Southampton. One of the properties was currently unoccupied. The obvious thing was for Bessie and Chris to move in after they were married and pay Fred and Flo a nominal rent.

★   ★   ★

James called one evening for Lewis and Albert to come and join him for a bike ride on the Common. He had something to tell them both and couldn't wait. The three cousins were still quite close at the age of fifteen, they shared everything they acquired and did everything together. Flo nicknamed them 'The Three Musketeers'. James would try to dominate the scene and give the other two orders. Albert would always give in and let James have his own way but Lewis wouldn't. He would stand his ground and say what he thought. He was a lot like Flo and had inherited her strength of character. He would always want to see fair play done and could not abide cheats. James grew more arrogant by the day and thought he was God's gift to women. At times Flo thought she would like to give him a good slap to bring him down a peg or two, but then thought better of it. I suppose he can't help it. He takes after his father, old man Leyton-Barrie. I wonder how many more young girls he has got pregnant since our Rose and got away with it?

★　★　★

'Come on you two, get your bikes from the shed. I've got someone I want you to meet. Hurry up or we'll miss her coming out of work.'

'Where does she work?' asked Albert.

'At the Leyton-Barries. You know, where Mum used to work before she had me. The big house near the Common.'

Rose had never told James who his father was. She said he was a seaman and had died a long time ago at sea, before they could be wed. She thought one day when he was grown up she might tell him the truth, but little good it would do him. Perhaps it was best left this way, with him accepting what she had told him.

James never once questioned what he had been told about his father, as the house was always filled with sailors anyway, drinking and playing cards. Rose still liked a good time with the men. He completely accepted the fact that one of them had probably got his mother pregnant and unfortunately died before he could marry her. He did tend to look down on her friends. He thought they were so common, always swearing smoking and drinking. He hated them and wished his mother could meet someone decent, who was not of a naval profession and settle down with him. So he did not have to come home to a room full of drunken sailors every night. Sometimes the air would be so blue from their smoking that you couldn't see across the room.

★　★　★

Rose had been thinking of Anthony a lot lately, mainly because James was a constant reminder of him. He had the same jet black curly hair, the same arrogance and stance. The way he wanted to take charge of things all the time, a born leader. No one could deny the fact that he was Anthony Leyton-Barrie's son, the likeness was quite alarming. She would turn around sometimes and James would be standing in the door way, the years would roll back and it was Anthony standing there. How different things could have been, if he had acknowledged James as his son. I wouldn't

175

have made any demands on him, I loved him too much. I was a virgin when I went to work for him, he just used me. I meant nothing to him and all these years later it still hurts. The only consolation I have is that his son Raith turned out to be such a twerp and Edwina wouldn't have any more children.

She found the pain of childbirth too much to bear. She would say to Anthony many times when he wanted to increase the family, 'Oh darling, it was just too awful to bear all that pain. It was just too horrid. I know you wouldn't want me to go through that suffering all over again and it would spoil my figure. You know how nice you like me to look for all your important functions. I have only just managed to get my figure back after all this time. No darling, not a good idea. We'll say no more about it.'

★　★　★

Anthony sighed in exasperation and thought of Rose. How good it would have been if she could have been mistress of my house. But if I had acknowledged her, my father would have cut me off without a penny. He would never have accepted a common maid as part of the family. She was twice the woman

176

Edwina is, even as young as she was. I did hear through the grape vine she had a son. I have never seen him and suppose I never will. Unknown to Anthony this was about to change.

★   ★   ★

Rose had heard through her friend Daisy, who still worked for the Leyton-Barries, how Edwina had refused to have any more children. She always was a selfish cow thought Rose. She does not know how lucky she is being married to Anthony. If I had been his wife I would have had a dozen children for him. She has never known in her life what it is to do a hard day's work. Selfish spoilt woman thought Rose, venomously.

The boys arrived outside the Leyton-Barries with 5 minutes to spare.

'What is this girl like? Who is she? What's her name?' asked Albert.

'Her name is Ellee, she is beautiful. She has blue eyes, lovely long blond hair down her back, and enormous tits. She's Irish, and she's going to be my girlfriend. I'm going to ask her to go to the pictures with me next week. I know she likes me.'

'What makes you so sure she'll want to go out with you anyway? How do you know her name, and that she's Irish?' Cocksure of himself as usual, thought Lewis. I expect he has exaggerated what she looks like as well.

'Veronica, Daisy's daughter, told me all about her and she hasn't got a boyfriend either. The family haven't been over here very long.'

★ ★ ★

They all looked up to see the two girls walking down the long driveway of the house. They had come from the servants' entrance at the back. Lewis just stared in amazement. He was speechless, she is beautiful. Know-all was absolutely right for once.

'Hallo Veronica and Ellee. Nice evening isn't it.'

'How do ye know me name and who are ye? asked Ellee.

'I'm James and this is my two cousins, Lewis and Albert.'

Ellee thought how handsome Lewis was with his lovely blond hair. She couldn't take her eyes off him and he felt the same about her. There was an instant attraction, love at first sight. For one awful moment Lewis had a horrible thought. What if she does want to go out with James. He seems pretty sure of himself.

178

'We were wondering if you girls would like to come to the pictures with us on your day off, and if we could walk you home?'

The girls conferred for a moment, then Veronica spoke up.

'Yes please, we would like to go to the pictures with you, and yes you may walk us home.'

Ellee stepped forward and took hold of Lewis' arm. He looked back over his shoulder and winked at James, who was by now seething with rage. Veronica not wishing to offend James or Albert, caught hold of each of them.

★　★　★

All this was being watched with much amusement by Anthony from a bedroom window of the house. Our new little maid Ellee certainly is a very pretty girl. Not just one boy waiting for her at the gate but three, and it looks like she had a choice of any of the three. All of them look smitten. I bet none of them were waiting for Veronica. Poor lanky Veronica, towering above all the boys and oh so plain. Still never mind, she's a willing and very good worker, just like her mother. If only I was twenty years younger. I mustn't think like that. That's how I got into trouble last time, chuckling to himself. Suddenly the boy with the black curly hair turned and looked towards the house with a face like thunder, having had Ellee stolen from right under his nose. He could hardly contain his anger.

Anthony was not expecting the shock he was about to receive as he looked straight at the boy. My God can it be? I can't believe it. It's me as a boy all over again. The resemblance is remarkable. Can it be, can it really be my son? He began to sweat and his hands were trembling. He sank onto the bed feeling weak from the shock. Edwina breezed into the room.

'Darling aren't you ready yet? We are going to be late. Why whatever is the matter? You look white as a sheet and you are trembling. Shall I call a doctor? Are you ill?'

'No, no I'm alright. Just a bit overcome by the heat. Did you see those boys at the gate, waiting for the girls? Who are they?'

'Yes, I'll speak to the girls tomorrow. We can't have any riff-raff hanging around outside. I'll tell the servant girls to keep their boyfriends well clear of our gateway.'

'No I'll speak to them myself tomorrow.'

'Oh very well, they can be very tiresome at times. I'll leave you to deal with them then darling.'

★ ★ ★

All through Colonel Barrington-Smyth's dinner party, Anthony was deep in thought.

'Everything alright old chap? You've been very quiet all evening.'

'Yes it's this darn heat getting me down. It's so humid, one can hardly breathe.'

He could not get the dark curly haired boy's face out of his mind. All evening it kept coming back to haunt him. I must find out who he is.

★ ★ ★

The next morning Veronica was summoned to the master's study. A little nervously she tapped on the door.

'Come in. Now Veronica don't be nervous. I need to ask you a few questions. Who were those boys at the gate yesterday evening?'

'Please Sir, they meant no harm. They were just friends. I'll tell them not to come again Sir. I'm very sorry Sir.'

'Now don't upset yourself girl. I just need to know their names. Tell me the dark haired boy, who is he?'

'That's James Ford, Sir. The other two boys are his cousins, Lewis Preston and Albert Burrows.'

181

'Thank you Veronica. That will be all. I only needed to know they were good respectable boys. As you know we have a lot of valuable things in this house and I had to make sure they were not burglars, but if you can vouch for them, then that's alright. Veronica not a word to your mistress about this conversation. She gets a bit nervous at times. Ask your friends to wait a little further up the road, away from our gate in future please.'

'Yes Sir.'

* * *

It's him, James Ford, my son. I knew the moment I clapped eyes on him. He has Leyton-Barrie stamped all over him, more so than Raith that weed of mine. He takes after Edwina's family, weak, no backbone, mother's boy. That James looked tough and angry, annoyed with the blond boy over the girl. That's my boy, a one for the girls. I must watch for him again this evening. Perhaps I'll take a stroll just as the servants are leaving, and see if I can get a closer look at him.

* * *

Days later James was still furious with Lewis. It was the first time in their lives that they had seriously fallen out. They had their squabbles as children but always remained friends, they were cousins. They were the 'Three Musketeers' and they soon shook hands, made up their differences and were friends again. This was different. How could Lewis do this to me? He stole the only girl I could truly love. How could he do it? He was my friend. He kicked open the garden gate and slammed the front door. Rose was sitting drinking a cup of tea when he came in.

'James for goodness sake, whatever is the matter with you these past few days? You are like a bear with a sore head.'

James related the story of how Lewis had stolen his girlfriend from under his nose.

'That doesn't sound like Lewis. It sounds to me like this girl preferred Lewis to you. If she took his arm and not yours.'

James had hoped at least his own mother would have been on his side.

'Where did you all meet this girl anyway?'

'She works for the Leyton-Barries.'

Rose nearly choked on a mouthful of tea and began to cough and splutter.

'Mother do be careful, you nearly choked yourself. Don't try to talk and drink at the same time.'

'What are you doing hanging around the Leyton-Barries? I would prefer it if you kept away from that lot.'

'Looks like I'm going to have to now Lewis has stole my girl.'

'James, she was not your girl. She wasn't walking out with you. I suggest you go and make it up with Lewis. It's not his fault if she prefers him to you. There are plenty more fish in the sea. Find yourself another girl.'

'But I only want her,' wailed James.

★ ★ ★

Rose went around to Daisy's house that evening to find out what had been going on. Daisy related how Anthony had called Veronica to his study and questioned her about James.

'My God Daisy. He's spotted the family likeness and realised James is his son. I always feared this would happen.'

'He was bound to bump into him one day, living in the same town.'

'But I never thought he would with him being so rich. We move in different circles. Have a different way of life altogether. It was ironic that the boys all went after the new maid and he saw them waiting for her. Thank God she preferred Lewis to James, or he would be hanging around their gate forever more, waiting for her to come out. God knows what would have happened then. What do you think Anthony will do next, Daisy?'

'I haven't any idea Rose. All I know is he wasn't best pleased with Mistress Edwina for not wanting any more children, and he's not very pleased with the son and heir he's got, Raith. If I know the master your James would be far more to his liking as an heir.'

'Well I'd better be going Daisy. Keep me posted of any events.'

★   ★   ★

James took his mother's advice and decided to bury the hatchet and be friends with Lewis again. Lewis was delighted and told James he had met Ellee's family and she had three sisters. One is already spoken for but perhaps they could all go out in a foursome with one of the other two. James was immediately interested.

'I think the best one for you James is Annie. She's sixteen, a year older than us, but that doesn't matter. The other one Bridie is only thirteen, a bit too young. The other one is eighteen, too old, but she already has a boyfriend anyway.'

James readily agreed and arrangements

were made for the four of them to go out together.

★   ★   ★

From the first moment Annie saw James she was immediately impressed with him. She thought him so clever and he seemed to know a lot about everything. She did not find him cocky or overbearing, as others sometimes did. To her he was wonderful, kind and generous. He seemed to have plenty of money to splash about. He must have a very good job to have so much money thought Annie. He never told her he was just a butcher boy in his Great Uncle John's shop. She prayed to God that he would want to see her again. James for his part was delighted with his blind date. He could see she was captivated by him and hung onto every word he said. She took him so seriously. It gave his ego a mighty big boost. At the end of the evening he asked if he might see Annie again. She jumped at the idea, then blushed thinking she had sounded too eager. James just smirked to himself. He had made a real conquest there. About time someone started appreciating me, he thought to himself.

★   ★   ★

Lewis invited Ellee to tea to meet his family. She was a little nervous at first but soon settled down. She liked Florence, Fred and Chris immediately and they all liked her, but what she did not like was the house. Although she enjoyed the tea party she couldn't wait to get away from the house. There is something terribly wrong here, she kept thinking. Florence picked up on her thoughts immediately. She is psychic and has sensed the bad atmosphere in this house. I can tell by the look on her face and the way she keeps glancing over her shoulder, like someone is watching her, thought Florence.

'Penny for them Flo. Well what did you think of her, you're very deep in thought?'

'I thought she was charming. Perfect for our Lewis.'

★   ★   ★

When Ellee arrived home Bridget was sitting in the kitchen waiting for her.

'Well how did ye get on? Was his family nice?'

'Yes Mother but the house was terrible.'

'What do ye mean terrible? Was it dirty, or falling down?'

'No, none of those things. The house was very neat and clean and well decorated. It was just dark and spooky. I didn't like being there. The sun was shining outside but it was so dark inside. It was like the sun couldn't get through the windows to brighten the place up, something seemed to be holding it back. Lewis took me outside to show me their pretty, long garden. We were stood at the very bottom of the garden when I heard a baby crying. It was such a pitiful wail, terrible it was. I've heard nothing like it in me life before. I said to Lewis, can ye hear that baby crying? Who does it belong to? He said he couldn't hear it and that I was as bad as his mother and Albert. They are always hearing a baby cry, especially during the summer months. That house really gave me the creeps and I was very pleased when it was time to go. I liked his family very much. They were all lovely, kind, generous people.'

'Perhaps the house is haunted Ellee, and ye have the gift that is only given to a few of us. I have the gift and me mother before me. It seems to be passed down through families. And because ye have this special gift, ye would know that a house was haunted as soon as ye walked in. I wonder what ails that house?'

★ ★ ★

Florence was still pondering over Ellee's reaction to the house. That girl didn't like the house the moment she walked in. She seemed to sense the strangeness of it all, just like that gypsy all those years ago. Her words have come to pass. She said Chris would marry a girl from over the water and Bessie is from the Isle of Wight, and I would have another son. Lewis also has a girl from over the water, from Ireland. The hauntings in the house seem far worse when there is a psychic presence. I do hope things are not going to happen all over again, now Ellee has come to our family. It has been so quiet lately. I've hardly been here on my own, I've been that busy. Fred, Chris and Lewis are totally unaffected by anything supernatural so it is unable to touch any of them, thank God. They just laugh and make jokes about the ghost all the time, which is good in one way to deny its presence, seems to render it harmless.

★   ★   ★

Lewis thought it time Albert found a girlfriend to walk out with and voiced his opinion.

'I have mate. Her name is Julie and she's the red head in the Fish and Chip shop.'

189

'You crafty devil. You kept that quiet. How long has it been going on?' James chipped in.

'Not long, only a few weeks. Just after you two started going out with your girls. I've known her by sight for a long time, but it was only the other week I plucked up courage and asked her out, and she said yes.'

'A red head you say. That means we have as girlfriends between us a blonde, brunette and red head. Not bad lads,' laughed Lewis.

'Ellee was telling me the other day, that the Higgins gang from St. Mary's had been bothering her sister Maggie because she wouldn't go out with the younger Higgins boy.'

'Do you mean that creep Charlie? We've had trouble with that gang before. Tell Ellee we'll soon sort them out, as we have done in the past.'

'I think it's all been sorted out James but we'll keep an eye on the situation. Any more trouble we'll be straight there. No one bothers our girls or their families and gets away with it.'

12

It had been two years since Anthony first saw James. The thought that James was his son and he had no claim to him, riled him.

I wonder if I should get in touch with Rose. No that's not good thinking. It would only show me up as the liar I am, in denying my own flesh and blood, and ever having had anything to do with a lowly parlour maid. Perhaps I could bump into Rose accidentally on purpose, and ask after her and her family. Yes that's what I'll do, take a stroll past Cedar Road in the hope of seeing Rose. I think Daisy was too dense to realise why I questioned Veronica about James, she wouldn't have passed it on to Rose. He did not know how wrong he was. In his snobbery he regarded all the servants as dense. Daisy might not have had a posh education but dense she was not. She had enough common sense to know what he was getting at, in questioning Veronica.

★ ★ ★

The next evening his luck was in. As he was walking down Cedar Road, Rose was coming up.

'Hallo Rose. How nice to see you.'

'I wondered how long it would be before you showed up. What do you want?'

He was taken aback that Rose had rumbled him.

'Why Rose I was just passing, out for a stroll.'

'Don't give me that Anthony. I wasn't born yesterday. Taking a stroll in this area, where your servants live. Slumming it are we. Don't you think there have been enough lies in the past? Just be straight with me. You owe me that much. What is it you want? As if I didn't know. It's James isn't it?'

Her sharp words stung him. She was lovely as ever. He felt all the old emotions stirring. He took her in his arms.

'Rose I . . . '

She pushed him away.

'Rose please let me come in and try to explain.'

Out of the corner of her eye she could see the net curtains twitching over the road, and not wishing to entertain the neighbours she let him in. Once inside she unleashed her spite on him.

'How dare you. Who do you think you are,

that you can just come here, after all this time and interfere with my life?'

The back door banged and in walked James, unaware anybody was in the house.

'Mum I'm going to need a new bike. This one is . . . ' his voice tailed off. Who was this tall dark stranger who looked slightly familiar, talking with his mother. He certainly wasn't one of her sailor friends. He looked too refined for that, more uppercrust.

'I'm sorry Mother I didn't know you had company. I'll just go up to my room.'

'No don't do that,' Anthony was quick to stop James leaving. 'I'm Anthony Leyton-Barrie. I used to be your mother's employer. I was just passing and bumped into your mother, whom I hadn't seen for years.'

Rose glared at him, still keeping up his lies. He was always good at making himself sound plausible.

'You need a new bike you say. Perhaps I can help.' Anthony took a wad of notes from his wallet.

'No Mr. Leyton-Barrie. It's very kind of you but we don't take charity. We can manage.' Rose almost hissed at him.

James was disappointed. He could really do with the money. He needed the new bike, to take Annie out to impress her further. How could Mum do it. Refuse his kindness. We

193

deserve the money. I expect she worked really hard for him once, for a pittance, and he wants to show his gratitude.

'Well Mr. Leyton-Barrie, don't let us take up any more of your valuable time. I expect you have important business to attend to. It was so kind of you to call,' Rose said rather sarcastically as she showed him to the door.

★　★　★

As Anthony wandered back home a plan began to form in his mind. That boy looked really disappointed when Rose refused the money. She always was a strong stubborn girl. That's what I liked most about her, how strong willed she was, and defiant too. She has done a good job in bringing up our son all alone. His manners were impeccable. Well Rose my girl, I'll not see our son go without or struggle over money anymore. Anything he wants he shall have. If he needs a new bicycle, he shall have one. I'll try to get him on his own away from Rose and give him the money.

★　★　★

The next day, as luck would have it, James had to make a meat delivery to one of the other big houses in The Grove. It was just a few doors away from the Leyton-Barries' residence and Anthony spotted him. Immediately he seized the opportunity to speak to James again. He was out the front door in a flash.

'Good morning James. How nice to see you again so soon.'

'Good morning Sir.'

'James, about the money for your new bicycle. I have it here. Please take it.'

'But Mum said . . . ' Anthony interrupted him before he could finish what he was going to say.

'Never mind what your mother said. Women don't understand these things. How sometimes us men need a little bit more money than we have for important things, and may need a little bit of help from our friends from time to time.'

'Are you our friend Sir? I don't understand. Why are you being so kind to us?'

'Let's just say, when your mother worked for us she was a very good worker. Perhaps we didn't appreciate her, or show our gratitude enough at the time, for services rendered. Now bumping into you has given me the opportunity to put that right. Tell me James. Have you a father?'

'No Sir he died at sea, before he could marry Mother.'

So that's what she's told him. As good a story as any I suppose, in the circumstances. Good old Rose. She didn't let me down by blabbing all around the neighbourhood who the father of her illegitimate son was. He handed the wad of notes to James.

'Now take this my son. I can easily afford it.'

James hesitated. Strange thing to say, my son. If only he were my father. I would have no worries over money anymore. I could buy all the things I've ever wanted, take Annie out, and buy her nice things as well. Even marry her one day.

'Go on take it,' forcing the money into James' hand, he left quickly before Edwina spotted what was going on. I hope she wasn't looking out of a window somewhere in the house.

As luck would have it she was nowhere near a window. She was sat in front of her dressing room mirror. Trying to make herself look glamorous and wondering what to do with herself today.

★ ★ ★

James wondered how he was going to explain the money to his mother. He knew she would be furious. If I bought the bike first, surely

196

she wouldn't make me take it back to the shop.

★   ★   ★

The following day while shopping with Flo and Ame, Rose related the story of how Anthony had turned up and tried to give James money, and how furious she was.

'Calm down Rose and just think about it for a moment. All these years you have struggled to bring James up alone and a fine job you have made of it too. Everyone says so, not for one moment did you consider giving him up for adoption. You took no notice of all the gossip. You didn't let it upset you one bit and gradually all those gossips have come to admire you. You've done your duty as a mother all these years. Now it's Anthony's turn. If he's suddenly found his conscience after all these years and wants to provide for James, let him. Don't you agree Ame?'

'Yes I do Flo. Take anything he has to offer Rose, for James' sake. Don't let pride get in your way.'

'Do you really think so?'

'Yes we do.' They both chorused.

'Do you think I should tell James, Anthony is his father?'

'That's up to you dear. You know your son

better than Flo or I. If you think it right to tell him, then do so. But if you think he'll be upset, then leave things as they are. It's your choice. We can't advise you on that Rose.'

★ ★ ★

When Rose returned from her shopping trip, a rather nervous James was waiting for her. She could see at once he was edgy.

'What is it now James? What have you done?'

'Mum please don't be cross with me. I saw Mr. Leyton-Barrie today and he gave me the money for a new bike. Please Mum don't make me take it back. I really need a new one. I've never had a new bike before. Just a load of old second hand ones that everyone else cast aside. The frame has gone on my bike. It's beyond repair.'

Rose could see how much the bike meant to him and didn't have the heart to upset him anymore. Still ringing in her ears was the advice given to her by her sisters.

'Well I suppose I'd better have a look at this new bike. Where is it then?'

'In the back garden, leaning against the scullery window.'

'James it's a lovely bike.'

'Mother thank you.'

'For what? I didn't buy the bike. Anthony Leyton-Barrie did.'

'For being my mum and letting me keep the bike. I have a few pounds left. I want you to have it Mother. I know how you struggle to make ends meet with your cleaning jobs, and my pay doesn't amount to much.'

'No, you keep the money. You deserve it. Buy Annie something nice for her birthday, which is coming up soon isn't it? I have my barmaid work two evenings a week. We'll manage so don't you fret and James, thank you.'

'For what?'

'For being my son and for being so kind and generous.'

Mother and son hugged one another. James smiled. He could not believe his luck. It was the happiest he had felt in a long time. He was expecting an evening of upset with his mother over the bike and was surprised at her change of heart. Things were really beginning to look up for the first time. He had money in his pocket to spare. He had his lovely Annie who adored him, what more could he want for.

★ ★ ★

The next day was Saturday. Florence, Fred, Amelia, Tom and Rose were all going on The Elm Tree annual pub outing. Lewis decided to have his cousins and the girls around for a game of cards and a few songs around the piano. Lewis was very good on the piano and could play any tune by ear.

'Come on girls, what Irish song would you like me to play?'

'How about Galway Bay. It's me favourite,' chirped Ellee.

Lewis began to play and everyone joined in singing 'If you ever go across the sea to Ireland . . . '. Then Annie suggested, 'I'll take you home again Kathleen', followed by 'Danny Boy'.

Lewis stopped for a breather and poured everyone another drink.

'It's a shame Julie isn't here. What time does she finish at the chip shop, Albert?' asked James.

'Quite late, but her boss said if they are not too busy she may be allowed out a little earlier.'

'Speaking of which, I'm starved. Does anyone else fancy fish and chips?' enquired Lewis.

'Yes' came the unanimous reply.

'I'll go and get them,' offered Albert. 'Cod and chips all round.'

'Don't let the chips get cold while you're chatting to Julie,' teased James.

'No I won't. I'll run all the way back with them, I promise.'

★ ★ ★

After half an hour, Albert had still not returned.

'I wonder what's keeping him? If there is one thing I hate it's lukewarm fish and chips. Do you think we ought to go and see what's happened to him, James?'

'No I expect he's chatting with Julie. I just hope he buys the fish and chips after his chat, and not before.'

There was a frantic banging on the front door. Lewis went to answer it.

'Albert why didn't . . . ' his voice tailed off. A very white faced Mr. Butler was stood on the step.

'Can I come in lad? I'm afraid I have some very bad news for you.'

'Yes of course,' his mind was racing. The charabanc had crashed with all their parents on board and they were all killed.

'It's your cousin Albert lad. He's dead.'

'Dead, no he can't be. He's gone to get some fish and chips for our supper. You must be mistaken Mr. Butler. It must be someone else.'

'No lad I'm not. He was running past our house by the alleyway up the road. Just as he was passing the alleyway, someone jumped out on him as a joke. It frightened him. He wasn't expecting it and he just dropped down dead. The ambulance man said it looked like he had a heart attack.'

Lewis was joined in the hall by James and the others. Everyone was shocked into silence, no one could find the words to speak.

'I'm sorry to be the bearer of such sad tidings. I'd better get back to Mrs. Butler. She's taken it badly, with it happening right on our doorstep so to speak.'

'Just a minute please. Who jumped out on him?'

'It was one of the Higgins boys, Charlie I think.'

'That does it. Charlie Higgins is for it. He killed our cousin. We're going to get him.'

'Now Lewis, I know you're upset but beating up the Higgins boy won't achieve anything. In fact he's in a bad enough state anyway. He kept muttering, 'It was only a joke. I didn't wish him any harm.' Then he got sick. He's just a shivering wreck and was taken off to hospital as well, to be treated for shock.'

He'll be in shock alright by the time we're finished with him, thought Lewis.

'How are we going to be able to tell Aunty Amelia and Uncle Tom, Lewis. What do we say?'

⋆ ⋆ ⋆

Amelia was inconsolable and shut herself away in their bedroom for days on end. She would not even come out to eat or drink. Tom feared for her life if she did not eat soon.

'You must try to eat, Ame. You must keep your strength up for little Alice's sake. Thank God she's away on holiday in Devon with my family. Poor love, losing her big brother will be a terrible shock, and her only six years old. I don't know how she will cope. She adored Albert.'

⋆ ⋆ ⋆

Florence was in a state of shock and could not concentrate on anything. All she could think of was the house. The curse that is on this house, it had got to dear sweet Albert. Albert who was always afraid of the house and never wanted to be alone in it.

She dared not voice her thoughts to anyone else, in case they thought her deranged. I wish we could leave this damned house. We can't leave just yet. Amelia and Tom will need us all close at hand, but one day maybe. It seems to me that all the special ones are taken. First Harry, such a good friend to Fred, and now Albert, who never did any harm to anyone. Such a sweet natured boy. He was so thrilled with his new girlfriend Julie, with her red hair and bouncy curls. They say she has not been back to work since it happened. She has been that distraught, people are saying she'll never get over it, but she's young. Please God, one day there will be someone else for her. I suppose I must tell our Mary the bad news. Her health has been steadily failing for years. It's the strain of living with that old devil she's married to. I swear he'll drive her into a mental institution in the end, with his demanding, domineering, cruel ways. She is a bundle of nerves all the time when he is around. She nearly jumps out of her skin every time he opens his mouth. To the best of my knowledge he hasn't laid a finger on her since our little talk.

★   ★   ★

Flo did not realize how true her thoughts would become. Within one month Mary was reduced to a blithering wreck. Had a complete breakdown and had to be institutionalised. Florence blamed Ernest totally and told him so. Little good it did her. It was in one ear and out the other. With Mary safely out of the way he was free to carry on his womanising, gambling and drinking with his friends. He never went near the mental home, or had any contact with Mary whatsoever. To him it was as if she never existed. Someone to be cast off when she was of no further use to him.

'He'll get his comeuppance one day. God doesn't pay his debts with money Flo, you should know that.'

'I know Fred but our poor Mary is in that dreadful place, all alone without any of her family near her. Do you think she will ever be cured?'

'I don't know my sweet. We shall have to see. Only time will tell.'

'The only consolation is that poor Mother is not here to share these very sad times we're all going through. She used to worry over Mary all the time. All Mother ever wanted for her was to see her settled in a good marriage. She loved us all, but knew the rest of us could take care of ourselves, but Mary needed kindness and someone to look after her, she's such a timid frail thing.'

★   ★   ★

Gradually Amelia began to pull herself together, for the sake of Alice. She cried daily for Albert, alone in her room. Tom was a tower of strength. He kept himself together and did not give way to his feelings by breaking down and letting all his sorrow out. Old Doctor Fisher had warned him, if he did not grieve for his son it would play havoc with his health later on.

Tom remembered when he had the breakdown after the war. How bad he had felt when he couldn't stop crying. I won't let that happen again. I owe it to Amelia and Alice to stay strong.

It was a year later before old Doctor Fisher's words had come to pass. It was the anniversary of Albert's death and Amelia thought they should all get away to Devon to Tom's family. They planned to leave early Saturday morning. Friday night everything was packed ready for their early start. Amelia was out of bed first. She threw back the curtains, the sun was shining.

'Come on Tom, get up the weather is perfect.'

There was no movement or reply from the bed.

'Come on Tom. Do move yourself or we'll miss the train.'

Still nothing. Tom's eyes were opened

staring at her. He couldn't move or speak. She screamed and Alice came rushing into her parents' bedroom.

'Quick Alice, fetch Aunty Flo and Uncle Fred. Tell them Daddy has been taken ill. Hurry!'

Flo and Fred had already heard the scream and were out of bed pulling on their clothes as fast as they could.

★   ★   ★

When Doctor Fisher arrived he confirmed what they had all feared. Tom had suffered a very bad stroke and was paralysed. He would probably be confined to a wheelchair for the rest of his life, if he lived through these next few hours.

★   ★   ★

Their world was shattered. Flo wondered how much more the family could take. Life could be so cruel at times. The family were very lucky financially. Other people were suffering through these very hard times. Men out of work and not a penny to their names to feed their families. Children begging in the streets for a few coppers, but none of Flo's family had suffered this fate.

Flo and Fred had managed to secure a third property and were currently renting it out to a poor family who only paid their rent when they could. Which wasn't very often. Flo just turned a blind eye to the money they were owed and thanked God that they were not in the same position. Fred was still working for Mr. Griffin and Lewis also worked for him, as an apprentice carpenter. Tom and Amelia were doing quite well until fate had struck this cruel blow. Tom had eventually accepted Great Uncle John's offer to manage the butcher's shop, with a lot of gentle persuasion from Amelia.

'Beggars can't be choosers,' she had often said to Tom.

Finally he had to agree. There was not a lot of choice. He had not learnt a trade while in the Regiment. He was not very talented with his hands, unlike Fred who could turn his hand to anything. Work was so scarce that in the end he had to give in.

Young James had joined him as a delivery boy and was learning the meat trade, quite enthusiastically.

★ ★ ★

John and Christine had never had any children and regarded Beatrice's children as their own. Amelia had always been his favourite. He thought her the prettiest of the bunch. Now he was well into his eighties and Christine her early sixties, he decided to make his will, leaving the butcher's shop to Amelia and Tom. Any money left after both of their deaths was to be shared amongst the remaining sisters.

★ ★ ★

Rose was also managing quite well with money. She had her cleaning jobs by day and two evenings per week behind the bar at The Elm Tree public house. James was extremely fortunate as well. His weekly wage was constantly being topped up by Anthony every time he bumped into him. Which was quite often these days. At least once a week, sometimes twice. He did feel slightly suspicious about the whole situation, as to why Anthony was giving him all this money. One day I shall find out no doubt. There is more to this than meets the eye. Still I must not look a gift horse in the mouth, so for the time being I'm quite content to accept Anthony's money.

13

Ellee was still upset by Albert's death. It was taking her a long time to get used to not having him around. He had always been there with Lewis and she could only imagine how bad Lewis must be feeling. Sometimes she would look at him and see tears in his eyes and know he was thinking of Albert. She had preferred Albert to James. With his show off ways, plying our Annie with gifts all the time. He's giving her a swollen head, with all the money he seems to have. She's getting as bad as he is. She can't wait to tell us all about her latest gift from him. The minute she is in the door, she never stops talking about him until she goes to bed. She's driving us all mad with the swank of her.

★ ★ ★

Ellee and Bridget were alone in the house. It was Ellee's day off. She decided to confide in Bridget about the night Albert had died.

'We were all stood around the piano. Lewis was playing and we were all singing. There was a terrible wailing sound, just like a

Banshee. Mother, it really frightened me. I said Jesus the Banshee. That means a death. Everyone laughed at me and said it was the dog up the road. Lewis said it sometimes made weird noises like that. I said, that was no dog. After that Albert went out to get the fish and chips and I never saw him again. Mother they didn't know what a Banshee was. They said they'd never heard of one before.'

'The English don't seem to know about these things. Ah to be sure they're a lot of non believers.'

'Mother I hate that house, I really do. There seems to be something bad about it. I don't know what it is. It just gives me the creeps every time I'm in it. I can't wait to get outside and away from it, and breathe in God's good clean air, then I'm alright again till the next time.'

'Does the family ever say anything about it, or feel the strangeness of it all?'

'None of the men do. They just laugh it off. Anything that happens, they always try to explain it away. I tink Mrs. Preston does but she never says anything to me.'

'Why don't ye ask her Ellee?'

'No Mother I'd be too embarrassed.'

* * *

Their conversation was brought to a close by the return of Annie and Maggie from work.

'Mother what's for me tea I'm starved?' shouted Maggie, as she hung her coat up in the hall. Before Bridget could answer, Annie was off once again.

'Mother just look what James has bought me. This beautiful blouse. He met me at dinner time and gave it to me. Won't I look grand in it? All the girls in the office will be so jealous.'

They won't be the only ones thought Bridget. No sooner had the thought crossed her mind, when Maggie let loose with a torrent of abuse.

'For God's sake Annie. Do we have to have another meal time of what James bought you and what James said. Anyway, where does he get all this money from? Does he come by it dishonestly?'

Annie was horrified at this suggestion. Not her darling James.

'How could you tink such a ting, never mind say it. You can be so cruel and jealous at times. You know what Pop always says about jealousy. It's worse than galloping consumption.'

Maggie raised her hand to strike Annie, but Ellee and Bridget were on their feet in an instant and managed to stop the blow.

'Let go of me,' screamed Maggie, 'I hate her.'

'Not till ye calm down and don't ye ever let me hear ye say ever again, that ye hate any of yer sisters.'

'Jesus, what the hell is going on in here?' shouted Willy as he entered the kitchen. 'Do I have to come home to me tea and hear this every evening. I can't stand much more of it. If it doesn't stop, ye'll all have to pack yer bags and get out of me house.'

'She started it Pop. Criticizing me and James. She's as bad with Ronnie, trying to talk posh with her you's and th's.'

'Enough! Stop now I'll have no more of it,' roared Willy.

★ ★ ★

Bridget had turned ashen and felt sick, she tried to get up and collapsed on the floor. The doctor was called in. It was her heart trouble once again. She was confined to bed and must have complete rest with no worries or stress. She had suffered another very mild heart attack. This time she refused to go to hospital. The doctor agreed she could stay home, although he was not at all happy with the situation but he did not want to distress Bridget further by insisting she went to hospital.

The girls were all on their best behaviour for the next few weeks. Never a cross word passed between them, but a few black looks did. Gradually as the weeks passed, Bridget began to regain her strength and was beginning to get about again. The doctor had warned Willy that her heart was in a bad shape and he should expect the worst at any time, but hopefully it wouldn't come to that and she might last for years. No one could predict for sure, how long she had to live. Willy decided to keep this information to himself. He would not tell the girls or Jack this upsetting bit of news, and certainly not Bridget. He would have to bear the pain of it all alone. He would have to keep the magpie in order. (His nickname for Maggie). That girl is far too headstrong and not too big to feel the back of me hand if she steps out of line again. I won't have Biddy upset by the likes of her.

★ ★ ★

Ellee was shopping in Portswood for the family late one Saturday afternoon, when she bumped into Florence.

'Hello Mrs. Preston.'

'Hallo Ellee dear. Are you coming to the

214

house this evening?'

She was quick to notice, although fleetingly, the look of fear on Ellee's face.

'I a . . . don't know if Lewis wants to take me out or not.'

As Florence looked past Ellee, she couldn't help noticing the house which they were standing outside. The brass plate on the wall read 'Madame Deveaux', Clairvoyant and Medium. On impulse Florence thought it would be a good idea to see Madame Deveaux and take Ellee with her.

'Look Ellee, whose house we are standing outside, a medium's. Shall we go in and have our fortunes told?'

'I don't know Mrs. Preston. I tink it's against me religion. I don't tink I should.'

'I don't think it is, but you could always ask the Priest when you next go to confession and if it is he could grant you forgiveness,' said Florence with a wicked twinkle in her eye. 'Come on Ellee, it'll be a bit of fun. I've never been before so it will be my first time as well.'

Ellee agreed very reluctantly. Not wishing to upset Mrs. Preston.

★　★　★

Florence knocked loudly on the door and it was opened by a lady in her early sixties. She had black hair and a dark complexion.

A bit of gypsy in her, thought Florence. Florence asked if they could make an appointment for a reading. Madame Deveaux had a cancellation and could see them right away. Florence was under the impression that they would have their fortunes told, and was taken aback when they were given messages from the other side.

She turned to Ellee first.

'I can see a young girl, who passed over many years ago. Her head is completely covered in bandages. She says she was your friend and she was very pleased when her mother gave you her few little trinkets. Do you know who she is?'

Ellee nodded her head.

'Ah good I thought you would. She is so pleased you are here. She says, you will marry a fair man and have a very happy life together. You will not be rich, but you will not want for anything. You will have enough money to live on through your lives together. She says be happy and sends you her love.'

Ellee was thrilled that Sarah had come back to her to wish her well.

★ ★ ★

Florence sat in stunned silence. She thought it was going to be a bit of fun on a Saturday afternoon. Not the accurate details they were receiving from the other side. She believed in God and an afterlife, but could not fully accept that people could see into the future and give messages from the spirit world.

She had assumed it was all a fake. I suppose there could be something in it. The gypsy on my doorstep all those years ago was pretty accurate in what she said, and I myself sometimes get a sense of foreboding before something bad is going to happen. Madame Deveaux was staring at Florence.

'Now my dear, it is your turn. I have a man with you. A strong stern looking man. He has a moustache and smoked a pipe. He said you didn't like him very much when he was alive and the feeling was mutual. He has a Yorkshire accent. He said he thought you had far too much to say for yourself and women should know their place. Can you accept this man?'

'Yes he's my father-in-law.'

'Good, good, I'll continue with him then. He says perhaps he was a little hard on you. He was very old fashioned in his ways. One of the old school who believed that the men should wear the trousers. He now realises he

217

was wrong. Times are changing and these days women have much more freedom. He thanks you for being a good wife to his son and mother to his grandsons. The baby boy you lost is with him, growing up in the spirit world. He says beware of the house. There is danger!'

'What does he mean, danger?' Florence shivered slightly.

'I don't know my dear. He has gone and I can't get him back.'

★ ★ ★

As they strolled home together, Ellee was elated, but Florence was pretty shocked.

'That was a grand reading we had Mrs. Preston. Shall we go again sometime?'

'No I don't think so dear.' Florence made the excuse it was a bit expensive and they must all save their money for her wedding to Lewis.

'But that's not for ages yet. We are not even engaged.'

'It is never too soon to start saving. The sooner you start, the more you will have later on Ellee.'

★ ★ ★

When Florence related the afternoon's events to Fred, he laughed his head off.

'Ee Flo, you've been 'ad. She was a fake. You never liked Father, or he thee. Why would he come back to you and admit he was wrong, never. If there was one thing he would never do, is admit he was wrong.'

Florence was slightly annoyed at Fred's attitude and thought it best to let the subject drop, and not argue with him any more.

She still felt uneasy. Madame Deveaux's words still kept echoing in her mind. 'Beware of the house! There is danger.' What could he have meant. Just like him not to tell you everything you need to know. She decided not to dwell on his words too much. She had been safe up to now, although others had not been so lucky. First the baby, it is nice to know he lives on in the spirit world. Even if he is with old Henry Preston, poor love.

Then our dear friend Harry and Albert, my darling nephew. I truly hope there will be no more bad luck.

★ ★ ★

After Tom's stroke Amelia tried to manage the butcher's shop by herself but found it all too much. She decided to make young James manager and hoped he would not upset the staff too much.

She needed to spend more time with Tom, not leaving him for hours on end while she was in the shop. She had to rely on Flo and the goodwill of the neighbours, to pop in and keep an eye on him while she was working. She found it all too hard to handle. She just wanted to be home with Tom and Alice, to grieve for Albert in her own home and in private. Not having to put a brave face on things all the time. Two years had now passed since his death and one year since Tom's stroke. He had regained the power of speech but not the use of his limbs. She prayed daily for his complete recovery but in her heart of hearts she knew this would never happen. Tom would be confined to a wheelchair for the rest of his days. She hoped she had not made a terrible mistake in leaving James, a mere nineteen year old, in charge of the shop. He was family after all, and he had promised faithfully he would do his best for her and Uncle Tom. She wondered how the rest of the staff would feel about taking orders from a nineteen year old, but it was too bad, not her concern anymore. Her duty was to Tom and Alice. The staff should think themselves lucky in having a job at all in these hard times.

★ ★ ★

Edwina and Anthony were growing further apart. She spent more and more time in London, at the fashion houses with her smart friends. Often she would stay there for several days on end, partying into the small hours. Anthony began to wonder if she was seeing anyone else. Knowing full well that if anyone took her fancy, she wouldn't say no. Spoilt bitch, always did want her own way and usually got it. I couldn't care less, if she is, or if she isn't. In fact it would suit me quite well if someone came along and took her off my hands, and that spoilt brat of a son of ours as well. I'm fed up bailing him out of debt all the time. It's time he stood on his own two feet and took some responsibility for his gambling debts. I won't be around forever to foot the bill, and to think all this will be his one day.

Father would turn in his grave if he knew the family fortunes would be going to a bounder and complete waster. Why should it all go to him. James is my son as well. Father would have been proud of him. He is a Leyton-Barrie through and through, there is no denying it. It's plain for all to see. Why should my own flesh and blood suffer poverty. I'll go and see the family solicitor tomorrow and change my will. Meanwhile I think I'll go and see Rose. I want her to tell James that I am his father.

★　★　★

Rose was sitting alone in her front room thinking. James was out with Annie and would not be back for hours. She could not get Anthony out of her mind lately. I must stop thinking of him like this. All the old feelings I thought had gone forever are still there. Seeing him again has stirred it all up. If only . . .

A sudden bang at the front door brought her back to earth. Who can that be this time of night she wondered? She opened the door and was startled to see Anthony. She trembled slightly. It was a shock seeing him standing there. It was almost as if her thoughts had brought him to her. She had wished so much she could be with him and now here he was standing before her.

Anthony was quick to notice the slight tremor and flush to her cheeks. Can it be true, he thought, does she want me, as much as I want her?

'Rose I . . . ' his voice was husky with emotion. 'I had to see you again, talk to you, be with you. Please let me in.'

She led him through to the front room, where she had previously been sitting thinking about him.

★ ★ ★

All the past years had suddenly been swept aside. He took her in his arms and kissed her. They were both young again. It was as if they had never been parted. Time meant nothing.

'Rose can you ever forgive me? I should have owned up at the time, that I was the father of your child. I was a coward. I was afraid my father would cut me off without a penny. Money and position meant a lot to me in those days, but I have suffered believe me. I have paid the price. I have not had a day's happiness or love from Edwina in all these years. I found out how wrong I was the hard way. I intend to divorce her and marry you if you'll have me. I want James to know who his true father is and take up his rightful place in my household.'

Rose was stunned into silence by this outburst. It seemed like all her prayers were being answered at once. She must be dreaming, or she didn't hear correctly. She still remained silent.

'Rose answer me please. Please say you'll do me the honour of becoming my wife.'

'Yes, yes Anthony I will.' Her usually strong steady voice was barely above a whisper.

'What about James, Rose, how will he view me as his father?'

'Well he likes you very much, and he's already suspicious of your generosity towards him. But I don't think the penny has dropped yet, as to why you have been helping him out financially.'

'When will he be back? It's quite late, shouldn't he be in by now?'

'No, being a Saturday night he may not be in till after midnight. What about Edwina? Won't she wonder where you've been till this time?'

'No she's up in London with her fancy man and won't be back until Tuesday. Rose, could I stay the night with you? Please say yes, then we could tell James the news together in the morning over breakfast.'

Rose agreed, and took Anthony's hand and led him upstairs to her bedroom.

★　★　★

The next morning Anthony awoke bright and early to the birds singing and the sun shining. Rose was still asleep. He decided to surprise her with breakfast in bed. He opened the bedroom door and walked straight into James who was coming out of his room. Working in the butcher's shop he was used to rising early, even when he only had a few hours sleep. There was a look of complete horror and disbelief on his face.

'What are you doing in my mother's room?' He didn't wait for a reply, but pushed past Anthony and rushed into his mother's bedroom.

'Mum are you all right? What's he doing here?'

Rose awoke with a start.

'It's all right James. Come downstairs and we'll explain everything. There's something you need to know.'

James wondered how long this had been going on. Is that why he was paying me, for my mother's services now, not long ago when she worked for him. He could hardly contain his anger. The bastard, I'll kill him. Taking advantage of my mother like this.

'Sit down James. Please listen carefully and don't be angry with me.'

'I'm not angry with you Mother,' glaring at Anthony as he said it.

After all had been revealed to James, he was in a state of shock. He could not believe what he had just heard. Anthony is my father, not some sailor lost at sea. As he looked closely at Anthony he could see the resemblance. He wondered why he had looked so familiar when he first saw him, now he knew. He was an older version of himself.

'Why didn't you tell me before, Mother?'

He always called Rose Mother, when he was annoyed with her, or when he wanted to impress someone. Rose was not quite sure which it was at that precise moment.

'Well I didn't want you to hanker after things you couldn't have, and to feel you should be living in the big house with your father. I thought it best you were brought up being happy with your cousins, leading a simple life with all the family around you.'

'Yes I do understand Mum.' He gave Rose a hug. 'I wouldn't have wanted my life any different from the way it was.'

'James, my son, will you give me a chance to make it up to you and your mother? Can you forgive me for the past?'

Anthony waited for a response from James. It seemed like he waited an eternity, but in fact it was only seconds. James stepped forward to shake Anthony's hand, but this was not enough for Anthony. He flung both arms around the boy and hugged him, tears streaming down his face.

'This is the happiest day of my life,' sobbed Anthony.

His mother was also crying, hers too were tears of happiness.

'As soon as I can get things on a legal footing, my divorce from Edwina, and marriage to your mother, you'll move into my house. The sooner the better as far as I'm concerned. I know we shall all be happy together. Neither of you will want for anything for the rest of your lives, and if you marry that pretty young Irish girl I've seen you with James, she will be welcome under my roof as well. There is enough room for all of us to live together quite happily without getting in each other's way. What do you think James? Will you give it a try?'

'Yes sir.'

'Do you think you could call me Father? It would mean a lot to me if you could.'

'I'll try sir, I mean Father.'

James was rapidly coming around to the idea of living in a big house and becoming one of the idle rich. Wait till I tell Annie. He was deliriously happy.

⋆　⋆　⋆

Edwina agreed only too readily to the divorce once she realised the game was up and that Anthony was not quite the fool she had taken him for. She would be free to marry her

Italian boyfriend Gino, and move to Italy to lead the cosmopolitan life she always craved. Raith of course must go with her, mainly to avoid the huge gambling debts he kept running up.

★ ★ ★

She knew nothing of Rose or James and Anthony had no intention of telling her about them. It was none of her business now they were divorcing. Soon she would be out of his life forever. It was like a heavy burden was being lifted from his shoulders.

The divorce was the talk of the town. Rose and James said nothing to anyone. They both agreed it best to keep quiet until the dust had settled — then they would come forward and take up their rightful place with Anthony. Rose did not relish the thought of being the centre of gossip once more but the end result would be worth it this time. She would be with the only man she had ever truly loved. The father of her son, what more could she ask of life. Rose found it hard to keep the secret from her sisters because usually there were no secrets, they shared everything together. James also found it hard to keep from boasting to Annie. However, he could not resist in telling her that when she married him, he would make her into a fine lady. She did not quite understand this but as she believed everything he told her, she readily accepted this latest notion and looked forward to the day.

14

It was 1933. Lewis was to marry Ellee. He had completed his apprenticeship 3 years earlier and was now a qualified joiner.

One of his parents' properties that was close by in Spear Road had become vacant and he and Ellee were to rent it. It would be their first marital home. Ellee was over the moon with the pretty little house and thought, thank God we don't have to live in the Betts Lane house. The house was bright with sunshine and she felt there had once been a lot of love in it.

She knew she would be very happy there, living with Lewis as Mrs. Preston. She loved the sound of it, Mrs. Ellee Preston. There was a bit of jealousy from Maggie and Annie, that she had made it to the altar first. Then Annie consoled herself with the thought, James would get them an even better house.

⋆　⋆　⋆

The day of the wedding dawned. They were to be married in the Avenue at St. Edmunds Catholic Church. Chris Preston was best man and Ellee's three sisters were bridesmaids. Poor little Ellee was so nervous when reciting her marriage vows, she said, 'I take this man to be my awful wedded husband,' instead of lawful wedded husband. Lewis thought it was a huge joke and didn't let her forget it for a long time.

★   ★   ★

Over the years the girls had lost a lot of their Irish sayings and accents. There was still a faint hint of Irish when they spoke. Florence thought this a shame, she thought their accents were charming but they all just wanted to blend in with the rest of the people of Southampton. Not to be different in any way.

★   ★   ★

Lewis and Ellee had been married just a few months when Rose decided to drop her bombshell about marrying Anthony. Florence was shocked to the core.

'When did all this happen Rose? You kept quiet about it all right.'

'We had to Flo. We had to stay silent until Anthony's divorce came through, because of all the scandal it would cause.'

'I understand Rose, but I'm a bit hurt that you didn't trust Amelia and me enough to tell us what was going on. We wouldn't have let you down.'

'I know Flo, I'm sorry, but I promised Anthony. You know what Father used to say 'My word is my bond' and I felt exactly the same. Having given my word to him not to say anything, I couldn't go back on it.'

'Are you sure you are doing the right thing Rose? You know he let you down before and wouldn't stand by you.'

'I know all that Flo but he's changed. He's older now and views life far more maturely. He says he never stopped loving me, in all those years we were apart.'

⋆   ⋆   ⋆

When Florence told Fred the news, he was amazed.

'Well, well, Leyton-Barrie came up trumps in the end, and has done right by Rose. I never would have thought it of him. I don't think the doorway will be big enough to let James in though. I bet he wasn't opposed to the idea.'

⋆   ⋆   ⋆

Annie was ecstatic when she found out James would be moving into the big house, and when he proposed to her as well, she thought she had died and gone to heaven. He would be taking his father's name and when married she would become Annie Leyton-Barrie, not just plain old Annie Ford. Although once she would have been happy to settle for that. Maggie could not conceal her jealous rage when she found out. Instead of congratulating Annie she stormed, 'It's not fair. I'm the eldest and have been going out with Ronnie the longest. I should have been the one to marry first.'

'Perhaps Ronnie doesn't want you after all. I can't say I blame him,' smirked Annie.

Maggie was on to Annie immediately, pulling her hair and slapping her face. She pushed her to the ground and sat on top of her, punching and slapping her relentlessly. Annie was screaming in pain. Willy rushed into the room and dragged her off Annie.

'Stop, ye little hell cat. What have I told ye before about fighting with yer sister. Be Jesus I won't have it.'

Maggie was screaming hysterically, she was totally out of control. Willy slapped her face hard. She was stunned into silence.

'Now get up those stairs to your room and don't come out till morning.'

'But Ronnie is coming around to take me out,' sobbed Maggie.

'To hell with Ronnie, yer not going out with him tonight me girl.'

Bridie appeared in the doorway.

'Hello Pop. What's all the noise about? Are me sisters fighting again?'

Willy was still enraged and could not calm down. Rounding on Bridie he let rip at her.

'What's this I hear about you hanging around with that Italian boy from the Valley. That family is trouble and I don't want you anywhere near him or any of them. Do ye hear me Bridie? I'll not have it.'

'But Pop, Roberto is all right. He's not like the others.'

'I said no Bridie and I mean it. Have ye got that no, n.o. no.'

Annie was busy snivelling into her handkerchief and trying to repair the damage to her face.

'I have a bruise starting to show already. I don't know what James or his father will say when they see my face. How can I explain that I have a savage for a sister. They'll think we're all so common.'

'Jesus help us,' Willy left the room in exasperation and retreated to his shed at the bottom of the garden.

234

'I'll help you with your face Annie. Have you any powder? We'll soon disguise the bruises with lots of make up. I don't know what possesses our Maggie at times. She is so eaten up with jealousy. It will destroy her one day.'

Annie produced a beautiful box of very expensive make up.

'James gave me this for me birthday. He said he wanted me to have the best so I could always look pretty for him.'

'Oh our Annie, this is so expensive. I didn't know he gave you this as well as the real fur coat. You didn't tell us.'

'No I couldn't because of Maggie. You know what she's like, she was jealous enough over the fur coat.'

Bridie nodded her agreement.

★　★　★

It was decided to hold a double wedding in the late Autumn. Anthony and Rose, James and Annie.

'May as well get it all over in one go, James old chap. Don't want all the fuss twice do we?'

'No Father, what a good idea.'

Maggie declined the offer of being a bridesmaid. Her jealousy wouldn't let her play any significant part. Ellee was matron of honour and Bridie the only bridesmaid, with Lewis as best man.

Fred gave Rose away and Alice was her bridesmaid. Marcus Hunter-Palmer, an old friend of Anthony's since their University days, was best man. He had his eye on Bridie all through the wedding celebrations. The fact that Bridie was young enough to be his daughter never entered into it. In his book all women were fair game.

★   ★   ★

Bridie thought she would go outside to cool down, and take the opportunity to have a look around the huge garden. She had never been in such a large garden before. She had only been sat there five minutes when she was joined by Marcus Hunter-Palmer.

'My you are a pretty thing, and no mistake.'

Bridie felt uneasy. She did not like this fat overbearing old man. She stood up to leave. He gripped her arm and pulled her backwards, she slipped on the mud and fell to the ground. He was on top of her in an instant.

'That's more like it. I bet you know how to make a man happy.'

She tried to scream but he put his hand over her mouth and stopped her. He was smelling of drink and his words were slurred, she couldn't move, she was helpless. He's stupid drunk, Jesus, God, he's going to rape me. Help me please, she prayed. Her prayers were answered. Willy was there dragging him off her. Fists were flailing in all directions, he fought like a man possessed. He had not fought like that since he lived with the Dunns. The rest of the guests had come out to the garden to find out what all the commotion was about. In one glance Anthony had taken in the situation. He knew Marcus had a reputation as a ladies man but never thought he would be so stupid as to try something like this at a friend's house.

'Leave my house at once, you cad, you bounder. Get out and never come back. I don't want to see you ever again.'

Lewis, James and one of the other guests had to hold Willy back, he still felt the urge to kill Hunter-Palmer. The feeling was so strong it took all the strength of the three men to hold him back. How dare he try to sully my daughter, and her still a virgin. To lose her virginity to such a rat would have been more than I could stand. He would have been a dead man that's for sure. Tears of anger were still in his eyes as he watched the women take

Bridie into the house to clean her up. Her pretty dress was in tatters and covered in mud.

★ ★ ★

Only one person enjoyed the incident that had just taken place, Maggie. She stood in the shadows smirking to herself. That'll teach them all. The stuck up lot with all their posh swanky ways. Serve them all right. I'm glad the day has been spoiled. It might teach our Bridie a lesson as well. She has been getting too big for her boots lately. Smiling and giggling with all the boys, giving them the eye. Pop's little pet.

The look of pleasure on her face did not escape Ronnie.

'What are you smirking at Maggie? Aren't you shocked at what has just happened to your sister? I thought you would be so upset for her.'

Quick as a flash Maggie answered.

'Oh yes Ronnie I am. Poor little Bridie. I was just thinking what a fine fight Pop put up in defending Bridie. He showed that Marcus fellow, us Collins are not a family to tangle with.'

Ronnie accepted this explanation and Maggie heaved a sigh of relief, thinking I'll have to be a bit more careful what I say to Ronnie. He's all for family loyalty. He wouldn't understand what a spoilt bitch our Bridie is, and always has been since the day she was born.

★ ★ ★

Anthony tried to make amends by offering money to Willy, who in turn was highly insulted by this gesture.

'Money can never make up for what my little girl has just gone through. How dare ye try to buy me off, Leyton-Barrie. If that is how the rich behave then I'm glad I belong to the lower classes.'

'Willy I'm so sorry, please forgive me. I didn't mean to insult you or your family. I only thought the least I could do was to pay for a replacement dress for little Bridie. She has looked so fetching all day in her nice new dress. Can we remain friends, and try to put this whole sordid business behind us? Please for the sake of our children, Annie and James.'

Anthony put out his hand, which Willy shook rather reluctantly.

★ ★ ★

Bridie soon forgot the terrible ordeal she had been through and was soon back to her usual bouncy self, full of fun and energy.

Thank God thought Bridget, it's had no lasting effect on her. It had shaken Bridget more than she cared to admit. She had been having palpitations again, and feeling weak and sick, since that night. She didn't tell any of the others for fear Willy would try and seek out Hunter-Palmer and do something he might regret. If he thought Hunter-Palmer was responsible for making her heart condition worse, there would be no holding him back.

★   ★   ★

Since Annie and James' wedding, Maggie had been dropping hints to Ronnie about it being time they tied the knot. He seemed a little reluctant to talk about marriage. Maggie put this down to his shyness. It never occurred to her that he may be having second thoughts. He could not get out of his mind the look of delight on her face, when she saw poor little Bridie in such a sad state. Although she had explained it away as pleasure in seeing her Father defending the family honour, he was still not convinced.

With two of her sisters now out of the way,

she seemed to calm down a lot. Bridie and Jack were much younger than her so there was not a lot to get jealous about with them.

★　★　★

Two years had passed before Ronnie finally popped the question. He had decided perhaps he had been mistaken about Maggie after all. The people of Southampton were celebrating Queen Mary and King George's silver jubilee. The streets were ablaze with colour, balloons and bunting hung everywhere at the street parties. Children wore paper hats and squealed with delight.

Ronnie thought this a very romantic time to propose to Maggie.

'I may not be able to offer you what James has to Annie, but Maggie, will you do me the honour of becoming my wife?'

'Oh yes, yes Ronnie I thought you'd never ask me.'

★　★　★

The wedding was a quiet simple one with just a few members of the family. Not the big lavish affair that Annie had, or even as big as Ellee and Lewis. All Maggie was interested in was getting a ring on her finger with the least

241

fuss and being able to call herself Mrs. Newman. Willy gave a secret sigh of relief when it was all over. She's his problem now, not mine any more. He felt at peace now she had left home, as if a burden had been lifted from him. Now he could enjoy his remaining two children Bridie and Jack, without the raging rows and jealousies which seemed to keep occurring from time to time. Nearly always these were down to Maggie and her jealous temper.

★ ★ ★

Jack had got a job in the docks as a rigger and was courting a girl from the sweet shop near to his works. Her name was Doreen Dennis. Her father owned the shop, as did his father before him. She had worked there since leaving school so she didn't have much of a social life, living above the premises with her parents and brother. She was thrilled when the dark haired Irish boy asked her for a date. It was her chance to get out and meet his family and friends. Willy thought she was a lot like Annie, very quiet and listening adoringly to every word Jack said. When he spoke she never took her eyes from him. In her book he was the most wonderful person in the world. Bridie was completely different from any of her sisters, she was full of fun and very flirtatious. She was not afflicted with shyness and had all the boys eating out of her hand. They crowded round begging her for a date. She just tossed her bobbed curls and turned them all down. She belonged to Roberto, the handsome Italian boy. Willy was not at all pleased with this liaison and told Bridie many times, not to associate with him. He did not like him or his family. He had the reputation of being a bit of a rogue, as did the rest of his family. Anything shady going on locally, and they always seemed to be in the thick of it. Nothing had ever been proved against them, but everyone seemed to know they were responsible for the petty crime in the area. They were always ready to fight anyone who opposed them. It reminded Willy too much of the fighting Dunns, and no way did he want his Bridie mixed up with a family like that.

★　★　★

Bridie thought Roberto was the most handsome man she had ever met and in her eyes no one could ever match up to him. That is until one day when a good looking Naval Officer walked into the café come cake shop where she worked. He wanted to order a cake for his mother's birthday and asked Bridie's advice on the shape and design of the cake. Then he sat down and ordered a cup of tea.

As the shop was fairly quiet, Bridie was able to chat with him for a while. He said his name was Alan Simmonds, and before he left he asked if he might see Bridie again. She snapped up his invitation and agreed to meet him the next night and go to the pictures with him. This would give her time to think up an excuse not to see Roberto.

★   ★   ★

The next evening arrived, Bridie was all a flutter with excitement at the prospect of her date with the handsome Naval man. He is so good looking thought Bridie. I do love men in uniform. He makes Roberto seem so young and foolish. Half way through the film, Alan slipped his arm off the back of the seat and placed it around Bridie's shoulders. She didn't object, she just snuggled closer to him. All thoughts of Roberto were gone, in her mind he had never existed. That was until the lights went on for the interval, and who should be sitting behind them but Phillipo and Luca Falleni, Roberto's brothers. She froze in horror not knowing what to do. For the first time she felt afraid of the family. All the things she had heard about them suddenly seemed real. Their violence and people saying 'never cross the family or you'll be sorry.' They both looked at her menacingly.

Alan had gone to fetch some sweets to eat during the second half and was completely unaware of what was taking place. Phillipo leant over the seat and grabbed Bridie's arm, he held it in a steel like grip.

'Hey what you doing with this guy? You're Roberto's girl not hees? You wait till Roberto finds out. You dead meat.' He ran a finger across his throat.

Bridie shivered with fear. Alan came back with the sweets and sat down.

'What's the matter Bridie, you look quite ill?'

'I don't feel well Alan. Can we go please, I think I'm going to faint.'

'Don't you want to see the second film?'

'No, can we go please?'

★   ★   ★

The next day Alan had to return to his ship. His leave was over. He was sorry he had met Bridie at the end of his leave and not the start. They both made a promise to write and always stay in touch, each feeling that this was the start of something really special. A tearful Bridie waved good-bye and watched Alan's taxi disappear into the distance. She walked home slowly wondering what she should do about Roberto. Should she tell Willy? He would be pleased, but the threat to her, he would not be pleased about. She definitely wouldn't tell Bridget. She had become so pale and fragile looking of late. The whole family was terrified of losing her. She must be spared any worry. Perhaps I'll just tell Jack. Oh I don't know what to do.

★　★　★

That evening things were taken out of her hands. She was in the house alone and feeling uneasy. Bridget and Willy had gone to spend the evening with Ellee and Lewis. Jack was out with Doreen. She was upstairs in her bedroom when she heard the loud banging and shouting at the front door. She peeped through the net curtains, then pulled back in horror. It was Roberto and his brothers.

'Come out Bridie Collins, we know you're in there. You two timing little beetch.'

'Whore,' yelled his brothers.

Roberto was brandishing a gun. Bridie didn't know if it was real or not but she suspected it was. Both his brothers had knives in their hands. She ran downstairs and hid in the cupboard under the stairs. They had started kicking at the front door. The swearing became much worse, both in Italian and English. Bridie prayed that if they broke the front door down they would think the house was empty and not look in the understairs cupboard. She began to pray to the Virgin Mary for help.

'Hail Mary full of grace. The Lord is with thee . . . ' She got no further when suddenly everything went quiet. Mr. Martingale, the next door neighbour came out. He was a big burly ex policeman. He towered over the Falleni boys.

'What's your game? I'll have the lot of you on several counts. One for disturbing the peace. Two threatening behaviour. Three abusive language. When I call my colleagues you'll be down the local nick so fast your feet won't touch the ground. While you are down there, perhaps you can help them with one or two others matters like theft and burglary.'

The Fallenis didn't need telling twice, they were off like a shot.

'And don't let me catch you back here ever again,' Mr. Martingale yelled after them.

Bridie came out in floods of tears.

'Oh thank you Mr. Martingale. Please don't tell Mother and Pop, she is so ill, any worry could finish her.'

'Now then Bridie, don't take on so.' He put his arms around her and hugged her against his big body. 'I'll have to tell Willy for your own good but Bridget needn't find out. I don't think they'll be back again. The police have been watching them for sometime. Looking for some evidence against them but they're a cunning lot. I think they'll probably lay low for a while till things cool off a bit.'

When Mike Martingale quietly told Willy of the happenings of the evening before, he was livid with Bridie for being so foolish in taking up with Roberto in the first place, against his express wish for her to stay away from the Falleni family. But when she put her arms around his neck and begged his forgiveness he soon forgot his anger. She told him about her new found love for Alan, her English sailor boyfriend. He seemed pleased and was looking forward to meeting him on his next shore leave.

'Well we have some news to tell. Ye are going to be an Aunty, Ellee is expecting. That's why we were invited around for the evening, to hear the good news.'

Bridie whooped with joy.

'You're going to be grandparents. Isn't it grand. Grandpop and Nanny Collins.'

Bridget interrupted, 'Florence wants to be

called Grandma, not Nanny or Granny.'

'Oh I say how posh,' laughed Bridie. 'When will it be born?'

'Next Easter,' answered Bridget. 'I hope our Maggie won't start playing up again, jealous that Ellee is having our first grandchild.'

'I can't ever imagine her having any, she's not the maternal type. Far too selfish, she thinks too much of herself.'

15

The following year Ellee gave birth to a beautiful little blond haired boy, who they named Edward, Lewis. There was much excitement in the family, even Maggie was thrilled. She doted on him, bought lots of presents and couldn't stop knitting baby clothes. Whenever she had a moment she would sit down with her knitting needles and it seemed in no time at all another beautiful garment was produced.

★   ★   ★

Bridget was so pleased that at last the family seemed happy and united. It was the first time she could ever remember this happening. She thanked God she had been spared long enough to see her first grandchild born. She felt at peace with the world, all her children had found partners and her duty as a mother seemed at an end, but her duty as a grandmother was just beginning. She smiled at this prospect, of all the new babies being born to her children. Ellee's baby was just the first of many, she hoped.

Willy insisted that all the male members of the two families should go on a pub crawl to wet the baby's head. Fred and Lewis were in complete agreement so a big tour of all the pubs in Southampton began. After closing time the men all arrived home to their respective wives, very much the worse for drink. They were singing, staggering about and speaking with slurred words. But all the wives managed to overlook this outrageous behaviour as this was really something to celebrate. The start of the next generation. They all wondered who would be next to produce a playmate for Edward.

★ ★ ★

The next day Fred was recounting the evening's events to Flo.

'I heard something in the pub last night Flo, that made me feel very uneasy. We got talking to a man who has a daughter that ice skates at the local rink. He was telling us, she costs him a fortune in skating boots and pretty dresses. She's an only child and he didn't seem short of a bob or two, so most of his spare cash goes on her. He usually sends abroad to Austria or Germany, to buy a

251

particular make of skating boot that she likes. He's been doing this for some years, since she was a tiny tot. I think he said she's about 10 or 11 years old.'

'She sounds a bit spoilt to me. He must have more money than sense I'd say. What made you uneasy about that Fred?'

'No, not that. It was the next thing that he said. He sent off to get her next pair of boots, as her feet were growing so fast, but he couldn't get hold of any. He said all the factories were making boots for the German army and had stopped producing skating boots. He thinks there is going to be another war with Germany. Everyone in the pub laughed but I didn't think it so funny. I tended to believe him. I don't think they ever got over their defeat in the last war.'

'Surely not Fred. It was so long ago 1918. This is 1936, there couldn't be another war, could there? That was supposed to be the war to end all wars.'

'I'm not so sure lass. Nothing surprises me anymore.'

'I have some news as well Fred. I heard today that Ernest Cunningham has died. Rumour has it that he died of syphilis he caught from all those women he went with while our Mary was in the mental home. Good riddance to bad rubbish I say. I remember him standing at our Mary's graveside two years since, pretending grief. The man was nothing but a hypocrite. It was all I could do then to keep my hands off him. I for one won't be attending his funeral. Unlike him I am no hypocrite.'

★ ★ ★

Bridget had become great friends with Aggie Martingale next door. Whenever she got the chance she was always popping in for a cup of tea.

'Bridget can you read tea leaves? They say the Irish are very gifted people that way.'

'Yes Aggie I can. It's a gift. It seems to run in families. Ellee has the gift and Bridie too, although they don't read the leaves. The other two, Maggie and Annie are too frightened to acknowledge it, and as for Jack, well . . . men don't talk about things like that, do they.'

'Oh Bridget, would you read my leaves please? Look at my cup, it is full of them. There's a lot there for you to see.'

'All right, if ye promise not to tell the menfolk, they don't understand.'

'I promise Bridget. Now what do you see.'

'I see a little windfall is coming to you, and a family wedding.'

'Oh that will be my niece. We heard this

morning she's getting wed. You are good Bridget. Can you see any more?'

'I also see, sadly ye have a funeral to go to. It's the loss of a friend. I can see clearly the happiness and sadness are close together. I'm getting a bit tired now. I can't do any more, perhaps I will another time.'

'Oh yes of course Bridget. Thank you. Now you rest, I hope I didn't tire you too much. Bye for now.'

★ ★ ★

It was the last time Aggie was to see her dear friend Bridget alive. Two days later Bridget was taken ill and rushed to hospital, sadly they could not save her. She had foretold her own funeral. The whole family were beside themselves with grief. Bridie was the worst of the lot. There was no consoling her. At the funeral she wanted to throw herself into the grave after her mother. Members of the family had to restrain her.

There were even tears in the eyes of the hardened grave diggers at such a sad sight. She thought she would never recover from the loss of her dear mother, truly a saint in heaven.

'Why was she taken so young Pop. 63 years isn't old is it?'

'I don't know Bridie. They say the good always die young, and your mother was surely that. Our lives will never be the same ever again without her lovely smiling face. The nearest we have left to her is Ellee. She is so like your mother was at that age.'

'Yes but she's not her is she.' Bridie felt outraged that he could suggest Ellee measured up to her mother.

'No one will ever be as good and kind as Mother was to us. She always put everyone before herself.'

She then burst into uncontrollable sobs. She sobbed and wailed for another half an hour. Willy was beside himself. He didn't know what to do with her. He was thankful for the loud knocking at the front door. Perhaps someone could help him with her.

When he opened it he saw a young man standing there in a navy uniform. Thank God, it was Alan.

'Alan come in. I'm so glad to see ye. We have some very bad news to tell ye. Dear Bridget passed away two weeks ago and I'm afraid Bridie has taken it very badly.'

Alan stood in the doorway, not knowing what to do or say. Bridie looked up with shock. She didn't know he was due home. The tears stopped immediately. It was like a tap was being turned off. Thank God, thought Willy, perhaps he can do something with her. I sure as hell can't. Bridie felt she had cried a river or even an ocean, and with the arrival of Alan the tears had temporarily stopped.

★   ★   ★

Ellee, who had been very close to Bridget, felt the loss of her mother quite badly but she was not so demonstrative in her grief as Bridie was. She grieved in private when no one was around.

Baby Edward had developed bronchitis and had given her even more worry to add to her loss. One evening she was alone with the baby in the bedroom. She cuddled him in her arms and prayed he would not be taken from her as well. It would be more than she could bear. First her mother and then her baby son. God would not be so cruel as to take Edward as well. She heard a movement by the door. She looked up and could hardly believe her eyes.

Standing in the doorway was her mother, smiling at her. She said, 'Keep him warm,' and then disappeared.

'Mother come back, please come back,' sobbed Ellee, but she was gone. The room was as before, still and dimly lit by the night light at the side of the cot.

* * *

The next day Edward seemed to make a remarkable recovery. When the doctor called he was amazed. He said it had been touch and go whether he lasted through the night or not. He had passed the crisis point and was well on the way back to good health. Ellee felt somehow her mother had helped him out of danger. She had sent some sort of special love and healing for her beloved and only grandchild she ever held.

* * *

After giving it a lot of thought Ellee decided to confide in Lewis. She knew he didn't believe in anything supernatural and she would never be able to convince him otherwise, but he was sympathetic to her beliefs so she felt she had to tell him.

'Are you sure you hadn't dropped off to sleep and were dreaming about your mother coming to you? I know how close you two were. It's only natural to think about her at a time like this, when we are both so worried about our son. The mind plays tricks on us sometimes, when we're under pressure.'

Ellee just smiled to herself and said no more about it. She knew she really had seen her mother so that was all that mattered.

★   ★   ★

Annie was the next of the sisters to give birth, just after Edward's second birthday. She also had a son. Jeremy James Leyton-Barrie. Everything was done in great style. An announcement in the newspaper. Baby clothes from the best shops. The pram was the most elegant of designs. One of the rooms near to Annie and James' bedroom was turned into a nursery and Annie could have a live-in nanny if she chose.

★   ★   ★

There was only one thing marring the happy occasion. Annie wanted the baby baptised a Catholic, but Anthony wanted him christened in the local church where all the family christenings, funerals and marriages had taken place for the past hundred years. Anthony was adamant on this one point.

'I don't ask much of you or Annie, but James please indulge me on this one point.'

'I'll speak to Annie, Father.'

'Thank you, I would appreciate that.'

In Anthony's mind the whole thing had been settled. He was not reckoning on his daughter-in-law's stubbornness. Annie who wouldn't say boo to a goose, stood her ground.

'No James I'm sorry. He must be baptised a Catholic. I don't want to go to hell when I die.'

'Don't be absurd Annie, of course you won't go to hell.'

Annie then burst into floods of tears. James for the first time ever began to feel anger and resentment towards Annie. He was surprised at the depth of these feelings. In the past he had only felt love for her. This was something new to him which he didn't much like. He began to see Annie in a different light. She was behaving like some religious nut. Perhaps he had made a mistake in marrying her. After all he was a Leyton-Barrie, he had inherited his father's good looks, he had money. What more could any girl wish for. He could have had the pick of dozens of girls and he chose Annie, what a mistake. This religious whimpering wreck is my wife. What have I done!

'Now then, what is all this upset about?' Rose came into the room. 'If it means so much to you Annie, having Jeremy christened a Catholic, then I'll have a word with Anthony and see what we can do about it.'

'Oh thank you,' sniffed Annie.

James looked on contemptuously. She just couldn't do this one thing for me or Father. Little bitch, she had to have her own way, creeping around Mother like that. Her religion means more to her than we do.

★ ★ ★

Eventually Anthony agreed to Annie's wishes, with a lot of gentle persuasion from Rose. He could never deny Rose anything ever again. He loved her so much, he would do anything for her.

From that moment on things changed between Annie and James. He began spending a lot of evenings out with his friends. Not Lewis and the old crowd they'd both had so much fun with, but his new posh friends. Anthony's friends' children. They were all rolling in money and very spoilt. Annie didn't much like any of them. She felt they looked down on her and were laughing at her behind her back. One day she walked into the library and heard them talking to James about her.

'I say James, it was a good night we had. How about that little Betsy. A real cracker.

How did you make out with her after you took her home? I could see you had her eating out of your hand. She would do just about anything for you, and did she? Come on you can tell Uncle Nick. We are all friends together.'

For a brief moment James thought of the three musketeers, all friends together, and he felt a little sad for the times gone by.

Albert gone from his life forever and he hardly ever sees Lewis these days. Mainly his own fault because he mixes with the rich people now. He soon brushed the thought aside. I have everything I want now and can do just as I like. I need never worry over money ever again. Nick was pressing him for an answer.

'How you can put up with that dull little wife of yours James, I'll never know. However did you come to marry her? Not your type at all. Now Betsy well, a different kettle of fish altogether. Come on James spill the beans, did you, or didn't you?'

Annie didn't wait to hear his answer. She knew what it would be.

She ran to their bedroom and dissolved in floods of tears. How could he. His marriage vows meant nothing to him. He has committed adultery. Jesus, he will rot in hell. I wish to God we had never come to this

261

place. I wish he never had all this money and we could just go back to how we were before Anthony turned up. Flashing his money and turning James' head. I hate him as well. James walked into their bedroom.

'What are you snivelling about now?'

'I heard what you and your friends were saying about me. Who is this Betsy you have slept with?'

James paled slightly. He was shocked she had found out so soon. His affair with Betsy had only just got off the ground.

'Don't deny it James. I know when you are lying. I can never forgive you for this.'

'I wasn't going to. All rich people have mistresses and I'm no exception. Just think yourself lucky, you're well provided for and if you want to remain living here you'll be quiet and accept the situation.'

'Accept the situation,' she screamed at him like a fish wife. She took off her shoe and beat him over the head with it. Blood began to trickle down his face. He pushed her away roughly and she fell to the floor. She felt weak with emotion. She was stunned at what had just taken place. She could not believe what he had just admitted. She heard a laugh from the despicable Nick as James joined him downstairs. The front door banged and she was alone in the house. She must leave before he gets back, and take Jeremy with her. He will never see either of us again, our marriage is over. Oh Mother, Mother what am I to do? I don't have you to talk to any more. Where shall I go, what shall I do? She packed as much of hers and the baby's things as she could carry on the pram. She shut the front gate and left without a backward glance.

★　★　★

She started walking towards the town, not knowing where she was going, or what she was going to do next. The first person she bumped into was Florence.

'Annie whatever's the matter? You look so pale. Have you been crying?'

'Yes Mrs. Preston.'

'Let's sit down on this bench and you can tell me all about it. I'm sure nothing is that bad, that can't be sorted out.'

After Annie had finished telling Florence the whole story of James' betrayal, she offered to put Annie up for a few days, till she found somewhere to stay.

'I expect James will track you down and beg your forgiveness, and take you back home.'

'No he won't Mrs. Preston, and if he did I wouldn't go.'

★ ★ ★

Annie had not paid too much attention to Mrs. Preston's house before. She had only been in it one other time. The night Albert had died. As soon as she stepped inside the door she disliked the house immediately. She could not find a reason for this, as it was clean, tidy, and beautifully decorated.

Fred Preston always took great pride in his home decor. I hope I don't have to stay here long. Our Ellee says the place is haunted. Immediately Annie felt guilty for thinking such ungrateful thoughts. Florence was a very kind person and would go out of her way to help anyone in need, and she surely was in need right now.

'I'll put you and baby Jerry in the back bedroom. It's nice and sunny there and looks out on the garden.'

'Can I see your nice garden Mrs. Preston please? I don't mean to be rude but can you call him Jeremy please. I don't like Jerry.' James used to call him that just to annoy me.

'I'm sorry dear, of course I will. I've heard your sister refer to him as Jerry. I thought that was what everyone called him.'

★ ★ ★

Annie put the sleeping Jeremy upstairs in the back bedroom, while she went to look at the garden with Flo.

'It's so pretty Mrs. Preston.' She felt much happier outside than in. 'Will Mr. Preston mind me staying with you both?'

'No of course not. He's a dear sweet man, he won't mind at all.' She noticed a cloud come over Annie's face and guessed she was thinking that James was like that once. That young man needs a good spanking. I've always thought so. Our Rose should have done it years ago. How could he possibly hurt this sweet innocent young girl. The mother of his child. It's all beyond me. It just goes to show, money does not bring happiness.

'I think I can hear Jeremy crying Mrs. Preston, shall we go in?'

'I can't hear him but we best check and make sure he's all right.' Flo felt slightly uneasy. Oh dear God not the baby crying again. The house has been quiet of late. It is the right time of year, August, when the ghost baby can be heard. I wonder if Annie is psychic like her sister Ellee?

★   ★   ★

Once inside the house Annie rushed upstairs. The baby was sound asleep but the room smelled terrible, like something was rotting in it. She opened the window to get rid of the awful smell and carried Jeremy back downstairs with her. She wondered if she would offend Florence if she mentioned the bad smell in the room.

'Here he is. He wasn't crying after all, he was asleep all the time. I must have imagined I heard him cry. I expect I'm over anxious with all the upset. Mrs. Preston I hope you won't mind me mentioning it, but there's a very bad smell in the bedroom. Please don't think me rude or ungrateful but I just wondered what it is.'

'I don't know dear. It just happens from time to time. In the past we've had floor boards up and done all sorts of things to try and trace where it's coming from. So far we've had no luck in finding the source of the smell. Mr. Preston thinks it's coming from the drains outside. From time to time when the weather is especially hot, like today, it drifts in through the open windows in the house.'

I hope that puts her mind at rest and she won't be bothered by the ghostly things that happen in the house periodically.

★   ★   ★

The next morning Annie was up first and thought she would go downstairs to make Jeremy a bottle. She was at the top of the stairs when she thought she heard a movement behind her. She thought it was Fred and turned to say good morning. There was no one there. Next minute she felt herself falling headlong down the stairs. She finished up at the bottom with an almighty bang. Fred and Flo were out of bed like a shot.

'Annie are you alright lass? Did you trip? I must make sure all the stair rods are secure and that the carpet hasn't worked loose.'

'Yes I think so. I thought someone was behind me. I turned around but no one was there. I must have lost my sense of balance when I turned quickly. If I didn't know better I'd have said I was pushed.'

'Ney lass, I think thee had better wake up properly in the mornings before thee goes wandering about half asleep in a strange house.'

Strange house is right thought Flo. I must get this girl away from here as quickly as possible, before she gets hurt badly, or even worse. I'll start trying to find her a place right away.

16

It was 1939. England had declared war on Germany. Annie had been alone for a year bringing up her baby son by herself. James seemed to shirk all responsibility towards his wife and son. Annie managed to rent a house near the bottom of the town. The further away from the Leyton-Barries the better. She scrimped and saved to make ends meet. She took on as many cleaning jobs as she could possibly handle in one day. She took Jeremy with her. He would be asleep in his pram in the gardens of the posh houses she cleaned. She would buy the cheap vegetables from Kingsland Market at the end of the day. Her clothes were patched and darned till there was hardly any material left that had not been mended. Ellee was very generous in passing on Edward's baby clothes that he had grown out of. Life was very hard for her but she could hold her head up high and be proud of how she was managing to support herself and her son without any help from James.

In the beginning Anthony had tried to send her money for Jeremy but she sent it straight back again by return of post. Eventually he gave up trying. He sent her a letter saying that if ever she or his grandson needed help at any time, she would only have to ask and he would be there for them.

★ ★ ★

Christopher Preston had not been well for a long time and eventually he was diagnosed as having tuberculosis. He had an operation to have a lung removed. He was making a good recovery but was far from well.

'Ee Flo, I said I never wanted our sons to go to war and suffer as I did in the last lot, but I would never have wished T.B. on our Chris. It's a dreadful illness and it's killing thousands. I hear young Ken Sherman who lives up the road has the disease, and his chances are not very good. Poor lad he's only 36 and has a wife and three youngens to support.'

'It doesn't bear thinking about Fred. It's just too terrible for words. Tomorrow I'll take Janet Sherman a bag of groceries to help them all out, and pick some roses from the garden to cheer her up. We're so lucky Lewis is in a protected trade and he doesn't have to go to war either. I pity all the poor young men that do. I wonder if it will be different from the First World War?'

'They say it could be a lot worse this time. Mrs. Pink at No.13 has a son in the navy. She was telling me the other day his ship is the HMS Hood. She's very proud that her Roy is serving his country in a time of war, but being a mother she's also very worried about him, which is only natural.'

'I've always liked Mrs. Pink, Fred. She is one of the nicest people in the lane. She has such a sunny disposition. Always a smile and a kind word for everyone. I do hope her boy stays safe.'

★   ★   ★

Alan Simmonds asked Bridie to marry him, and she accepted without hesitation. She was head over heels in love with him, and the idea of being a war bride and marrying Alan in his naval uniform appealed to her. They planned a small quiet wedding with just a few family and friends, before Alan had to return to his ship.

'It's nice to know we've had the last of the big posh weddings in the family. We don't have to suffer any more of them. It only ends in tears anyway. All that swank, and what it's all for, nothing, I ask you.'

'Now Maggie, that is uncalled for. I don't want you causing trouble on Bridie's special day. I won't stand for it. I think you need something else to take your mind off other people and what they are doing. I think it is time we started a family.'

Maggie was horror struck. Although she was a bully to her sisters and always had far too much to say for herself, she would take on anybody in an argument and stand her ground. Nobody could frighten her or get the better of her. Her Achilles heel was that she was really frightened of any physical pain. The thought of going through childbirth was just too much for Maggie to take.

'Ronnie I don't really think it's the right time to start a family. There is a war on. I don't think it right to bring a baby into the world when we could all be blown sky high at any moment.'

'Your sisters don't seem to share your view about the war. You have two beautiful nephews which I know you adore, especially Edward. You can't stay away from him. Yet you don't seem to want our children. I don't understand you at times Maggie, I just don't.' Ronnie walked away shaking his head sadly.

★   ★   ★

Ronnie wanted to join the army and do his bit for his King and country but was turned

271

down on medical grounds. He had extremely poor eye sight and it was also discovered that he was suffering from a duodenal ulcer, as well as having very flat feet. He took the rejection quite badly. He wanted to prove he was a man. Make Maggie proud of him. Maggie had rejected him and now the army didn't want him either. Secretly Maggie was overjoyed, being the selfish person that she was. Let the others go and get their heads blown off. I'm happy to keep my Ronnie at home with me. Who would look after me if he went off to war and was killed. I wouldn't want to end up like Annie, struggling to make ends meet.

★   ★   ★

James had no excuse not to go to war. Even Anthony's money couldn't save him from call up so he decided on an Air Force career. Anthony hoped to pull a few strings and get him into a ground job but James had other ideas. He wanted to be part of the dashing young air crew, the ones that all the girls went after. Annie was adamant that she would never divorce James.

It was against her religion. Catholics don't get divorced, she told him time and time again, whenever he contacted her with a view to divorcing her.

'But you don't love me anymore, or I you, so what is the point of hanging on to this sham of a marriage. I just don't get it.'

'No you wouldn't would you. You with not an ounce of religion in you. You haven't even asked to see your son, or how he is getting on.'

'How is Jerry anyway.'

'Don't call him Jerry. Wouldn't you like to know. Well you're not going to see him, so there.'

'Really Annie, you can be so childish at times. I'm not staying here any longer to play your stupid games.'

He left banging the door behind him. He heard a cry from Jerry as he walked up the road. It pulled at his heart strings. He was relieved that he did not see the child. He found it all rather painful and didn't want to give Annie the satisfaction of seeing him hurting inside. He missed his son a lot more than he cared to admit, even to himself. That blasted woman has my son and won't allow me to see him. Yet I'm stuck with her being my wife, till death do us part, huh. Wait a minute, it may turn out alright after all. Just think, all the fun I can have with the girls, without making a commitment to any of them, because of my selfish religious wife who won't give me a divorce as it's against her religion. I shall be honest with them, let them know from the start I'm married and can't get a divorce, and how unhappy I am. They will feel so sorry for me that they will end up doing anything for me. Thank you Annie, thank you very much. You have just handed me the passport to true happiness without marriage and all it entails. Boy what a time I'm going to have. Air Force here I come. He entered the house head held high and whistling a catchy tune. He suddenly felt much better.

Rose was in the hall as James came through the front door. She couldn't help noticing how much happier he looked.

'Well you've certainly cheered up. Did you make it up with Annie?'

'Certainly not Mother. She was as difficult as ever and refused to let me see Jerry.'

'And that has made you so happy? I don't understand.'

'I'm happy Mother because on the way home I made a decision, to not let Annie get me down anymore. I'm going to get on with the rest of my life and enjoy it. You never know what's around the next corner.'

'I'm pleased to hear it James. That's the spirit, don't let her get you down. Perhaps one day she will come to her senses.'

I sincerely hope not Mother, thought James.

'She has been a very silly girl. I'm sure we could have sorted things out. If she would have let us.'

'Yes Mother I'm sure you are right.'

By this time James had become bored with the conversation and escaped to his room.

★　★　★

The next day Anthony and Rose waved goodbye to James as he set off for his new life with the Air Force. Anthony felt very proud of him. Rose dabbed away the tears from her eyes. It was the first time she had ever been parted from him since he was born. She looked at the proud look on Anthony's face and thought men don't feel these things as deeply as us women. She thought of all the women all over the world having to say goodbye to their men folk as they went off to fight a war that none of the ordinary people wanted anyway.

★　★　★

Annie didn't know James had joined the Air Force and felt a pang of regret when she found out. She had denied him seeing their son. What if he is killed. I was so horrible to him and may never see him again. That evening she went to church and prayed for his safe deliverance. So strong was her faith, she felt so sure God would look after him and he would return safe and sound after the war. She still loved him, although she didn't like to admit it.

★ ★ ★

Southampton was coming under heavy bombardment. As Alan was away, Lewis took it upon himself to keep an eye on Bridie. After he finished work in the docks he would meet her from the cake shop and escort her home. One day when the air raids had been particularly bad, Lewis was making his way to the shop. He got to the park and was quite shocked to see bodies strewn everywhere. What was even more shocking was that they had no clothes on. He couldn't make out through the gloom why they were all naked. As he got closer he couldn't stop laughing. They weren't people at all, but tailor's dummies. The outfitter's shop had been hit. When Lewis told Bridie who had a very infectious laugh, she couldn't stop laughing all the way home. The whole family were going to Florence and Fred's house for tea, to discuss the possibility of evacuation to the country with the younger members of the family. Ellee was against going and leaving Lewis and her Father.

'Now Ellee you must think of Edward, you'll be with Annie, Jeremy, and Doreen. You'll be a great help and comfort to her when her baby is born.'

'But I'll be worried sick all the time, about Lewis working in the docks, and Jack as well. It's being bombed daily, and then there's Pop. He's so lonely since Mother died. He seems to be drinking more and more to drown his sorrows. I don't think he'll ever get over her loss. We can't all desert him.'

'I promise you Ellee, we will look after Willy for you. He is welcome in our house any time. I'll check on him daily and make sure he has a decent meal inside him.'

'Please say you'll come Ellee, my parents will make you very welcome. Since selling the shop and moving to the country, they miss seeing people so much. They only met you briefly at our wedding and would welcome the chance to get to know Jack's family better.'

Ellee eventually and very reluctantly agreed.

★ ★ ★

A few days later the three women and two little boys set of for Tangley, a village just outside of Andover. Mr. and Mrs. Dennis welcomed them with open arms. There was a roaring fire in the grate, and home made cakes and tea awaiting their arrival. They had only been there a week when Doreen gave birth to Jack's baby, a little girl. She decided to call her Mavis, after her grandmother.

★   ★   ★

One evening Lewis called around to see if Willy was alright. He was not in. So he decided to look in various pubs to see if he could find him and bring him back for supper with his parents.

Eventually he found him, drunk as a lord in one of the pubs in Bevois Valley. He was propped up against the pub stove. He was so drunk he didn't feel the intense heat, the stove was so hot it had melted his belt. A fact he was totally unaware of till Lewis tried to move him away.

'Ah Lewis me boy. Will ye not take a small drink with me.'

'I think you've had enough for one night. I'm taking you home.'

Some of the regulars helped Lewis get him

outside. He was singing at the top of his voice.

'I'll take ye home again Kathleen . . . '
After he had finished that song, Lewis was immediately treated to his rendition of 'Danny Boy.'

Lewis eventually got him safely back to Betts Lane and left him in the charge of Florence and Fred, while he returned to his Home Guard duties. They tried sobering him up but he promptly fell asleep on the settee so they decided to leave him there till the next morning to sleep it off.

★　★　★

Tom Burrows was getting more and more nervous as the air raids on Southampton were becoming more intense. The bombs seemed to be missing the docks and landing more and more on the residential areas of the town. His main concern was the difficulties he experienced in getting to the air raid shelter. Being wheelchair bound made it virtually impossible. He was a big man and having spent many years immobile he had gained even more weight. Amelia had tried many times to lift him to the shelter when the air raid siren sounded, but was never successful. Fred and Lewis always helped whenever they were available but there were times when they were not around. So Amelia would have to push the wheelchair under the stairs and hope to God they didn't receive a direct hit. Tom tried hard to put a brave face on things but he was growing decidedly more jumpy as each day went by, and there was no let up in the bombing. He felt so inadequate not being able to fend for himself and having to rely on others all the time.

'Go Ame and go quickly. Get Alice to the shelter. I'll be alright here under the stairs.' He tried hard to sound brave and in control.

'But Tom I feel so guilty leaving you here all alone. What if the house is hit.'

'If it is I'll be alright here under the stairs. You said yourself when houses have been hit around here, the only part left intact seems to be the stairs.'

No sooner had Amelia and Alice left him when he heard the drone of planes overhead which was deafening. He began to shake from head to toe. He heard explosion after explosion as the bombs found a target. The whole house shook to its foundations. He felt sure the next bomb would be for their house. The sweat on his brow glistened in the darkness. He held his breath as he heard the next bomb falling, it was so close. It was surely coming for him. He shut his eyes and waited for the inevitability of his death. Being blown into hundreds of little pieces, never to be found again. As the bomb exploded the whole house shook once more, even worse than last time. He breathed a sigh of relief as he heard the planes flying off into the distance.

That last one was close. One of the neighbours must have been hit, not too far from here. My name was not on that bomb this time. I wonder which poor devil's name was. The all clear sounded and Amelia and Alice rushed back into the house in floods of tears.

'We thought the house had been hit,' they both sobbed simultaneously.

'I'm alright, but some poor devil close by has been hit. Let's hope everybody was out of the house and safe in their shelter.'

'I wonder whose house it was?'

'We'll know soon enough when the dust settles and you're able to go out and about again.'

The house that was hit close by was Lewis and Ellee's. Mercifully no one was in it at the time. Ellee was still away in the country and Lewis was at work at the time of the air raid. When he arrived home he was very shocked to find their pretty little home had been hit by an incendiary bomb. It had landed in

Edward's cot and the whole of the bedroom had been ablaze. Their beautiful double bed with the oak headboard had been destroyed, and had Edward been in his cot he would now be dead. In fact they all would be dead. He was so thankful Ellee was still away and his little family was safe. I don't know how I'm going to tell her. She loved this house so much and now it is uninhabitable, virtually destroyed. Tears glistened in his eyes. He felt a hand on his shoulder, he turned and it was Fred standing there.

'Come on lad. Come home to us. Your mother is waiting. We'll put thee up for as long as thee like.'

'I was going to see if I could salvage any furniture. Poor Ellee, she loved this house so much.'

'Ay I know lad. Later, we'll come back later, and see what there is to be saved. Right now thee needs a stiff drink.'

★ ★ ★

'Tom, it was Lewis and Ellee's house that was hit. I have just been outside to the dustbin and Fred was bringing Lewis up the garden path into Flo. He looked pretty white and upset. It must have been a terrible shock for him. Coming home from work and finding

282

his home gone and all their possessions strewn about the garden like that. After they had gone indoors I nipped out the back cut and over the road to have a look. It was devastating, seeing his home in ruins.'

'It is only bricks and mortar Amelia. The main thing is that they are all safe. So many poor people in Southampton have not been so lucky. They have lost their lives as well.'

'I know Tom. I don't know how much more of this I can take.'

'Me neither Amelia. I've given it a lot of thought lately and I think I've come up with a solution. There is no reason for us to be suffering here when we could all be in Devon with the family. Where it's a lot quieter than here. My brothers would be on hand to help any time we needed it. You only have to say the word and we can leave straight away.'

Amelia flung her arms around his neck.

'Yes Tom, yes we will definitely go. I don't know why we didn't think of it before now.'

★   ★   ★

Amelia went next door to tell Florence the good news. She would miss her sister terribly, but she must think of Tom and Alice.

Their safety must come first, she was sure Flo would understand, and she did.

'You may have the answer to our problem. Lewis could move into your house with the bits and pieces he has managed to save from the other house. It will give him time to replace the ruined furniture before Ellee's return. I don't think he ought to mention what has happened until she gets back. Knowing will only upset her even more.'

★ ★ ★

Ellee was feeling restless and wanted to come home. She hadn't had a letter from Lewis in ages and she began to feel something was terribly wrong. Mr. and Mrs. Dennis had been really kind to her and she felt slightly guilty at being so ungrateful. She didn't care what danger she would be in by going back. She took the view that if they were going to be killed, they might as well all go together as a family. She missed Lewis so much, she couldn't bear to be away from him any longer. She packed her bags, her mind was made up, nothing anyone could say would dissuade her.

★ ★ ★

Annie was the exact opposite. She had a little part time job helping out at the local post office and loved every minute of it. Mrs. Dennis looked after Jeremy while she was at work, she and Doreen had become great friends. No one in the village knew her business or anything about her and James. Unlike Southampton where the tongues never stopped wagging. Saying what a fool she was to give up her position and all that money. She must have been potty. She should have turned a blind eye to her husband's wild ways and enjoyed her privileged position. The villagers just thought her man was away at war, the same as everyone else's were. They never questioned it for a minute. If anyone asked which of the services her husband was in, she would just answer, the Air Force.

★ ★ ★

Ellee set off for home the next day. She didn't even bother to write and say she was coming. None of the mail seemed to be getting anywhere very fast so she thought she might as well just turn up. She was not expecting the sight that greeted her when she got back. Her home destroyed and the few possessions they had left had been moved next door to Flo and Fred. She tried so hard to conceal her disappointment from Flo, who had been so kind.

'I know it's upsetting for you dear. To come home and find your home gone like that. But every cloud has its silver lining. If you and Edward had not gone away to the country you wouldn't be standing here now talking to me, and Lewis would now be a very sad man. God has been merciful to us all.'

In her heart of hearts Ellee knew Flo was right but she still couldn't help feeling the despair of it all. She hated the house from day one. Just as she had done when she stepped over the threshold of Flo and Fred's house next door. I think the two houses must be cursed. I have the same bad feelings in both of them. She sat down and began to cry. Amelia and Tom never had any luck in this house either, and as for poor Albert well . . . The thought of him made her cry even more.

★ ★ ★

She must pull herself together and not let Lewis see how unhappy she is. He has done his best, he couldn't have done any more. She dried her eyes and began to prepare the evening meal, with the thought that perhaps this is only temporary, and we won't have to stay here very long.

Florence had had the very same thoughts over 40 years ago when she first moved in. It is like the house won't give you up easily. Every time Flo and Fred managed to purchase another house it was immediately snapped up by someone in need, and they ended up renting it out. Fred had become very set in his ways and didn't want to move. He had been very happy in the house and had never sensed anything unusual at all. Every time Flo brought the subject up, he would just smile, nod and say.

'You ladies have an over worked imagination. It's a good job us men aren't like that or nobody would be living anywhere. Ney this is a good sound house, strongly built, and I'll be happy to end my days here.'

Florence would groan inwardly and give up the conversation, as she was getting nowhere fast with him and his stubbornness.

17

May 1941 was a very sad time for the people of Betts Lane, when the news arrived that the H.M.S. Hood had been sunk off Greenland. There were 14,020 on board and only 3 had survived. Unfortunately Roy Pink was not one of the three. Everyone in the Lane shed a tear for young Roy, the only son of Ted and Gladys.

'They say it was the Bismark that was responsible for the sinking. She hit the ship and the fire quickly spread to the ammunition. She blew up and was gone within 2 minutes. Those poor devils never stood a chance Flo.'

'I don't know how Gladys and Ted will ever get over it. They have no other children to comfort them in their time of need, only a lot of good neighbours who care for them. She was so proud of him. I remember her telling me all about the Hood. How it was built at John Brown shipyard on Clydebank, and was named after Admiral Hood who was killed at the battle of Jutland. It put me in mind of the other ship built there all those years ago. The Lusitania, and dear Harry our good friend.'

Flo dabbed a tear from her eye. 'I think it must be bad luck to have a ship built at the John Brown shipyard. They don't seem to survive.'

'Ney lass, you and your superstitions. It's war, both ships were lost because of the aggression of the German enemy in war time. Nothing to do with bad luck. Go on with you.'

'We all used to be so happy then. Harry used to come around every week. Tom was a fit man. Not the shadow of a man he is now. Confined to a wheelchair for life.'

'Speaking of Tom, I keep forgetting to tell thee Flo. Before they left, he was telling me apparently last year there was a meeting at Caxton Hall in London. O'Dwyer, the man alleged to be responsible for the Amritsar Massacre was shot dead by a survivor of the Jallianwala Bagh. The man responsible has since been hanged. Tom said he wished he'd thought of it and shot him at the time. Someone had waited 21 years to take revenge and now he's dead as well. It just goes to show people have long memories and don't forget that easily.'

'I know one thing, Tom never will for as long as he lives. We are living through terrible violent times Fred. When is it all going to end?'

'Ee I don't know lass. It's a bad business all round, war. There are no winners, just dreadful losses on both sides. A lot of good men killed who didn't want to go to war. They just want to be home with their families living a normal life. All the politicians should be put in a field with rifles and let them fight it out between themselves and leave innocent people who don't want war, out of it.'

Florence smiled at the thought of it. All the fat politicians slogging it out in a field. Fred always knew how to cheer her up when she was down.

★　★　★

Bridie and Alan had moved into the Lane only a few doors up from the Prestons. Willy was like a wandering nomad. He would stay a while with one daughter, and not to out stay his welcome or cause any jealousy he would move onto the next. The one he was always glad to leave was Maggie. I don't know how poor Ronnie puts up with her. Pete Finnegan was right. I should have drowned her at birth in the harbour at Cobh, not brought her over here and inflicted her on the poor people of Southampton.

No one deserves that, not even the English, he thought chuckling to himself. He was off to Bridie next, his favourite. Dear little Bridie, as Alan is away at sea I'll be able to stay there the longest and help her with all the jobs she needs doing.

The thought cheered him up no end. Sometimes he felt he couldn't go on without Bridget. She was taken far too young. We should have had years ahead of us together, watching the grandchildren grow up.

⋆ ⋆ ⋆

By the end of 1941 there was a turn of events in the war. The Japanese had bombed Pearl Harbour, thus bringing the Americans into the war. The Japanese had scored a direct hit on the Arizona, killing all on board. The previous day the musicians on the ship had secured a prize in a band contest and as a reward they were allowed to sleep in late the next morning. All the crew were on board, most still asleep in their bunks at the time of the air raid. There was an appalling loss of life after the bombing of the harbour. When the American service men arrived in Southampton it was to change a lot of people's lives forever.

⋆ ⋆ ⋆

By the Spring of the following year Ellee was pregnant again. She was soon followed by Bridie a few months later.

As the end of Ellee's pregnancy approached the doctor and midwife tried hard to persuade Ellee to have the baby in the East Park Clinic, as she did not have an easy time giving birth to Edward. She had suffered so much she vowed not to have any more children and was surprised to find herself pregnant once again. She soon settled down to the fact and was quite looking forward to the new addition to their family. The doctor offered to find a foster home for Edward while she was giving birth, and for the weeks afterwards till she was back on her feet again. Ellee was appalled at this suggestion. She was fiercely protective towards her family. No stranger would care for them as much as she did.

'My son suffers badly with bronchitis and I can't allow strangers to look after him. I will look after him here for as long as I can and when the time comes for the baby to be born my mother-in-law next door will help out. I also have a sister a few doors up the road who adores Edward. She will help as well. I have plenty of family around to care for us. I am definitely having this baby at home.'

At this point the doctor and midwife gave

up trying to persuade her any different.

'She is a very strong willed woman, Nurse Smedley. I hope all goes well for her.'

★ ★ ★

A very large tired Ellee was sitting in the front room with Lewis that evening, telling him of her decision to have the baby at home. He agreed with her at once. He didn't like the family separated any more than she did. He loved her so much and anything she wanted or wanted to do was fine by him.

'Lewis when do you think this war is going to end? It seems to have been going on forever.'

'I don't know, but now the Americans have joined us it may come to an end soon. One of the saddest things I've seen while on duty in the Home Guard was the bombing of Edwin Jones department store. All those poor people dead. I can't get it out of my mind, and the poor manager of the shop, well he'll never be the same again.'

'Didn't you know him quite well?'

'Yes I always used to see him when I was in the darts team, and I used to play matches around the pubs. I'd always have a laugh and a drink with him. He's not the same man he used to be since that dreadful day. He blames himself you know, for the death of all those people. He feels guilty that he was the only one left alive.'

'Surely not. No one is blaming him. He was only doing his duty as store manager.'

'That's what I told him. Anyone would have done the same in his place. He led all those people to safety as he thought, to the store air raid shelter in the park opposite. He was only following company procedure. When he went back to check the store to make sure all customers had left the building, the air raid shelter received a direct hit killing everyone in it.'

'I think he was quite brave to return to the building after he got all the people out. Not many in his place would have gone back, poor man.'

★ ★ ★

Two weeks before Christmas Ellee and Lewis were the proud parents of a little girl. Weighing in at a hefty ten and a half pounds, with a mass of blonde hair.

'You've given birth to a child Mrs. Preston, not a baby. She's enormous and all that hair she has. She looks more like a 3 month old than a new born baby,' commented the midwife.

Lewis thought she looked like someone had sat on her head, with her chubby cheeks and red face, and crying so hard she would bring the house down. After a few days her head seemed to take on a normal shape and he thought she was quite beautiful and was very proud of her. Six year old Edward asked when she could be sent back to where she came from, much to the whole family's amusement. When Willy saw her he was pleased as punch. She was just like Ellee and Bridget.

'Hello little Katey,' were his first words to her, as he held her in his arms. 'She's the image of Bridget's sister Katey.'

Ellee and Lewis hadn't decided on a name yet. That was as good a name as any, so that is what she would be called, Katey.

*   *   *

Five months later Bridie gave birth to a little girl who was the exact opposite to Katey in every way. She had dark curly hair and was much smaller in size. Alan and Bridie decided to call her Polly. Willy pondered over how different the two little girls were. Bridie's baby definitely takes after my side of the family. She has the Spanish look of my grandparents and Ellee's baby takes after

Bridget's Norwegian grandparents. Lewis was telling me the other day his grandparents were French. Jesus what a mixture. As long as neither of them take after our Maggie, we'll all be alright.

★ ★ ★

Ellee and Bridie spent hours together with their babies, shopping and talking for hours on end. Bridie was a born giggler and knew all the local scandal.

'Did you know Ellee that 'dirty Gertie' scents her knickers.'

'Oh Bridie, whoever told you that?'

'Bob the milkman, and one of the Yanks told Pop.'

'How does Bob the milkman know? He must have been into her.'

'He has, but not to deliver milk.' Bridie screamed out laughing.

Ellee blushed bright red. 'You know what I mean Bridie. He must have been inside her house to find that out. She must have her underwear hanging everywhere indoors.'

'Well it has been raining a lot lately, so I suppose she has to dry her clothes indoors the same as the rest of us.'

'She has no shame. Fancy the Yank knowing that as well.'

'Half the American forces know. She's a very generous woman with her hospitality to our allies, or anyone else come to that.' Bridie collapsed with laughter again.

'You ought to be careful of that young Bob. He's so cheeky, give him an inch and he'll take a mile. You don't want to be getting a bad name through him. You know what the gossips are like in the Lane.'

'I am careful Ellee. I never let him in. I only talk to him at the door but I can find out an awful lot about what is going on around here. I was talking to him for so long the other day his horse wandered off dragging the milk cart with her. It was so funny to see him running down the road after it, cursing and swearing at the horse, who seemed to be running faster the louder he swore. Luckily it stopped before reaching the main road so no harm was done.'

★　★　★

Willy enjoyed the American service men's company very much. He'd spend hours talking to them and would always end up bringing one or more home to one of the girls for tea. Lewis liked their company as well but found most of them yarn spinners. They were all very rich and owned large properties and

297

businesses back home. One showed Lewis a picture of the garage he supposedly owned back home in the States. It was a beautiful big building and he was standing outside wearing a white overall. Lewis' immediate thought was that he worked there, not owned the place. He felt the owner of this place would not be in overalls, but he went along with it not to cause offence. If it made this man feel better in war time to brag and boast about who he was and what he owned, it was alright by him. After all who gives a damn. Some of us might not be here tomorrow. We could all be blown sky high any time. There was one American that Lewis liked very much, Larry Weston. He was a tall handsome fellow, very quiet and appeared quite intelligent. He was different from the rest of the braggers and boasters. He was in love with a girl from Earls Road, June Stone, and promised that after the war, if he should make it through to the end alive, he would come back, marry her and take her back to the States where they would set up home. Lewis felt he was a real genuine guy and meant every word he said. June was a lovely quiet girl and anyone could see by the way she looked at him, she felt the same way.

★   ★   ★

It was not only the Americans that were out for a good time. Some of the local women were as well. They took the view that their men were away fighting the war and some may never return, so they might as well enjoy themselves while they can. Our American cousins were very generous, with chocolate and nylons, so why not. One young woman Norah Lines, waved good-bye to her sailor husband in the morning sobbing into her handkerchief, and in the evening was in the local with the Yankee service men. A few months later she found out she was pregnant.

★　★　★

Bridie as usual was first with the gossip.

'What do you think Norah Lines told me today Ellee? She's pregnant and scared stiff what will happen when her Alfred comes home. He might kill her. He has a terrible temper when roused.'

'Why would he do that? He was home on leave a couple of months ago. It takes two to make a baby. It's as much his fault as hers.'

'No Ellee, you don't understand. She's frightened of the colour the baby will be when it's born. Her American boyfriend could be the father, and if so, it could be born black.'

'God help us Bridie. Is her boyfriend the one who is black as the ace of spades?'

'Yes, I think his name is Abraham. She asked me if she should drink a bottle of gin and jump off the kitchen table, would that get rid of it. Someone told her it would. I said Jesus no Norah, don't do anything silly for God's sake.'

'Doesn't she usually drink a bottle of gin in an evening?'

'Yes.'

'Then it won't make any difference.'

Both women collapsed with laughter.

★   ★   ★

When the baby was born some months later, her worse fears were confirmed. He was coloured. She was thinking up all sorts of excuses to tell Alfred when he came home. The most favoured one being someone left him on her doorstep and he was so sweet she decided to keep him. But would the neighbours let her down and tell him the truth? She was sure they would. Especially that old dragon up the road. Her friends would back her in anything she said, but the old women in the road had nothing better to do than peep from behind their net curtains, and spread gossip. No, that was no good. She must think of something else. I could tell Alfred I have Negro blood in me, four generations back. Yes that's it. He won't be able to disprove it.

★ ★ ★

Ellee and Bridie were chatting at the gate one afternoon, when Norah ran screaming up the road, baby in her arms and Alfred in hot pursuit brandishing a carving knife. They just looked at one another quite shocked, then Bridie said, 'I suppose he didn't believe her about the Negro blood in her veins.'

★ ★ ★

They carried on talking for a while and finally Alfred Lines came back down the road alone. He glared at both women. Bridie whispered to Ellee 'There's no blood on the knife, he couldn't have caught her.'

'I suppose you two know all about Norah's black little bastard?'

'Watch your language Alfred Lines. We know nothing, do we Ellee?'

'Who's this black man that got my wife in the family way? Come on tell me. I bet the pair of you know. I'll kill him when I find out who he is. The gum chewing Yank.'

301

'Why don't you believe your wife's story.' Bridie did not realise the slip she had made.

'Ah Ha, you admit it was a story concocted to pull the wool over my eyes. How dare she insult my intelligence. That's her lot, I'm through with her. I'm getting a divorce. I'll not bring up another man's child. I can't even pretend it's mine. For God's sake, it's black. Trust my wife, she couldn't even get this right. I'm well shot of her. Me Ma was right, she said she was a little slut and wasn't good enough for me. But did I listen to her? No I didn't.'

There were tears in his eyes, all his anger had abated. Ellee immediately felt sorry for him. After all he had been dealt a bad blow. He left the two women, head bowed, a broken man.

★   ★   ★

'I think we need a cup of tea after all that excitement. Are you going to come in for one Bridie?'

'Yes I've loads more gossip to tell you Ellee.'

'I don't think I could stand to hear any more.'

Bridie ignored this last remark and launched in with the next bit of scandal.

'You know the French woman, Francine, who lives opposite me. Well Gerald the rent man called on Tuesday for the rent and she didn't have it. Her husband Gilbert has given her the rent money every week without fail and she spends it. God knows what on. She had fallen behind and owes several weeks. She was crying and pleading with Gerald. 'Pleaze don't tell my Gilbert he'll keel me.' The next minute Gerald put his arm around her and went in. He came out about 20 minutes later, all red in the face and straightening his tie. She was all smiles waving good-bye, calling out see you next week darleeng.'

'What a disgraceful carry on, and him married with two little girls. He'll be lucky if he's able to keep that secret, knowing what they're like around here. Another marriage will be on the rocks.'

Willy came up the garden path with a little white and brown mongrel dog.

'Pop where did you get him from?' enquired Ellee.

'The Yanks gave him to me. They're shipping out somewhere and can't take him with them. His name is Skip. I thought he would make a nice playmate for Katey and Polly.'

'Jesus, Mary and Joseph.' Ellee uttered the

prayer in exasperation. 'Pop we've only just found a home for the cat, because it kept sitting on Katey's face. I thought she would be smothered in her pram. Now you bring home a dog. What am I to do with you. They are far too young for a dog.'

'Ah to be sure, they are growing fast. They'll be crawling around in no time at all and they'll love him.'

★ ★ ★

James was home on leave from the Air Force and brought a fellow officer with him, Julian Hargreaves. They had become great friends. As his parents both lived abroad, and he was not married or spoken for, he had no one to spend his leave with.

'Come on back with me old chap. The parents won't mind a bit.'

'Are you sure?'

'Yes of course I am. Bags of room in the old house you know.'

Since moving in with Anthony, James soon adopted the rich way of talking, as if he had been born into this very privileged life. He seemed to forget his lowly beginnings and had turned into a right little snob and show off. He liked nothing better than to show off his parents' big house and invited friends home at every opportunity.

'I say old man, I have to do something really boring tomorrow. I have to see the wife and my son in the country.'

'You call that boring James? I wish I was in your shoes and had a wife and son.'

This pleased James that he was being envied.

'Well not boring from my son's point of view. Jerry is a great little chap, but my wife drones on and on all the time. I was wondering if you could amuse yourself while I'm gone? It could take all day, getting there and back.'

'How old is Jerry?'

'He is six years old.'

'A great age. You must miss him very much.'

'I do.' As he answered, James suddenly realised how much he did miss little Jerry. I'm missing him growing up, but what can I do? I won't have that miserable little hag back, at any price.

★　★　★

From the first moment Julian saw Annie he fell in love with her. He never before believed in all that rubbish about love at first sight, but now it had happened to him. He knew what everyone else was talking about. James must be mad not to want her. She is so beautiful with her short dark hair and blue eyes. She is so small and slim. She looks so fragile like a china doll, and if I hugged her she would break in two. James is insane. I always knew he fancied himself with the ladies but to pass up this beautiful girl for a good time is beyond me. Why does he do it? I would give my eye teeth to have what he has, and I don't mean his wealth. He just doesn't realise how lucky he is.

'Annie this is my friend Julian Hargreaves, a fellow officer.'

Showing off as usual thought Annie, 'A fellow officer indeed'.

'He has very kindly driven me down here in his spivving little sports car. Nice little number don't you think?'

I wish you'd shut up James before you make an even bigger fool of yourself, thought Annie.

'Pleased to meet you Mr. Hargreaves.' As Annie shook his hand and looked into his face her heart missed a beat. My God he is so handsome. He looks a quiet, genuine sort of person. Not the usual rich riff-raff James knocks about with.

'Call me Julian please.'

James was not slow to notice the instant

attraction between the pair of them. This both surprised him and pleased him. Once again he revelled in the envy in Julian's eyes, every time he looked at Annie.

★ ★ ★

Julian was very quiet during the drive back.

'I hope my wife didn't bore you too much Julian. She can be a real pain at times, going on about this and that.'

'On the contrary I thought she was very nice, and your little son is absolutely adorable.'

'Yes he is a super little chap isn't he?'

'Tell me to mind my own business if you like, but what went wrong with you and your wife? She seemed really nice to me and pretty as well.'

'Look I don't want to go into all that now old chap. Basically she is a religious nut and preferred her religion to me. You can take her off my hands if you like. I wouldn't mind at all. Really I wouldn't.'

Julian was quite shocked by this last remark.

'You mean you wouldn't mind if I contacted her again?'

'Of course not. I'll give you the address when we get back. It's been over for ages, only she won't give me a divorce. Perhaps you can change her mind for me. I doubt it though. Religion will rear its ugly head again, you mark my words.'

Julian could not comprehend the callous off hand way James referred to his wife all the time. If I had a young wife like her, there would be no way I could ever hurt her like James obviously has. Religion or no religion, I'd have her at any cost. I will definitely write to her and thank her for the lovely afternoon and nice tea we had. I suppose I will just have to take it from there and see what her response is. As soon as he got back to base he wrote to Annie, and waited, and prayed for a reply from her. She answered his letter by return of post. It was a short little letter saying how much she enjoyed meeting him, and perhaps they would meet again sometime.

18

Ellee and Bridie were having their usual afternoon cup of tea together, the children playing at their feet.

'It was a shame the Ice Rink got bombed, Ellee. Lewis used to enjoy going for a skate.'

'Yes he was in the back garden when it was hit. He said, the bomb that came down on it looked like a big dustbin falling from the sky. I never forget the time he first took me skating, before we were married. It was my first and last time on the ice. I was petrified. Lewis was hanging on to me and said 'don't worry I won't let you fall.' He no sooner said that, then the girl in front of us fell back and hit her head on the ice. It was such a loud crack. I knew she had been hurt bad, just by the sound. She was taken to hospital and we heard afterwards she'd died. I was off that ice like a shot and never wanted to go back again.'

'It was unfortunate that happened when you were there, you being so scared and all. I should think it was one of those freak accidents that doesn't happen very often. Still nobody will be skating there again for a very long time. I suppose it will be rebuilt after the war.'

★ ★ ★

Willy came rushing up the garden path.

'Something big is happening this time. There are British, American and Canadian troops everywhere. More than I have ever seen in me life before. Every time the siren sounds the docks is covered with smoke to hide all the vehicles and equipment. Did ye not hear the tanks rumbling down The Avenue? There were transporters, jeeps and bulldozers as well. All heading for the docks. No one is allowed in or out of the town. I tell ye it is something really big this time. Everywhere you look there's barbed wire closing off the docks, the Common, and some streets.'

'That's why the Yanks gave you Skip. They said they were shipping out somewhere and couldn't take him with them this time. We heard the rumbling noise but thought it was thunder, didn't we Bridie?'

'Yes we did. What do they want the bulldozers for Pop?'

'They're using them to level blitzed sites and then using the sites for parking military vehicles.'

310

★ ★ ★

On the morning of 6th June 1944 it became clear what was going on. A brief official statement was issued.

'Under the command of General Eisenhower, Allied Naval forces supported by strong air forces, this morning began landing allied armies on the northern coast of France.'

Top secret military orders had been handed down from Prime Minister Winston Churchill to Lord Louis Mountbatten.

'The South Coast of England is a bastion of defence, you must turn it into a springboard to launch an attack.'

Southampton was at the centre of the biggest invasion force the world had ever seen. The D-Day Normandy landings were under way.

★ ★ ★

Julian had started writing to Annie on a regular basis. Saying he hoped she didn't mind him writing to her as he had no one else to write to and enjoyed receiving her letters very much.

Annie began to fall deeply in love with Julian and felt the hopelessness of the whole situation. Being a Catholic she could never have a divorce. I can never be his wife. Oh why couldn't I have met and married him, instead of James? She wrote to each of her sisters telling them of her dilemma and asking their advice. Annie was the most deeply religious of all the sisters. Although the others were good Catholics and went to church regularly, they were not so devout as Annie.

Maggie's reaction to the letter was, 'Our Annie is a bloody fool Ronnie. Look at this letter she's sent me. If she wants to marry this man she should divorce that stuck up James. I've never liked him, and marry this Julian fellow. I don't know why she's hesitating or asking my advice. She's frightened of committing a mortal sin and going to hell, that's her trouble.'

'I don't really understand the Catholic religion on divorce Maggie. I'm sure God wouldn't want a good person like your Annie to spend the rest of her life alone and unhappy.'

Ellee and Bridie were of the same opinion. She should divorce James and grab a little happiness where she can, while she's still young. Soon her looks would be gone, along with her chance of making a fresh start with someone else.

The letters from Julian were becoming more and more passionate. When the letter finally arrived with a proposal of marriage, as she knew it would, she turned him down. In spite of her sisters' advice and much to everyone's disbelief, except James. Julian was heart-broken and couldn't believe she had rejected him.

'I did warn you old chap, that she's a religious nut. Religion comes first with her every time. Now perhaps you will see things from my point of view, and what I've had to put up with all these years.'

Julian was inconsolable. Even James felt concern for his friend. He had taken Annie's rejection badly. Annie dear sweet little Annie Huh. Sometimes I could tear her apart with my bare hands, James raged. How dare she upset my best friend like that. Who does she think she is? Anthony and Rose thought it best if they stayed out of it all. So they did not pass an opinion, or were asked for one.

★　★　★

The war was over. There were street parties all over Southampton. Everyone was happy and rejoicing, except Annie and Julian. Even

Willy couldn't understand how she put her own happiness second to her religious beliefs. Perhaps I let her spend too long with Fay Finnegan when she was a child, Willy pondered. She has turned out just like her. She used to drive poor Pete to distraction. He said she spent more time in the church than she did at home. She was always on her knees either praying or scrubbing. When she finished the cleaning she would do all the flower arranging. One thing's for sure, when they die there will be a place in heaven for Fay Finnegan and our Annie. I tink I'll be going to the other place meself, chuckled Willy.

★   ★   ★

Larry Weston came back to Southampton for June Stone, as he always promised he would. He married her in Southampton so she could celebrate their wedding with all her friends and relatives. Then he took her back to the United States to meet his family and see their new home, where they would be spending the rest of their lives together. Lewis always felt he was one of the genuine ones. When he said he would return, if he made it through the war, Lewis somehow knew that he would.

* * *

Lewis felt really pleased that he had kept his word, and remarked to Ellee, 'Not like some girls, left holding the baby, so to speak. Poor Norah Lines with her little coloured child. She's paid dearly for her war time antics. Now Alfred has divorced her she has to bring the poor little child up on her own, and is finding it really hard. Do you think Annie will move back to Southampton now the war is over?'

'I don't expect so. She likes living in the village and enjoys the surrounding country-side. When she isn't working she takes Jerry for long walks in the fresh air. I think she's staying down there, keeping out of Julian's way and avoiding temptation. She's scared stiff of giving in to her feelings. She's a fool to herself.'

* * *

James came home from the war with a W.A.F. girl named Pearl Reeves, who he had been knocking around with. He wanted to move her in with them all. This was frowned upon by Anthony.

'James I thought you might have made it up with Annie by now.'

315

'Not a chance Father.'

'She's the mother of your son.'

'I can't help that Father. She won't divorce me and there is certainly no hope for our marriage. Look if it makes you feel any better and stops the neighbours from gossiping, we'll say Pearl is my secretary. No one can dispute that. We have plenty of rooms in this big house. They are not to know she is sleeping with me.'

Anthony very reluctantly agreed. The neighbours were not fooled for one moment. 'A likely story', they were all saying, 'and him with a young wife and little boy, it's disgusting. I don't know how he could do it, and as for her the brazen hussie, with her red painted lips, and peroxide hair. She looks like a right little tart.' Pearl couldn't care less what the neighbours were saying about her, as long as she was around money, and James certainly had lots of that.

'They can all go to hell,' she laughed.

'Try not to be so coarse Pearl.'

'Sorry ducks.'

'And don't call me ducks. You sound like a common barmaid.'

'But dearie, that was what I did before I joined up.'

She was already beginning to irritate James. He realised he had made a dreadful mistake and must get rid of her at the first opportunity. She sensed he was tiring of her. She must think quickly, what she could do to keep him. She must try not to be so common. She must try and be posh like him. That will do for a start.

'James darling, I was wondering if we could start a family? I know how much little Jerry means to you and it would be super if he had a little half sister or brother.'

James was horrified at this proposal.

'I love children so much.'

James doubted this last remark. She continued on in a sickly sweet voice, 'I would just love to give you another child, and I really don't mind at all about not being married. You know me I don't care what people say.'

Don't I just, thought James.

'No sorry, it's out of the question. In fact now is a good time to tell you it's over. We have come to the end of our relationship. I would like you to get your things together and please leave as soon as possible.'

'You don't get rid of me that easily me lad. You can't just use me then cast me aside. You'll be sorry for this, I promise you. Just you wait and see.'

The torrent of abuse that poured out of her mouth shocked even James. Swear words he had never heard a woman utter before. All the people in the Grove heard them as well. Being a warm sunny day all the windows in the house were open. Rose returned from shopping to witness the terrible scene. James was throwing all Pearl's belongings out of the bedroom window, and she was in the front garden screaming and crying. Rose thought she was crying more for the lost meal ticket than James. Now he had thrown her out she would have to find herself a job and stop living off the family.

'James, can you please be very careful who you pick for any future liaisons. That girl has really embarrassed the family with her swearing and common foul mouth. She makes Annie seem like a saint next to her.'

'You can say that again, and Mother before you start. No I'm not going back with Annie.'

'But James why? She's respectable, hard working and good.'

'No Mother. The subject is closed.'

★ ★ ★

Florence received a letter from Amelia asking if she and Alice could come up and stay for a few weeks holiday. Alice needed to go into hospital to have her tonsils removed, and they could combine the two things at once. She had not seen Flo for several years and had missed her very much. Both Flo and Fred were delighted.

'I'll answer the letter by return of post Fred. It will be so lovely to see them both again. Alice seems to be a little old to have her tonsils out. Don't you think?'

'Aye, but I suppose the doctors know what they're doing. They wouldn't be doing it if it wasn't necessary.'

★ ★ ★

Amelia and Alice arrived a week before the hospital appointment for the operation. The four of them spent the week visiting people and having lots of days out, taking advantage of the late Summer weather before the Autumn set in. Amelia was quite shocked at the devastation of the bottom of Southampton, near the docks. There was hardly a building left standing. The following day they all decided to take a day trip to Bournemouth. They caught the early morning train to enable them to spend as much time as possible there, enjoying both the beach and shops.

★ ★ ★

Bridie was in with Ellee enjoying her usual afternoon chat and finding out what was going on next door.

'Why are they back from Devon Ellee? Are they back for good? And where is the husband, why isn't he with them?'

'Alice has to have an operation and Tom has stayed in Devon with his people because it's such hard work travelling with the wheelchair. They've all gone out for the day again. They've been going somewhere every-day since Amelia and Alice first arrived.'

'Did you hear that Ellee?'

'Hear what?'

'Heavy footsteps next door. Walking down the passage and up the stairs. They must have come back.'

'They won't be back yet. It's still early, only 3 o'clock. They said they would be catching the half past eight train home this evening.'

'Perhaps it's a burglar.'

'No I expect it's the ghost. I hear him all the time when they're out. Certain times of the year it's worse than others.'

'Jesus, that's a creepy house next door. I'm going home.'

'What's the matter Bridie? You look as white as a sheet.'

'I've a bad feeling Ellee. Something awful is going to happen. I'm going. See you tomorrow, same time. Bye, bye for now.'

Ellee felt uneasy. Bridie knew things, and had feelings as she did of impending doom.

★   ★   ★

Amelia, Florence and Fred were at the hospital awaiting the news that the operation was a complete success and they could all go home to get some rest. They were never to receive this news. A grave faced doctor appeared and before he opened his mouth, Florence feared the worst.

'I'm sorry to have to tell you Mrs. Burrows, your daughter died a few minutes ago on the operating table.'

Before the doctor could finish, Amelia was screaming hysterically.

'No! No! . . . Please God not my Alice. You took Albert. Why take Alice from me as well.'

The doctor continued. 'We did all we could to try and save her but there was extensive bleeding which we couldn't stop.'

'Can you tell us Doctor in simple terms what she actually died of?' asked Fred.

'To put it simply, she choked on her own blood. We were unable to stem the flow. There was just so much of it. Unlike children, when adults have their tonsils removed they bleed far worse. Although the operation is basically the same the risk is much higher with adults. Your daughter was just unlucky Mrs. Burrows, I am so sorry. There was nothing more we could have done.'

He quickly turned away and was striding down the corridor at a fast pace. Fred was left to console the two sobbing women. A nurse appeared and offered a cup of tea which everyone declined. Amelia asked if she could see Alice. This was agreed and after a short wait the three were taken to see her. Florence looked on the young face which was white like marble. She looked so peaceful, almost as if she was asleep, except for the awful whiteness of her skin. There was no sign of the trauma she had just gone through. The nurses had done their job well, in making her presentable. To Florence it was almost like she was looking at a statue of Alice. It was not her. The Alice that everyone knew and loved just wasn't there anymore. She was gone to a far better place. Perhaps she was with her brother Albert, even as we stand here. I do hope so. Fred was speaking and gently leading the women from the room.

'It's time to go now. You'll be able to see Alice again later on Ame.'

Someone had called a taxi at Fred's request and it was waiting to take the three of them home.

Ellee was sitting in the front room with Lewis when the taxi pulled up.

'Good God, Dad's splashing out. A taxi home!' Lewis joked.

Ellee interrupted, 'Lewis I think something must have happened.'

No sooner had she uttered these words than Amelia started crying and wailing again. Fred came and knocked the door to tell them the bad news.

★ ★ ★

'Flo I fear this will be the final straw with Tom. The shock of it will finish him off, and then all my family will have gone. I'll be totally alone at the age of 66 years. That's not old is it Florence? I could have years ahead of me alone, without my dear family at my side.'

'Now Ame, don't take on so. Tom is stronger than you think. He could go on for years yet. With all the modern science going on these days, who knows, perhaps one day they may find a cure and he'll walk again.'

Florence didn't really believe this but she had to calm Amelia somehow, she couldn't really think of anything else to say that would help.

$\star$ $\star$ $\star$

Three months to the exact day since Alice's funeral, Amelia's words had come true. Tom Burrows had died peacefully in his sleep. After his funeral she decided to remain living in Devon as Southampton held too many painful memories for her. Flo will just have to come and visit her more often. Devon was a beautiful county and the little village church yard where Alice and Tom were buried was so pretty. There was a certain peace and tranquillity about the place. Although she was very sad, she was happy too, living in such a lovely place. It seemed to help her to cope with her grief. She visited the grave every day and wished that Albert could have been buried there as well. He was buried in the cemetery on Southampton Common. If only she had the money she would have had him reburied down here, so he could have rested with his sister and father. Then her little family would have all been together. This troubled her deeply, that he was so far away.

$\star$ $\star$ $\star$

A Spiritualist man in the village tried to give her a crumb of comfort by telling her, 'Your family are not there in the ground. Their spirits are all free. They're with God. They have no more need of their earthly body. It was like burying an old cast off overcoat. They walk beside you day by day. They are here with you in this pretty little cottage. Not out there, in some cold cemetery. So you see, it doesn't matter that your son is buried far away. He's here with you now.'

Although Amelia was never religious. She had never thought much about God, even when Albert died. But this man's words did give her some grain of comfort. He also said that if she felt like any company she could come along to their little meetings each Sunday evening. She would be most welcome.

★　★　★

She had written to Flo and told her about her meeting with Mr. Fitzgerald. How she had taken him up on his offer and visited the Spiritualist Church in the village, and how comforted she had felt afterwards. Flo was pleased she had made some new friends and was gaining some comfort from them. She had a few misgivings about the Spiritualist angle of things, as she knew little about Spiritualism. Beatrice had brought them all up as strong Church of England believers.

Still if it helps our Ame to cope in any way at all, it can't be bad, pondered Florence. When she told Lewis about the letter, she got the reaction she might have expected from him.

'Christ Mum, Spiritualism. I hope it don't send her off her head like it has some people. Don't they get messages from the dead or something?'

'I don't know much about the subject Lewis but I'm prepared to keep an open mind. If there's anything in it, when I die you'll be the first one I'll come back to.'

'Right Mum I'll wait to hear from you then, shall I? But I hope it won't be for a very long time yet and if I should go first I'll do the same for you.'

They both laughed but were quite serious about the pact they had just made.

'Seriously Mum, I hope Aunt Amelia will be all right?'

'Yes I'm sure she will. She's not a silly person who's easily led. She has her head screwed on all right.'

'Suddenly all my family seem to be turning to religion. First my sister-in-law Annie has just thrown away her last chance of happiness, and now Aunt Amelia.'

'A little bit of religion wouldn't do you any harm either.'

'I used to go to Sunday school some of the

326

time, when you sent us.'

'What do you mean Lewis, some of the time?'

'I must go Mum. I've just remembered something.'

'You come back here. You haven't answered my question.'

Flo smiled to herself. Lewis had her mischief and sense of humour in him. She could see it time and time again. Whereas Christopher, dear sensible Christopher was just like Fred. Very serious and studious. He looked like Florence but definitely had Fred's way of thinking and approach to life. Lewis was the image of Fred with his blond hair and good looks, but definitely took after the Ford family in every other way. Funny how nature mixes up the qualities of both parents in the children, mused Flo.

★ ★ ★

'Polly do you want to come next door to my grandma? She'll tell us a story and give us one of her lovely pasties to eat. I think she's just started baking them.'

'Yes all right then.'

Florence's front door was always left unlocked and open so anyone could walk straight in.

'Grandma, it's me Katey and I've brought Polly with me. Will you tell us a story please?'

The two little girls ran down the passage to the scullery where Flo was just finishing her baking. She turned and smiled at the two little cousins. Polly so dark with thick black curls and Katey the exact opposite, with her blonde hair and ringlets.

After the story and they'd eaten a pastie each, Florence had to sort out some clothes for a jumble sale. They were in a box in the back bedroom.

'Can we help Grandma, please?' squealed Katey.

'Yes if you like.'

'Can we try them on?' asked Polly.

The girls strutted around trying to balance in high heels and dresses that trailed along the floor. Polly seemed to have better balance in the high heels than Katey did. Flo suspected she had worn them before, probably her mother's.

'My mum is expecting a baby Mrs. Preston. Next year I could have a baby brother or sister.'

That's something I didn't know, thought Florence. You can trust children to let the cat out of the bag. I'd better stay quiet until it is common knowledge. I don't want to get Polly into trouble.

'That's nice dear.'

'What's that horrible smell Mrs. Preston?'

'I expect it's these old clothes. I think I can hear your mother calling you, Katey. We'd better go down stairs now.'

Florence felt the urgency to get the girls away from the back bedroom as quickly as possible without alarming them. Katey was first at the top of the stairs and started to descend. She was half way down when she fell. Flo held on tightly to Polly before she met the same fate. At the bottom of the stairs a howling Katey was sobbing, 'Someone pushed me, and touched my shoulder.'

'We never did. No one touched you. You just made it up,' said a very indignant Polly.

'Hush girls. I'll just get some butter to put on that bump on your head Katey. Then I'll take you in to your mum.'

Polly was still muttering about Katey telling a lie which made her cry even more.

★   ★   ★

Florence was worried. All these years have gone by and things are still happening in this house. August is the time when things are worse. The mention of a new baby by Polly seemed to trigger things off again. First the smell, then Katey being pushed down the stairs. When Fred came home Florence told him what had happened.

'Christ Flo. How many more people are going to fall down our stairs? Katey is just the latest one of a long succession of people to fall down the blasted stairs. I fail to see why they all keep doing it. I've checked the stair rods and carpet, time and time again. None are loose and the hand rail is secure. What on earth is the matter with everyone?'

Flo knew the annoyance he showed was covering the upset he felt that his little granddaughter had been hurt. I wonder where all this is going to end, thought Flo despairingly.

19

Annie was devastated to hear that Julian Hargreaves was to marry Peggy Arrowsmith, his childhood sweetheart.

'It's still not too late our Annie. Go on write to him before it is. Tell him you didn't mean it,' Bridie urged, as she cradled her new baby son.

'Annie I want you to be Godmother to Kenneth, William, and it would be wonderful if you made it up with Julian. He could be Godfather. It would make me so happy. Please say you will.'

'Nothing would make me happier as well, but the answer is still no. I haven't changed me mind. Besides he's marrying someone else now.'

Bridie sighed in desperation. Then tried again.

'You know as well as I do, he's marrying second best. He really wants you. You'd only have to snap your fingers and he'd come running. He stayed in touch with you all through the war, it's been over for 3 years, and he's only recently given up on you. He must have the patience of a saint. You look like you've been crying a lot lately, and look absolutely worn out.'

'I've been arguing with Anthony.'

'What over this time?'

'He wants to send Jeremy away next year to a private school, to get a good education, but I won't have it. He stays with me. There's no way I'll send him away from home to live with strangers. Good education or not. He'll be eleven by then but I still think it's too young to leave home.'

'So do I. That's the most sensible thing you've said all day. You stand your ground Annie. I suppose all this was the 'Don' Anthony's idea. He sits at the head of his big family table. Doling out money and giving orders, and everyone jumps when he speaks. He puts me in mind of the Falleni family. Old man Falleni was in the Mafia, so they say, and he used to order his boys about. They were all scared stiff of him. He would only have to open his mouth and they'd all come running.'

'With Anthony it's money he rules with, not fear. He just has to ask James to do something and he will. He would jump through hoops for Anthony. He idolises him, and knows that if he keeps on the right side of him all that money will one day be his.'

'I think that's awful. I suppose Anthony was packed off to boarding school at a very young age. Missing out on family love and everything. So that's all he knows. Well he's not going to do the same to my little nephew. We'll all back you on this one Annie. You're not alone. We might have grown up poor but we never lacked family love, and neither will Jeremy. He will grow up in a proper family, among all his cousins.'

Annie flung her arms around Bridie and knew she meant every word.

★ ★ ★

The battle with Anthony and James raged on for ages. In one way Annie was pleased. It kept her occupied and helped keep her mind off Julian. Eventually Anthony gave up the fight. He was worn down by her dogged persistence. Rose half agreed with Annie but dared not say. She too was brought up within a good loving family and could not comprehend why anyone would want to be parted from their offspring.

★ ★ ★

It was Maggie's turn to have Willy stay with them. As he sat down in the chair by the window, his favourite spot, she could not help noticing a grimace of pain on his face.

'What's the matter Pop? Aren't you well?'

'It's nothing, just a bit of pain in me back.'

'Pop you should go to the doctor, and have a check up. You haven't seen a doctor in ages, and look how thin you're getting.'

'Will ye stop your nagging woman, or I'll be after leaving right away.'

'I'm only telling you for your own good, Pop,' Maggie persisted.

'Leave it Maggie. Don't pester your poor old dad.'

While staying with Maggie and Ronnie the pain in his back grew progressively worse, till one night he awoke screaming in pain.

Maggie called the doctor immediately, without any further reference to Willy. When he arrived he gave Willy an injection to ease the pain and said he must attend the hospital and undergo some tests. An appointment would arrive shortly for him to attend the Outpatients Department.

★   ★   ★

When all the tests were concluded everyone's worst fears were confirmed. Willy had cancer of the spine and nothing more could be done. Within two months Willy was dead. He was laid to rest with his dear Bridget. He had never really got over the loss of her.

★   ★   ★

A week after the funeral, there was a tap at Ellee's door, and who should be standing there but Pete Finnegan. Willy had not seen or heard from him since they had left Queenstown all those years ago. He thought he would come over and surprise his old friend. Desmond O'Leary had given him Ellee's address as he was never quite sure of Willy's true abode. Desmond and Willy would enjoy an occasional game of dominoes or crib in the local pub of an evening. He knew Pete would be over at sometime and had promised to keep it a surprise for Willy.

'I'm afraid you're too late Mr. Finnegan. We buried Pop last week. I'm so sorry you weren't in time to see him. He never forgot you. He would often talk of you, and wonder how you were getting on.'

Pete was both saddened and stunned by the loss of his old friend and wondered why the hell he hadn't contacted Willy sooner. Now I'll never see me old friend again.

'Where are you staying Mr. Finnegan?'

'With the O'Leary's. Fay and the boys are wid me as well.'

'You must bring them over and I'll take you to meet all the family. Although we're still grieving over the loss of Pop, we mustn't let it spoil your holiday. I'm sure everyone will be so pleased to see you all again.'

All the family were pleased to meet their old neighbours again after all these years. Especially Maggie, who could still not resist tormenting Pete.

'It's grand to see you again Mr. Finnegan. Do you ever see anything of me dear friend Sadie? You know, she lived next door to Kathleen Devlin?' There was a sneer on Maggie's face as she asked the question.

Pete reddened and looked distinctly uncomfortable under her scrutiny. He hoped no one had noticed his embarrassment, especially Fay, but she was too busy fussing over the girls.

'No I haven't heard of her in recent years. She married and moved away somewhere.'

'A pity that. I would have liked to have got in touch with her again and chewed over old times.'

Thank God Sadie has moved, or that little bitch could still break me marriage up. The pair together were a terrible combination. Always out to cause rows and make trouble. Even though Maggie is a grown woman she still has that malicious streak in her and would be quite happy to make mischief for me. Perhaps it was a mistake coming over here after all.

Ronnie, Patrick and Dennis Finnegan had all noticed how uncomfortable Pete was with Maggie. Ronnie had seen that smirk of triumph on Maggie's face before. The night poor Bridie was nearly raped. I'll have it out with her when everyone has gone, and see what she is playing at. Patrick and Dennis were both of the same mind.

'Christ Maggie has someting on the old chap. I've never seen him scared like that before, have you Dennis?'

'No but if she doesn't button her lip she'll be sorry.'

Jack asked the boys if they would like to sit in the garden, away from all the women's chatter. They both jumped at the idea. They were pleased to get Jack alone.

'Well Jackie me boy. What have ye been doing with yer life?'

'I work in the docks. It was a bit frightening during the war, with bombs falling all around you. I'm very lucky to still be here, and as you know I'm married with two children and another on the way. What about you two, are you married or courting?'

'No, we don't have time for all that. We are too involved with the cause, and you being a good Irishman we were wondering if you'd like to join us as well? We could do with more men based over here.'

Jack was shocked at Patrick's suggestion.

'You mean join the IRA? I couldn't do that. I've me family to think of. Anyway I thought everything was peaceful over there now.'

'It tis me boy, it tis, but you see the Irish Army has to be ready in case of any future trouble that might occur. So ye see, ye wouldn't have to fight or do anything. You would be a secret member we could call on, if we should need information or anything later on. Perhaps you could provide a safe house for our soldiers who are being hunted down, or take messages to the other members who are over here from time to time.'

'Was yer father not a member then?' asked Dennis.

'No, no he wasn't.'

'Ah I find that strange you see, our father was a very active member in fighting for Ireland.'

'What did your mother think about that?'

'Ah to be sure, she never knew. Even to this very day she has no idea of his activities, and your pretty wife need know nothing either. It's not for the women to know anything. Secrecy is of the utmost importance.'

'No sorry. I'm still not interested in joining. My answer must be no, and of course I will treat with confidence what you've just told me.' Jack was really scared now. Fearing they thought he knew too much.

'One last question Jackie boy,' Patrick quizzed. Has your sister Maggie got something on me Da? If she has, is she likely to use it?'

Jack was becoming increasingly frightened.

'No, take no notice of our Maggie. She knows nothing against your family. She has an unfortunate way with her, she annoys us all at times. After all, what could she know? She's been over here longer than she was in Ireland.'

'Can you be sure to pass on to her Jackie, that we wouldn't want our Da upset atall. At his time of life it wouldn't be good for his health.'

'Or hers,' laughed Dennis.

★   ★   ★

The next day Jack was at Maggie's house banging on the door.

'What the hell do you think you're playing at? Baiting old man Finnegan. Are you trying to get us all killed or something?'

'I'm not scared of any of them Finnegans. Especially the old man.'

'You would be if you knew what Patrick

and Dennis were saying to me in the garden. They gave a warning to lay off the old man or else.'

Maggie laughed in his face, which made Jack even more angry.

'Listen Maggie, and listen good to what I'm telling you. It's not a joke. They are dangerous men and mean business.'

'Dangerous, them two, ha. I remember them playing chalky gods in the road and crying when I smashed them. I'm not afraid of them.'

'Why can't you get it into your fat head. They're not children anymore. They are grown men and not prepared to take any nonsense from you. Now promise me, you'll act naturally when we see them again, and for God's sake be polite to the old man.'

'Never, I'm not kow-towing to Pete Finnegan.'

By this time Jack was getting both exasperated and panicky. He looked at Ronnie pleadingly for support.

'Anyway what is it you know about Pete that no one else does?'

'Only that he was carrying on with Kathleen Devlin behind Fay's back. Sadie and I used to watch them through the window. Sometimes they would forget to close the curtains and if they did close them we still knew what they were doing.'

Ronnie thought it was time to intercede.

'Maggie you must listen to what your brother is telling you. I didn't like the look of those two either. I think they would be capable of almost anything.'

★   ★   ★

Annie took Fay off to Sunday Mass before they caught the afternoon train to Fishguard to get the boat home. Fay was very fond of Annie, knowing she was a woman after her own heart, and she was filled with pride when she heard how Annie had given up Julian because of her religion.

'You did the right thing Annie, in the eyes of God. It doesn't matter what anyone else says. Your dear mother, God rest her soul, would be so proud of ye. Now ye must stay in touch and give me all the news. At least once a month I'll expect a letter from ye.'

'I promise Fay, I'll write to you and stay in touch.'

The two women hugged each other, and Fay wiped a tear from her eye.

'I'll write to you as well Fay,' offered Maggie. Looking at Pete and his sons defiantly. 'I'm sure we'll have lots to talk about, going over the old days.'

Jack felt fear grip him once more. He thought he was going to pass out on the spot. He saw the look of anger on the two brothers' faces. He knew they had not heard the last of this.

The brothers were not going to let things rest there. They were fiercely protective towards both their mother and father.

'I wouldn't count on a letter from our Maggie, Fay. She's always saying she'll do something and never does. Annie is far more reliable in keeping up correspondence.'

He hoped this would appease the brothers but one look at their faces told him he had not succeeded. As the train pulled into the station they both stepped forward to shake hands with Jack.

Their grip was like steel.

'Good-bye Jack, you will be hearing from us again quite soon,' they whispered menacingly in his ear.

Jack felt sick with despair. He tried to reason with himself. They're gone now, what can they do once they're back in Eire? Then their words came flooding back to him. 'We have plenty of people already over here. We only have to contact them if we need anything.' He felt Maggie was in grave danger, and she wouldn't listen to him. He took Ronnie aside and tried to warn him.

'Watch out for our Maggie all the time Ronnie. She doesn't realise how stupid she's been in upsetting the Finnegans. She could be in real danger. Whatever you do, don't let her write to Fay.'

'I'll try Jack but you know how headstrong she is, and only ever does what she wants. When she gets a bee in her bonnet about something she won't listen to anybody.'

'Then all we can do Ronnie is pray we've heard the last from the Finnegans. Of course Annie will keep up the letter writing to Fay, as she promised, but they'll only be talking about the Church. The Saints days and holy days of obligation and going on retreats. Perhaps we should send Maggie on a retreat to keep her out of harm's way,' Jack tried to joke, but the joke sounded hollow and neither one of them laughed.

'Do you really think Maggie is in danger Jack?'

'I don't know Ronnie, I just don't know. I sincerely hope not but I feel very uneasy about the whole situation.'

Now the Finnegan family were safely back in Ireland, Pete sighed with relief. Thank God, that bloody bitch Maggie didn't let any cats out of the bag. I'm not out of the woods yet. If she starts writing to Fay, she could say anything. She has never liked me, or me her,

343

and now there is no Willy to keep her under control. When the first letter arrived with an English stamp on, Pete was on tenterhooks. His sons spotted the apprehension on his face and the shaking of his hand as he handed the letter to Fay. He didn't have a chance to intercept the letter. Fay was there at his side when the post arrived. She tore open the envelope, and began smiling as she was reading.

'It's from Annie telling me all the latest news since we got back. How pleased she was to see us all again, and how well little Jeremy is doing at school.'

'What are we going to do about this situation Dennis? Da can't go on like this. Jumping every time the post arrives.'

'It will be taken care of Paddy, never fear. A wee message over to England should do the trick.'

'But we tried frightening her before and it didn't work. She doesn't frighten easily.'

Dennis just smiled his knowing smile and said, 'Tings are under way to take care of the situation permanently Paddy. Trust me, all will be well. Da need not have any fear of her anymore.'

★   ★   ★

'Maggie can I ask you something? You wouldn't really tell Fay Finnegan about Pete, and ruin their marriage after all this time, would you?'

'No of course not Ronnie. I just wanted to see him suffer a bit, as he made me suffer as a child. Always telling tales to Pop about me and getting me into trouble. Anyway I can't stand here talking, I'll be late for the early morning Mass at St. Boniface. Now when I get back we'll pack some food and go for a picnic, the weather is so nice. We could go to the Common or sit down on the Pier. We'll decide when I get back.'

She slammed the front door and was gone in an instant. She was hurrying along the pavement, not wanting to walk in when Mass had already begun. There were not many people about, most of the church goers were already inside. She should just make it in time if she was quick. She didn't see or hear the big black car that came from behind, mounted the pavement and ran her down. It didn't stop and was gone from sight in seconds. Only poor old Hilda Langhorn saw what had happened. She just stood there screaming and waving her walking stick in the air. Soon people were running from all directions to see what all the commotion was about. Some of the parishioners who were sitting at the back of the church heard the bang and the screaming and rushed outside to see what was going on.

'Quick fetch the Priest out,' shouted John O'Connor, 'and someone phone for an ambulance, and hurry up.'

'It's too late for an ambulance, she's gone,' said a voice from the crowd.

As John bent down and took a closer look, he was shocked to find he knew the person laying dead on the ground.

'Oh Jesus, it's Maggie Newman.'

Hilda screamed all the louder, after hearing Maggie was dead. Father Kennedy rushed out from the church to administer the Last Sacrament. The sound of the ambulance bells could be heard in the distance, getting closer. The police were close behind.

★　★　★

Ronnie thought he would water the plants in the front garden while Maggie was at church. He heard the ambulance bells ringing in the distance. As he looked down the road he saw a large crowd had gathered outside the church. Oh dear some poor soul has been run over or collapsed outside the church. No doubt I shall hear all about it when Maggie gets back. He went inside and closed the front door.

★   ★   ★

'Did anyone see what happened?' asked the police officer.

'I think Hilda did.' Someone had sat her on a chair brought out from one of the houses nearby and wrapped a blanket around her as she was shivering with shock.

'Who is Hilda?' Someone pointed the policeman in her direction. 'Now Hilda can you tell me what happened?'

'He drove up on the pavement and deliberately ran her down.'

'Are you sure that's what happened Hilda?'

'Yes and he never even stopped. He just kept driving on down the road.'

'Did you see the driver Hilda?'

'No, only poor Maggie left lying there covered in blood. Poor Maggie, a good Catholic woman who never did no one any harm. Her poor husband. What will he do without her. It's murder I tell you, bloody murder!' Hilda started sobbing and wailing all over again.

Another policeman had joined the constable taking down Hilda's statement.

'It looks like we have a hit and run on our

hands. It was a big black car. The old lady didn't know the make. He must have been drunk to mount the pavement and mow her down like that. Does anyone know where she lives?'

John O'Connor stepped forward. 'Yes I do. She lives up the far end of Shirley, a few doors down from the shops. She has a husband, Ronald.'

★   ★   ★

Ronnie was in the kitchen getting the food ready for their picnic when he heard the loud knocking at the door. Crumbs Maggie is back early. I hoped to have this food ready before she got back. She must have forgotten her key.

'Just coming. Did you forget . . . ' his voice tailed off as he opened the door and saw a policeman standing there.

'Are you Mr. Ronald Newman?'

'Yes I am, what is it?'

'I'm afraid I have some very bad news for you Sir. May I come in? I'm very sorry to have to tell you, your wife has been knocked down and killed in an accident outside the church.'

Ronnie could not take in what he was hearing. The policeman's voice seemed to be coming from far away, and had nothing to do with him.

'Not Maggie, not my Maggie. You must be mistaken. It must be someone else.'

'It was very quick Sir. She didn't suffer. Her death was instantaneous, she wouldn't have felt a thing.'

★ ★ ★

The big black car was found later, dumped at the bottom of the town. It had been stolen the evening before from one of the big houses on the outskirts of Southampton.

★ ★ ★

'Patrick, are you there?' Dennis called to Patrick, who was at the bottom of the garden digging the vegetable patch.

'I'm here, just getting some vegetables for Ma. What is it?'

'I've just heard some very sad news from Southampton. Maggie Collins that was, has been killed in a road accident. Tis a sad day for her husband to be sure. It's a blessing she has no children to mourn her passing. We must send a wreath with our condolences.'

'This means Dennis, that Da need not fear her anymore. Was it an accident? Or was it . . . ' Dennis put up his hand to silence him.

'Ah now, we mustn't dwell on the whys or wherefores. We'll just say it was divine intervention and the good Lord saw fit to take our friend Maggie into his safe keeping.'

Pete was quite shocked when he heard the news. He was not at all sure how much his sons had to do with any of this. If anything at all. Perhaps it was an accident, a pure and simple accident. He decided not to dwell on it too much. At least he was free of the blasted woman and her veiled threats. Fay was very upset, she made the sign of the cross and went down on her knees in prayer. 'Eternal rest give unto her O Lord, and let perpetual light shine upon her. May she rest in peace. Amen.' 'Amen,' echoed the men.

'I'll be away down to St. Colman's and have a Mass said for her this evening. We'll send a Mass prayer card over to the family. Oh that poor family. Thank God Bridget and Willy aren't alive to see this sad day. Poor Annie, first she loses her dear parents, then her husband, and now her sister. Dear God, life is so hard to bear at times.'

'Yes to be sure it tis Ma,' sighed Dennis, who by this time was getting bored with the pretence of it all.

20

The whole family was devastated by Maggie's death. Although she caused trouble and upset people from time to time, she was their sister and they loved her dearly. The one who was upset most by her death was Jack. He could not get it out of his mind, that this was not an accident. He felt sure the Finnegan brothers had something to do with it but he had no proof so what could he do. The police wouldn't believe him, they would think he was just upset, and looking to lay the blame at someone's door. Supposing I was next, perhaps they think I know too much. We must move away from this house. They know where I live. Panic began to set in. I must get Doreen and our children the hell out of here, and pretty damn quick.

★   ★   ★

When Jack saw the wreath from the Finnegan family at the funeral, the rising anger he felt was hard to control. The hypocrisy of it all was too much to stomach. He felt he couldn't even confide in anyone. Ronnie was the only one who knew anything but he was a wreck, so he couldn't talk to him about it at the moment. He would get right away from Southampton. To another town, or even county, as far away as possible, and no one should know their new address. The only one I'll leave it with will be Ellee and Lewis. I can trust them not to pass it on to the others. Our Bridie talks too much. Anyone can buy her a drink to loosen her tongue and she'll tell all. As for Annie, she thinks the sun shines out of the Finnegans. She would lead them straight to me, and not see any danger in it.

★ ★ ★

Doreen kicked up merry hell when she was told they would be moving.

'But why Jack? I like it here in our little house. We have everything we want here. Mavis and Jennifer are settled at school, and I have only just had little Victor. I need time to recover from his birth, and the dreadful shock of your sister dying like that. To think I was giving birth to Victor around the time she died. It's all too distressing, and on top of that you want to take us away from our family and friends, who are such a comfort in these sad times, and set up home among strangers in Plymouth. Why Plymouth for God's sake?

No Jack, I'm sorry I'm not going.'

'You'll do as you're told woman. I am the man of the house, and what I say goes.'

Doreen had never seen him like this before and immediately burst into tears. 'Oh Jack, why are you being so cruel to me?'

Jack softened a little. 'Please trust me darling. It's for our own good. I can't tell you any more. It's really important to me that we move now. Later on I may tell you more so you will understand, but not now. Plymouth is a lovely city, and I'll be able to get work in the dockyard. There's beautiful scenery in that area. Lots of good fresh air for the children so they can grow up fine and healthy. We may be able to afford an even nicer house than this one. Who knows it might even have sea views, like we had back home in Queenstown. I really miss waking up and looking out of my bedroom window at the sea, instead of the houses across the road.'

Doreen was coming around to his way of thinking. It would be an adventure, starting again in a new place. She loved Jack so much, and after all it didn't matter where they were, as long as she was with him and the children. Finally she agreed, much to his relief.

'Thank you darling,' he hugged and kissed her. 'You won't ever regret it, I promise.'

*   *   *

Next he went to see Ellee and Lewis, and told them the whole story from start to finish. What he had told them seemed to have a ring of truth about it.

'That is incredible Jack. The police don't seem to be getting anywhere in finding the person who did this to your sister. Whoever it was seems to have vanished into thin air. Someone from the church told poor Ronnie that the old lady who saw it all happen was screaming murderer at the time, and said he had driven the car at Maggie deliberately. It's hard to take it all in. I must say, I wasn't too keen on those two Finnegans either. I didn't like them the first time I saw them.'

Jack shook hands with Lewis, and hugged Ellee, and then he was gone.

*   *   *

A week later Bridie went to see Doreen and Jack, only to find their house empty and a 'To Let' board outside. She knocked on one of the neighbour's doors to ask if they knew where Jack and Doreen had gone. Mrs. Sheldon answered the door.

'No I don't, never a word to any of us. They stole away in the middle of the night.

We woke up one morning, and they was gone. If you ask me there's something fishy going on there alright. You're his sister, and he didn't even tell you. Yes definitely fishy.'

Bridie rushed straight around to Ellee to tell her the news.

'What do you think Ellee, our Jack has done a moonlight flit. Do you think he owes money?'

Bridie found it all rather amusing, and couldn't understand why Ellee didn't find it amusing too.

'No I don't think he owes anyone anything. He just had to get away after Maggie's death. He said he didn't want anyone to know where they have all gone. He has taken her death really badly.'

'I didn't think he was especially close to her. She wouldn't let anyone get that close to her. She was always telling us off and hitting us when we were young. I suppose he'll turn up again eventually.'

★ ★ ★

Christopher and Lewis were having a good old chat with their parents one Sunday morning when Fred suddenly stood up, looking quite pale.

'I don't feel too good lads. Do you think

355

you could help me upstairs?'

They were both on their feet instantly, and helped Fred towards the stairs. Half way up the stairs they felt his body go limp and heavy.

'I think he's gone Lewis.'

'No, no, Fred,' Florence screamed touching his face and trying to bring him around. The two brothers struggled to the top of the stairs and carried their father into the bedroom, where they laid him on the bed. The doctor said he had suffered a very bad stroke, and there was nothing anyone could have done to save him.

'Mum you must come next door and stay with us.'

'No I want to stay here on my own. Please leave me now, I want to be on my own to grieve in private.'

'Alright Mum, if you're sure that's what you want. You know you only have to bang on the wall if you want us and we'll be straight there.'

The two brothers left Florence alone staring into space. She was in deep shock trying to come to terms with the fact that, one moment they were all laughing and talking together, and the next her darling Fred was gone. He had died on the stairs, the very stairs he always used to curse, because so many people had fallen down them and hurt themselves. He could never understand why people should keep falling down his stairs. He checked them over a dozen times and could find nothing wrong with them. 'It's a real mystery to me Flo,' he used to say. I can hear him saying it now, as if he's still with me. I feel him so close to me, as if he's not gone. It felt like he just patted me on the head, like he always did when he came home from work. How am I ever going to get over this. Life will never be the same again. I know I have my two sons, who mean everything to me, but they have their own families, and I mustn't be a burden to them.

★   ★   ★

Katey and Polly were sitting on the front door step playing together as they did every day. They had become very close and told each other everything, young as they were.

'My granddad has just died Polly. Now I have no granddads left to talk to. They are with Jesus in heaven.'

'You can still talk to them Katey, in your prayers. When you kneel down to say your prayers tonight, say a prayer for your granddads. Mum always makes me say a prayer for Grandpop Willy.'

'Yes I will then.' This made Katey feel much better.

'Look at that horrible face at the bedroom window over the road, who is it Katey?'

'She's a witch, and Mum says if I'm not a good girl, she will come and get me. There's also a horrible tiger in the joinery works window. If you come upstairs with me, I'll show you. We can see him from the back bedroom window.'

'I'm glad I live up the road. It's really frightening living down this end. Has your grandma's house really got a ghost in it? I heard your mum telling my mum it was haunted.'

'Yes it is. He pushed me down the stairs that day, but no one believed me. They all said I tripped. You believe me don't you Polly?'

'Yes, I do now.'

'Look there he is. Can you see his eyes shining?'

'Yes, I think I'd better go home now. I can hear Mum calling me.'

'I didn't hear her.'

Edward came bursting into the room.

'Get out of my bedroom. What are you doing here? And stop touching my things.'

'We only wanted to see the tiger in the joinery works window, and we didn't touch any of your things, so there.'

'There is no tiger, you dopey girls.'

'Yes there is look. See . . . '

'That's something stood on the bench, that shines when the sun comes out.'

'It's a tiger, you don't know anything you're stupid.'

Both girls headed for the door quickly, pausing only to poke their tongues out at Edward. He chased after them, down the stairs in hot pursuit. Ellee called out.

'Mind the stairs. We don't want any more accidents, in future come down the stairs slowly.'

'We're alright Mum, it's only Grandma's house people get pushed down the stairs,' called Katey over her shoulder as they dashed out into the street and headed for the safety of Polly's house.

'Eddie stop chasing the girls.'

'But they're calling me names.'

'For goodness sake, you're much older than them. Take no notice.'

* * *

'Grandma look what I've made for you at school, to cheer you up. It's a tin of coloured spills, so you can light your cigarettes. We had to take to school a tin and some wallpaper to cover the tin. Then we painted some paper lots of pretty colours, and cut them up for the spills. Do you like it?'

'Oh yes, thank you darling. I will hold it up so Granddad can see it.'

Florence held the brightly coloured tin up to the window, quickly brushing a tear from her eye.

'Are you very lonely Grandma, without Granddad? You can come and live with us if you want.'

'I don't think there would be enough room for all of us in one house. I'm only next door, so I can come and see you all any time. I'm thinking of taking in some lodgers to live with me. So you see, I'll have some company after all.'

★   ★   ★

Dolly and Reg Grimes were in The Elm Tree having a drink, when they heard one of the regulars mention Florrie Preston was looking for a lodger.

'Did you hear that Dolly? It could be just what we're looking for. I hear the old girl is not short of a bob or two. We could hole up there for a while, till the heat cools off in London.'

Florence answered the door to Dolly and

Reg Grimes. On first sight she did not like the look of them. He looked like a spiv with his flashy tie, and her a gypsy with her tanned skin and dark sultry look. But after talking to them for a few minutes, they appeared to be very nice and friendly, and since no one else had applied she decided to let them have the room. She was really looking for one person, but as they were husband and wife, it didn't really matter.

'I don't like the look of your mother's lodgers, Lewis. I wouldn't trust him one bit, and she looks like a gypsy.'

'I know, he looks like a spiv. He comes from London, and you can bet he's had dealings on the black market. We'll just have to keep an eye on them. He said his brother had a stall in Petticoat Lane, and if you ever go there, keep your hand on your wallet at all times. It's full of pickpockets up there. Your wallet would be gone in a flash and you wouldn't even know.'

'Does that go for down here too, when he's around?'

'Now Ellee we must give him a chance, before we condemn him. He may be alright. It's the first time I've heard Mum laugh in ages. He's always telling her jokes and stories about London. He's a bit of a gambler. He's always in the bookies. I hope he doesn't try to

361

tap up Mum for money. I must warn her not to lend him any. She's so kind to everyone and now she's getting older she could be taken advantage of.'

★ ★ ★

Polly and Katey were playing in the road, waiting for Alan to come home from a trip to America. Since leaving the navy he had served as a chef on both the Queen Mary and Queen Elizabeth. Bridie came out the front door to check on the girls, and to see if Alan's taxi was in sight yet. The taxi was just pulling up. Alan was greeted by squeals of delight and hugs and kisses from both girls. He handed the two little girls a basket of flowers each, tied up in a dark blue ribbon. Printed on the ribbon were the words 'Bon Voyage'. Once inside he opened up his case and there were even more presents. Katey and Polly each had a gold cross necklace. Edward and his two sons Kenneth and Matthew all had beautiful fountain pens made from mother of pearl, with a picture of the Queen Mary on. Bridie had a set of beautiful silk underwear.

'We'll put the pen away for Matthew until he's older. He's a bit young yet. I've bought him a book of nursery rhymes as well. Now tell me, what have you all been doing since I've been away?'

'Nothing much Daddy. Mrs. Preston has two lodgers. A spiv and a gypsy.'

'Polly you mustn't say things like that. Whoever did you hear that from?'

'Katey, she said Uncle Lewis said they were, and they go to somewhere called a black market. Where is the black market Dad? And can we go and see it? I've never been to a black market before, only to Kingsland Market down town.'

Bridie and Alan looked at one another and had a job to keep a straight face.

★   ★   ★

As Lewis had feared Reg Grimes was beginning to run up heavy gambling debts at the local bookies. He had been denied any further credit until he cleared the outstanding amount he owed.

Reg wondered if he could approach Florence for a loan yet, was it too soon, or had he gained her trust? He decided to wait a bit longer, and ingratiate himself a little more before asking for money. He saw Lewis in the garden and called to him over the fence.

'Hey Lewis, I'm glad I caught you. I hear you play quite a tune on the old joanna. Hows about if we give your Ma a bit of a do on Saturday evening, to cheer her up. We could get some booze in and a few of the family and have a good old sing song. We could ask your sister up the road, she's always game for a laugh and a bit of a knees up. What do ya say?'

'She's not my sister, she's my sister-in-law. I suppose we could, if you think it would cheer Mum up a bit.'

⋆   ⋆   ⋆

Saturday evening came and the family all gathered round the piano. Lewis sat down ready to play.

'Any requests?'

'Dad play that angel song please . . . ' pleaded Katey. 'It's my favourite.'

Lewis smiled, he began to play the first few bars, then started singing. Soon everyone in the room was singing along.

'You may not be an angel, because angels are so true, but until the day that one comes along, I'll string along with you.'

At the end of the song, everyone applauded.

'You're not at all bad my old son. Do you know 'Tip Toe through the tulips'?'

Lewis began to play once more, and Reg bowed to Florence and took her hand. They tip toed together around the front room, much to everyone's amusement. Flo was really enjoying herself. Lewis was grateful for that.

★ ★ ★

The party finished around midnight, all the young children were asleep, and had to be carried home. Florence could hardly keep her eyes open. She hadn't enjoyed herself so much, since before Fred had died. That Reg is a real card. Since they've been here there have been no ghostly happenings. I think the ghost dare not show his face with Reg around. I don't think the pair of them has ever had a psychic thought in their lives. They are much too down to earth and materialistic. Oh well I'm not complaining. They're doing me a power of good, better than any tonic the doctor prescribes.

★ ★ ★

The next morning Reg thought the time was right to strike.

'Did you enjoy last night Mrs. Preston?'

'Oh yes Reg I did.'

'I'd like to do it again sometime but at the moment I'm a bit skint. I'd like to take you

365

out for a day at the seaside but funds are so short at the moment. I just can't afford anything else. You put me in mind of me dear old mum, just like you she is, a lovely person, lovely person.' He pretended to wipe a tear from his eye.

'Don't get upset Reg. Can I do anything to help you? Please say if I can.'

'No Mrs. Preston you can't, but thank you. You have a heart of gold. But what I really need right now is some money to send to me ma. You see, she's a very sick lady, and I have to pay people to look after her, while I'm trying to earn a living to keep her. I sends her all I can but it never seems enough. The greedy vultures up in London just keeps asking me for more and more money all the time. I couldn't possibly take money from you. It would be like taking it from me dear old mum, and that I could never do. Besides what would Lewis say if he found out I'd accepted money from his ma.'

'Nonsense. Here you take this, and Lewis need never find out.' She handed him £20 in one pound notes.

'Mrs. Preston, this is too generous of you. I couldn't possibly accept all this.'

'Yes you can. You'll only offend me if you don't. Now go on, take it and make an old

366

lady very happy. I don't need much these days. As long as I have enough to buy a packet of Craven A cigarettes and my Guinness, I'm happy.'

'Well if you're sure, and only on the understanding it's a loan. I will pay you back as soon as I get straight and that's a promise.' He kissed Flo on the forehead and went to find Dolly.

'Christ Dolly the old lady is loaded. I wonder how much more she has stashed away. I think we need to see what else she has in the house.'

'Oh yeah, and how we gunna do that with her there all the time?'

'You my sweet, are going to offer to do all the house work for her.'

'Not bloody likely.'

'You'll do as I say me girl, or feel the back of my hand. This is far too good an opportunity to miss. When you're going around cleaning you'll really be going over the place with a fine tooth comb to see what we can nick. She probably never looks at half the stuff she has in here anyway. So she will never miss it.'

'I suppose so.' Dolly rather sulkily agreed.

★   ★   ★

The next day Florence thought she would take a walk to the shops. She was feeling quite pleased with herself, at having helped Reg out with his poor old mother. Dolly had volunteered to do some housework while she was gone, in gratitude for the generous loan.

'Look at this lot Reg. Some of her old man's medals. They should fetch a bob or two down the pawn shop, and look at all her rings. Look at this ruby ring. It really suits my finger, don't you think?'

'Put it back Dolly, she'll miss that one. It's her engagement ring.'

★   ★   ★

Systematically over the months a lot of Florence's possessions began to go missing, and whenever she asked if anyone had seen them, the answer was always the same.

'Now Mrs. Preston love, you are getting really forgetful in your old age. Just like my dear old mum bless her. I expect you've put it down somewhere and it'll come to light soon. So don't you fret. Or perhaps Dolly put it away somewhere safe, in case of burglars. You do leave a lot of valuables lying around you know. You really must be more careful. Still as long as you have us here to look after you, you'll be alright.'

Florence was reassured for the moment.

★ ★ ★

Lewis was still suspicious of the wide boy lodging next door with his mother.

'What is his job Mum? How is he keeping them both? I hope he hasn't fallen behind with the rent.'

'He works in the docks I believe and she is a barmaid somewhere. He is just a little bit behind with the rent, but then the dear boy sends all his money up to London to his old mum. He says I'm just like her.'

'How much behind with the rent?'

'Well . . . just a couple of months. Not a lot really when you consider what a good son he is.'

'How many Mum? If you don't tell me, I'll have it out with him myself.'

'Don't do that please. I don't want to upset them both. Five months behind.'

'What!' Lewis exploded 'Five months! They have only been here six. That means they've been living here rent free, and eating all your food for the last five months. I'll soon put a stop to that. Is there anything missing Mum?'

'I don't think so. I've mislaid a few things

lately, but Reg put that down to my age and forgetfulness.'

'What things Mum? Think carefully please.'

'Well I can't seem to find your dad's war medals. Reg said Dolly has probably put them away for safe keeping.'

'Where is the Shakespearean clock that usually stands on the mantelpiece?'

'Dolly has taken it to be repaired.'

'Have you given them any money?'

'Only twenty pounds. They've promised to pay me back as soon as Reg gets straight.'

'Only twenty pounds. That's a lot of money Mum, and I'm afraid you'll never see it again. They are con merchants, and it looks to me like a lot of your antiques have gone, as well.'

Florence began to cry, 'Oh don't say that, please don't upset me anymore.'

Lewis put his arms around his mother and kissed her.

'Don't you worry Mum. I'll sort it all out for you. You go to bed. I'll just wait here till they get home. Now off you go.'

When the pair returned from their evening of drinking with their friends in several of the local pubs, they were quite startled to see Lewis sitting in the kitchen waiting for them. Drunk as they were, Reg was immediately alerted to the trouble they might be in. He feigned an air of complete innocence.

'Hallo Lewis, what you doing here? It's not your dear mother I hope. She hasn't been taken ill or anything. God forbid.'

'No Mum is alright. I've sent her on to bed. I don't want her to be upset by what I'm going to say to you. The pair of you have been sponging off Mum, borrowing money, not paying the rent, and some of her rings and antiques have gone missing. What have you got to say for yourselves?'

'Lewis how could you think such a thing. It cuts me to the quick to hear you speak about us like that. We've only ever had your mother's best interests at heart. She means a lot to me, just like me old mum.'

'You can cut the bullshit Reg. It's me you are talking to, not a poor trusting old lady who believes everything you say. Now I want some answers from you, and pretty damn quick. First of all, where has the clock gone from the mantelpiece? Secondly when are you going to pay back the money you owe? And where are my father's war medals, and several of Mum's rings appear to have gone missing? If you don't come up with the goods I'm going to the police first thing in the morning.'

'Now steady on Lewis son.'

'Stop calling me son. I'm not your son. Well I'm waiting.'

'I can explain everything.' Dolly thought,

Blimey, how's he going to do that.

'First thing in the morning, I was going to give your mother the first instalment of my loan.' He pulled out a bundle of £1 notes. 'I was going to give her £5. I've managed to save it up, and at the end of my debt, I was going to give her a little extra for her trusting kindness.'

'Saved up indeed. More likely you won it on the horses or dogs,' scoffed Lewis.

'She will have the money first thing in the morning.' He started to put the money away.

'I'll take that. Thank you very much. Just in case you have a little memory lapse, over night.' Lewis relieved Reg of the £5. 'Now about the clock on the mantelpiece.'

'It's due back tomorrow morning from the clock repair shop in the Valley. Dolly will fetch it first thing, and as for all the other things, well Dolly has put most away for safety. You tell us all the things you want to see, and they will be out on the table by lunch time, and an apology would be in order when I prove to you our innocence.'

'I'll be back in here first thing in the morning, and I'll be keeping a close eye on the pair of you from now on.' Lewis left the two alone to ponder on what he had just said.

'Crikey Dolly, we've been rumbled. Let's scarper. Get your things together and quietly.

We don't want to disturb the old girl. We'll leave through the back garden and out the cut way, and for God's sake get some sensible shoes on. If we're spotted we may need to do a bit of running.'

21

Ellee was telling Bridie details of all the stolen property the Grimes had got away with.

'We were really sucked in by that pair, the whole blooming lot of us Bridie.'

'I can't believe it meself. Reg was such a good laugh, always joking and full of fun. It's hard to believe he could do such a thing.'

'I know, Lewis is reporting it to Portswood Police right now.'

They heard the click of his key in the front door.

'Here he is. What did they say Lewis?'

'They don't hold out too much hope of catching them. They've had several hours start before we discovered they were gone. They've probably caught a train to God knows where and that'll be the last we'll see of them.'

'How is Mrs. Preston taking it?'

'Not too badly. She said they can rob me of my possessions but not my memories. No one can take them from me. I think she's quite upset about Dad's medals. I expect they only got a few bob for them but they meant an awful lot to her. Also the rings he'd bought

374

her over the years, they've all gone as well. Mum used to be such a strong person. She could see through people, take on anyone in an argument. No one could ever get the better of her when she was younger, and now look at her. It's so sad growing old. I suppose we'll be like that one day and our children will be worrying over us. I suppose the police will never catch them unless they show their faces in Southampton again, and that's not very likely.'

'You never know, they might catch them.'

'I don't hold out much hope Bridie. They never caught the person that killed your sister, did they.'

* * *

Katey thought she would go and cheer up her grandma.

'Grandma it's me, Katey.' Flo still left her front door open so anyone could walk in and out. In spite of how she had just been robbed, she still trusted people.

'Can I help you tidy up Grandma?'

'Well I was just going to tidy the bedroom now Reg and Dolly have gone.'

The pair went up stairs to change the sheets on the bed. Katey was busy changing the pillowslips when she let out a scream.

'What is it Katey? Did something frighten you.'

'When I looked up, I saw a man standing in the doorway, I thought it was that nasty man Reg, come back to get you.'

'There's no one there look. It must have been the sun casting a shadow over the door way, making it look like a man.' So little Katey has seen him as well, she has the gift just like her mother.

'The other day, when I was eating my dinner, I heard a baby crying in your house Grandma. Did you have a baby in here? I was going to come in and see it but Mum wouldn't let me. She said I had to go back to school. Then another day I thought I heard a big girl crying, not a baby, someone about my age. She cried and cried, really upset. I wanted to come and ask her what was the matter.'

'I expect it was some people Reg and Dolly had in here when I was out.'

'Will you be alright Grandma, in here on your own?'

'Yes, I'll just bang on the wall if I want anything, and later on I'll probably get another lodger.'

★   ★   ★

'Mum, Dad, Grandma is going to get another lodger. Then she won't be lonely anymore.'

Ellee and Lewis looked at one another.

'Oh no not again,' sighed Ellee. 'I wish she wouldn't. I don't know why she bothers, it's not as if she needs the cash. It seems like she doesn't want to be in that house on her own. She could come in here and live with us.'

'She said she doesn't want to be a burden to her family, Dad. I've already asked her to come and live with us but she won't, she said there wasn't enough room.'

'We could always move to a bigger house and then there would be room.'

Ellee's face lit up at the thought of moving. She never liked either of the houses.

'I wouldn't mind that at all. I've always got on with your mother. Do go and have a word with her Lewis, before she moves someone else in and it's too late.'

The word that Florence was looking for a lodger again, soon spread. The landlord of The Elm Tree approached Florence and asked if she would consider his brother-in-law Lionel as a possible lodger. He had recently been widowed and wanted to move away from where he lived, and be near his sister. He didn't fancy living over the pub. It would be far too noisy for him. He just wanted a bit of peace to grieve, knowing his sister was not too far away when he needed her.

'He wouldn't be any trouble to you Mrs. Preston. He's a very quiet man who keeps himself to himself.'

'I'm sure he'll be admirable, Mr. Williams. Tell him he can move in any time he wants. The room is ready and waiting.'

'Thank you Mrs. Preston, I'll go and tell Ethel the good news and she can get in touch with her brother right away.'

★ ★ ★

Lewis remonstrated with Florence but she would not budge.

'No Lewis, I have given my word and my word is my bond. Lionel Wheeler will be welcome here. The poor man has recently been bereaved.'

When Lionel arrived Katey and Polly were playing in the front garden. The taxi pulled up outside Florence's house and out got the most enormous man the two little girls had ever seen. They ran back indoors to tell Ellee of the arrival.

'Mum, come quick. Grandma's lodger has arrived, and he is so big. I have never seen a man that big before.'

'Shush Katey, or he'll hear you.'

★　★　★

When Ellee looked out of the window she saw a man of about eighteen to twenty stone struggling with two suitcases, and there were two more to be brought inside.

'I'm just going to help the new lodger with his cases, girls. I won't be long.'

Florence was at the front door looking pleased as punch.

'Come in and welcome Mr. Wheeler. How kind of you to come and help, Ellee. Mr. Wheeler, this is my daughter-in-law Ellee and granddaughter Katey, and her little cousin Polly.'

Curiosity had prompted the girls to follow Ellee next door.

'Pleased to meet you Mr. Wheeler,' said Ellee.

'Call me Lionel please, all of you.'

'Children you can call Mr. Wheeler, Uncle Lionel,' Florence said beaming at the two little girls' serious faces.

Once outside both the girls decided they didn't like Uncle Lionel. He was far too big and scary.

'I'm not going to call him Uncle Lionel. He's not our uncle, we have lots of uncles of our own, and we don't want any more. Do we Polly?'

'No we don't, but what shall we call him then?'

'Nothing, we aren't going to call him anything. If he talks to us we we'll just answer him and that's all.'

'Oh look Polly, who's coming down the road. It's the rag and bone man. I'm frightened of him, with his horrible black beard. Quick let's go indoors and hide under the table. I hope he doesn't knock the door.'

They ran inside slamming the front door behind them, and were under the table like a shot. The clip clop of the horse's hooves could be heard getting closer and closer, and the cry of 'rag and bones . . . ' They clung on to one another tightly, till they could hear him disappearing into the distance.

'Katey, Polly, where are you both, and why is the front door shut? I had to go all the way around to the cut and through the back garden, to get in.'

Two little heads appeared from under the table cloth.

'Is he gone yet?'

'Who?'

'The rag and bone man.'

'He won't hurt you, come on out the pair of you.'

'We don't like Lionel either, he's scary as well. He's so big Mum.'

'Did he get that big through eating too many dinners, Aunty Ellee?'

'I don't know. I hope you won't be rude to him. I expect he's a very nice man really.'

★ ★ ★

The weeks went by and Florence was very pleased with her new lodger. He was a good conversationalist, and they could have a good old debate together. Ellee was a bit concerned about it all getting too much for Florence at her age. She seemed to be waiting on him hand and foot. He would spend hours sat in the armchair with his feet on a foot stool, with Florence pandering to his every need.

'Katey I must come and meet your grandma's new lodger. I haven't seen him yet.'

'You won't like him Aunty Bridie, Mum says he's like a big fat Raja. Sat in the armchair all the time, being waited on.'

Bridie could not contain her laughter.

'Then I think I'd better come and have a look for myself.'

'What's a Raja?' enquired Polly.

'I think it's an Indian man,' answered Katey knowingly. Try as she would, Katey could not take to Grandma's lodger. She could not for the life of her think why

Grandma liked him so much. She resented the fact that there were no cosy little chats between the two of them anymore. He was always there, listening and watching everything that went on. I wish he would leave my Grandma's house, then we could be as we were before he came. After thinking it, she immediately felt guilty because Grandma would be on her own again, with the ghost.

'Grandma, look what we were given at school today. This lovely blue beaker, with a gold rim. It has a lion and a unicorn on it and says 'Coronation of Queen Elizabeth II, June 2nd 1953'. Isn't it lovely. Mum and Dad are taking us to the pictures at the Broadway to see the Coronation in colour on the Pathe News. I'm so excited.'

As she finished speaking her heart missed a beat. There he was again, watching, listening, from the armchair. In her excitement, just for a moment she had forgotten his existence.

She immediately went quiet as soon as she saw him, which he was quick to notice.

'That is really lovely dear. Now let me see what is written on the other side. Presented by the town of Southampton. I think that's a really splendid commemorative gift for the children of Southampton. Don't you think so Lionel?'

'Can I see it please Katey?' She handed it

to him rather reluctantly.

After a moment or so she said, 'I must go, I haven't shown it to Mum yet. I wanted you to see it first Grandma.'

'That was very nice of you dear. Run along and show your mother. I'll see you later.'

She glared at Lionel as she took the beaker back from him.

'I don't think your granddaughter likes me very much Florrie.'

'Nonsense Lionel, she's just a bit shy with strangers.'

'Well I hope I'm more than that. I've been here quite a time now. Time enough for her to get used to seeing me around.'

★ ★ ★

Jack and Doreen were well and truly settled in Plymouth. Jack was working in the dockyard. The two girls were settled at school and had made lots of friends, till one day Mavis came home and asked if her new friend could come home to tea.

'Of course she can darlin. What's her name?' asked Jack.

'Mulleen Sullivan, she's Irish. She comes from Southern Ireland. I think it's the same part that you came from Dad. Which day can she come to tea then?'

Jack nearly exploded with anger.

'Jesus Christ is there no peace for me. Is there nowhere I can get any sanctuary. I thought we would be safe enough down here. Do we have to go on running for the rest of our lives?'

He ranted and raged on for another few minutes. Then he gripped Mavis tightly by the arm.

'Now you listen to me my girl. I don't want you being friends with or bringing home to this house anyone who is Irish. Do you understand?'

Mavis didn't understand and was mystified by this outburst.

'What did I do wrong Dad? I thought you'd be pleased that I met an Irish friend.'

'Well I'm not and when you're older I'll explain it to you but right now you're too young. Did you tell her I was Irish? Did you, answer me?'

'No I didn't, I thought you could tell her when she came to tea. It would be something nice to talk about.'

'Don't you ever tell anyone I'm Irish, or that you have relations in Ireland. Not ever, do you hear me? And I don't want that girl in this house. You have lots of other friends, you don't need her.'

At this Mavis began to cry, 'But she's so

nice Dad. I really like her.'

'I said no Mavis, and I mean no, and the same goes for you too Jennifer.'

Both the girls were frightened by this outburst. They had never seen their father like this before.

'Jack I think you're being hard on the girls. I think you're going over the top with the Irish issue. If certain people wanted to trace you I think they could have by now. The fact that no one has proves we're safe. They're not bothered about you. They're probably thinking they're safe as well. If you wanted to cause trouble for them you would have by now.'

Jack calmed down a little.

'You may be right but I'm not taking any chances. You don't want a message from the dockyard one day, saying I've met with an accident do you? There are a few Irish working there but I keep right away from them.'

★ ★ ★

'Grandma, Polly and I are getting bikes for Christmas. So we'll both be able to cycle to school. It seems such a long walk sometimes.'

'Do you like your new school Katey?'

'Not very much. The nuns are a bit strict.

One of the girls was in the cloakroom the other day and she said 'damn', and a nun heard her. She made her wash her mouth out with soapy water. I think that was a bit cruel. Don't you Grandma?'

'Yes I do.'

'Because after all she didn't say a really bad swear word. I sometimes say damn when I'm cross but I shall make sure I never say it at school. Polly and I went ice skating last Saturday afternoon, in the new Ice Rink. We were terrible at it. Our ankles were tipping over all the time. Polly dared me to skate out to the middle. I said I dare you as well. So we both struggled and struggled, and when we finally got there we both fell over and couldn't get up again. Then a man's voice came over the loudspeaker and said, 'Clear the ice please for the dance interval.' We still couldn't get up so we crawled all the way back to the barrier, and all these clever skaters were dancing by us. It was really embarrassing.'

Florence found this highly amusing.

'But neither of you hurt yourselves did you? That's the main thing.'

'No, we were alright.'

'I think you ought to ask your father to give you a lesson sometime, in staying on your feet.'

Katey was really enjoying the conversation and the laugh she was having with Grandma, when Lionel came back from his shopping trip.

'Must go Grandma. It's nearly teatime. I'll see you tomorrow.'

'What's the matter with her? She left a bit quick, as soon as I entered the room. I told you Florrie, for some inexplicable reason she doesn't like me.'

'No, she was here ages before you came in. Telling me all her little bits of news, and what she and her cousin have been up to. She's growing up fast, and just getting to that age when she likes a bit of female gossip. I expect she thinks you might find her silly and giggly. Now think no more about it. I have a nice piece of fish to cook for your tea.'

⋆ ⋆ ⋆

Bridie and Ellee were deep in conversation when the two girls came home from school.

'What's for tea Mum?' enquired Katey.

'Never mind tea for now. Listen to me, both of you. You are not to ride your bikes on the Common anymore.'

'Oh, why not?' chorused the girls.

'There's been a man exposing himself to children. He may be dangerous so keep well

387

clear of the Common in future.'

'Oh . . . Where can we ride them then?' sighed Polly.

'Anywhere else, except the Common or lonely places where there aren't many people about.'

'When we were train spotting at St. Deny's station yesterday, Kenny and Matt said a man was flashing outside the toilets.'

'What! Why didn't you tell us this yesterday?' Bridie exploded. 'Did you see him, and where were you two? You know you must keep an eye on your younger brothers at all times.'

'Katey and me were up on the bridge waiting for the 2.30 London train to pass through. The boys wanted to go to the toilet. It was only just down the steps and along the platform, so we let them go. They came running back saying a man had flashed at them. We didn't know whether to believe them or not. You know they sometimes make things up. Then they said he was a great big fat man, so then I thought they were probably telling the truth. When we all got down the steps he'd gone. Then we came straight home.'

'So you two never saw him at all?'

'No Mum we didn't.'

'Perhaps it was Lionel,' suggested Katey.

Both girls began giggling.

'Katey, it's not funny. It is a very serious matter indeed. I'm going home to send Alan straight up to Portswood police station to report this. It seems like this man is exposing himself all around Southampton and our children aren't safe anywhere till he's caught.' Bridie stormed out dragging Polly behind her.

Ellee was pondering on what had just been said. A big fat man. I wonder how many big fat men there are in Southampton? Katey may have a point about Lionel. Still we can't go around accusing anyone. We'll have to leave it to the police. He does have a creepy look about him, and Katey has never liked him from the first day he moved in.

★   ★   ★

A policeman and a W.P.C. arrived at Bridie and Alan's house to question the boys. When they had finished talking to them, they said their description matched the one given by the children in the Common incident and they hoped to track him down soon.

★   ★   ★

389

Ellee thought she would pop next door and tell Flo about what had happened at the railway station. Lionel was there, sitting in the best armchair as usual, feet up on the foot stool. This always annoyed Ellee immensely. Flo fussing over him all the time, and he can't even be bothered to lift a cup to help her, and as for the back garden. It's turning into a jungle the grass has grown so high. I felt so embarrassed on Monday when I heard the dustbin men calling out, 'Watch out for the tigers'. Lewis and I must try and do something with it at the weekend. At least get the grass hacked down. It used to be such a pretty garden when Fred was alive. How he loved his roses. Poor Flo is getting on a bit now. She just can't cope with it all, and as for that lazy so and so, sat on his fat ass all the time doing nothing. It makes my blood boil.

$$\star \quad \star \quad \star$$

When Ellee related to Florence what had happened and how the police were looking for this big man, she looked directly at Lionel who went quite pale, his fat hands began to tremble. There were beads of sweat on his forehead. It's him thought Ellee. I knew it, Katey was right. Florence was speaking.

'You'd better stay indoors Lionel. In case

you get mistaken for this man,' said Florence jokingly. Lionel was not laughing. 'Come on Lionel. I'm only joking, of course the police won't think it's you.'

Lionel tried to smile but Ellee could see how badly shaken he was.

★ ★ ★

'Lewis, I was in with your mother this afternoon. Telling her all about the big man the police are looking for, and Lionel looked guilty as hell. He was real jumpy and nervous.'

'I expect the poor man is. He thinks because he's a big man everyone will jump to the same conclusion as you women. Leave the poor bloke alone for goodness sake.'

★ ★ ★

'Florrie I have some news to tell you. I'm afraid I'm going to have to leave you. My sister Winifred in Brighton has been taken ill. She needs me, so I must go to her at once, today.'

'But this is so sudden, Lionel. How did you find out she was ill?'

'A letter came in the post this morning and as you know it's impossible for Ethel and

391

Cedric to go. They have their pub to run. I do hope you understand, and forgive the short notice I'm giving you.'

'Of course you must go Lionel. Family must come first every time and don't worry about giving me any notice. You go to your sister at once, she needs you. My loss is her gain. There will always be a welcome here for you, should you want to return anytime. I'll keep you room vacant.'

'No don't do that, Florrie. You get another lodger and forget about me. It looks like it'll be a long stay down there, nursing her back to health. I've been happy here Florrie. Thank you very much indeed. You've shown me nothing but kindness. You're a good woman.'

★   ★   ★

Florence was amazed at the speed in which he packed his four cases. A taxi was called and he was gone in no time at all. Promising to write to her as soon as he had arrived and assessed the situation. As Flo stood at the gate and watched the taxi disappear into the distance, she had the distinct feeling that would be the last she would hear from him ever again.

★   ★   ★

That evening Florence thought she would go to The Elm Tree and find out if Lionel had arrived safely. The pub had a phone so he would be sure to call to let them know how Winifred was.

'Good evening Flo. What can I get you? Your usual is it?'

'Yes please Cedric, a Guinness. Did Lionel arrive safely at Winifred's?'

'Arrive where? Winifred who? Sorry Flo, you've lost me.'

'Winifred, Ethel's sister in Brighton. She's been taken ill suddenly and he's gone to take care of her. I thought he might have phoned to say he'd arrived safely and how she was.'

'I think you must have got your wires crossed Flo. Ethel doesn't have a sister in Brighton or anywhere else. There's only the two of them, Lionel and Ethel. No other sisters or brothers. Yes sir, what would you like?'

He left Florence to serve another customer. She was speechless. He had lied to me, but why? If he wanted to leave, he only had to say so. Not concoct a cock and bull story like that, he seemed so happy with me. I cooked all his favourite food and we used to have long conversations of an evening. He was thrilled to bits when I said I was thinking of buying a television. He couldn't wait for it to be delivered, and now he's gone without even seeing it arrive. I just don't understand.

Florence went home feeling very upset. A gloom seemed to have descended over the house once more. She felt her heart sink as she entered.

22

When Katey heard the news that Lionel had gone she was elated. I must go and see Grandma right away. She went next door hurrying down the long hall, calling for her grandma.

'Grandma it's me Katey. I've just heard the news about Lionel leaving you. Don't worry Grandma. You won't be lonely. I'll spend lots more time with you. I will come in every day when I get home from school and sit with you. You're not frightened being alone with the ghost are you?'

'No of course not. He hasn't hurt me in all the years I've been living here, so I don't think he will now.'

This cheered Katey up no end. Although she was highly delighted that horrible man Lionel had left, she was very concerned about Florence being alone in the house. Yes Grandma is right. She will be alright. I'll make sure of it.

★　★　★

Ellee and Bridie thought they should report the disappearance of Lionel to the police but

Lewis didn't think this was a good idea. Bridie went ahead and reported it anyway. The police were very interested in tracing him, and if they could catch up with him he would be put in an identity parade to see if any of the children would pick him out.

'Best not tell Mum. It will only upset her further.'

Everyone agreed with Lewis, to keep quiet. At least till he was found and charged.

★　★　★

Katey kept her word to Florence. She was popping in to see her morning, noon and night.

'Our Katey spends more time in next door with your mother, than she does in here. She might as well move in with her,' commented Ellee.

'I think she worries about her being alone. She seems to have this fear that something will happen to her when she's not around.'

'Nothing will happen to her. Old Doctor Fisher said the other day she's strong as an ox. Her heart is sound, and she will outlive us all. She will probably be around to receive a telegram from the Queen on her 100th birthday!'

'Well that is good news,' laughed Lewis.

★　★　★

One lunch time Katey did not call into see Florence, and she became anxious. Something has happened I just know it. There was a bit of a commotion outside in the road earlier, but she hadn't bothered seeing what it was. She thought it was nothing to do with her. She went outside to see if Katey was about.

Several neighbours were stood around talking in groups. She called to one of them.

'What has happened?'

'Mrs. Preston it's Katey. She's been rushed to hospital. She came off her push bike and hit her head on the curb. She was taken to hospital unconscious.'

'But why did she fall off her bike?'

'I think she was cycling with only one hand on the handlebars. She was carrying her mack. Her saddlebag had a pair of wellingtons in it so there was no room for a mack as well. The workmen that were digging up the road thought she hit a stone, and the mack she was carrying caught in the wheel, throwing her off her bike. The back of her head struck the curb.'

'Oh no, no, not Katey. Please God no.'

'Mrs. Preston, don't distress yourself. I'm sure she'll be alright. I'll come indoors with

397

you, and wait till her mother gets back from the hospital. Come along dear and I'll make you a nice cup of tea to steady your nerves.'

★ ★ ★

Katey awoke in hospital, suffering a memory loss. All she kept saying, over and over again was 'where's Polly?' It was 4th July 1957 but all she could remember was her brother's wedding 3 months earlier in April. The past 3 months of her life had been wiped from her memory. When the doctor had the result of the X rays it was confirmed Katey had suffered a fracture at the base of the skull and concussion. She would not be allowed to do anything strenuous for the next 6 months, but she was going to be alright, and gradually her memory would return.

'It's a good job your daughter had a big thick pony tail Mrs. Preston. It helped to cushion the blow to the back of her head. If she had very short hair, or was a boy, I'm afraid she might not have been here now.'

Gradually Katey's memory began to return. She remembered Polly had been kept in at lunch time by the nuns for talking in class. She had not had the chance to tell Bridie, before the accident happened, that Polly would be late for lunch.

* ★ ★

It was August and the summer holidays. As Katey was not allowed to join in the mad frantic sports and activities Polly and all their other friends were anticipating doing through the holidays, she spent much of her time with Florence, sat in the garden.

'Doesn't the garden look nice Grandma, now Dad has hacked down the high grass?'

'Yes dear. It looks very pretty.'

As they both looked back towards the house, they were both horror struck to see it shrouded in a black mist. Florence had only seen it look that bad once before. All those years ago, when she and Fred had first moved in, and now Katey had seen it as well. She could tell by the look on her face that she was seeing the same thing.

'Oh Grandma the baby is crying. It's such a sad, mournful cry. Why does it cry like that? And why does the house have a black mist around it when it's such a bright sunny day?'

'I don't know dear, try not to be afraid. It'll pass in a few minutes, and won't hurt you.'

'But I don't understand. There were no clouds in the sky and yet the house had a dark shadow all over it, as if someone had thrown a black cloak on top of it. Dad says there are no such things as ghosts and we'll all end up in loony bins if we keep saying there are.'

Florence laughed at this suggestion.

'That sounds like my son. Now as things are back to normal, let us carry on our conversation. Before your accident I saw you talking with that young butcher boy from Lodge Road, Malcolm Bennett. Is he your boyfriend?'

'Oh no Grandma,' Katey answered in a shocked voice. 'I couldn't go out with anyone who cuts up dead animals for a living. You know how much I love animals. I would give up meat only Mum won't let me. She says I need the protein. He's just a friend from school.'

'Are you sure he's nothing more than a friend? There is nothing wrong with being a butcher. Your great Uncle John used to own the shop that Malcolm's father owns now.'

'Yes I'm sure. Besides I have a boyfriend anyway. His name is Philip, and he's a joiner like Dad. He works at a boat yard at Northam. When he calls this evening I'll bring him in to meet you.'

'I'll look forward to that.'

★　★　★

When Philip called, Katey was as good as her word and took him next door to meet her grandmother. Florence was immediately impressed by this tall, fair, quiet young man.

'Katey if I was twenty years younger I would try and take him off you.'

Katey was delighted at the response she had received from Flo, and Philip was likewise impressed by this dear old lady who had a great sense of humour, was intelligent and seemed to have all her marbles.

★ ★ ★

Lewis rushed in from work clutching an evening paper.

'Look at this.'

Ellee and Katey both craned their necks to see what was so interesting in the paper. There in the centre pages of the paper, was a picture of Lionel. His big, ugly, fat face and jowls staring back at them. Above the photo a headline read, 'Police Catch Peeping Tom.' Lewis continued to read from the paper.

'Apparently he was apprehended by the police in Bristol, so he never went to Brighton at all. It goes on to say, when he left Southampton, he caught a train to Bristol, where he took up lodgings with a Mrs. Rudge who had a mentally handicapped daughter. She complained to the police that she came home one day and caught him kissing her daughter. At first they didn't take too much notice, but they were receiving an increasing number of reports from women about a peeping tom in the area, and also of a man exposing himself to women and children. A trap was set with a police woman walking the streets late at night and they eventually caught him. You were right about him all along Katey.'

'Yes, I always thought he was a bit creepy. I never liked him from the first day I saw him. Oh that reminds me Grandma is getting some new lodgers.'

'Oh God not again,' sighed Ellee.

'No it's alright I've met them. They're a really nice young couple. His name is Ralph Brooke and he's an ambulance driver. His wife Linda is really sweet. She's not working and now they have somewhere to live they want to start a family. I've met her mum and dad, and they are nice as well. I think it might be third time lucky for Grandma.'

'I hope so,' groaned Lewis. 'I do hope so,' he walked away shaking his head.

★ ★ ★

Ralph and Linda soon settled into their new home with Florence. They had not been there more than a few months when Linda became pregnant.

'You look positively blooming my dear. Have you some happy news to tell me?'

'Oh yes Mrs. Preston. You're the first to know. I haven't even told Mum and Dad yet.'

'And when can we expect the happy event?'

'Next April. We're both so excited. We can hardly contain ourselves. We want to shout it from the roof tops.'

Linda began knitting baby clothes every chance she got. Knitting needles could be heard click, clicking. Ellee and Katey caught the knitting fever, and added their contribution to the ever mounting pile of baby clothes and bootees.

★ ★ ★

Florence sensed the house seemed to be taking on its sinister air once again. Whenever she was alone the walking would start. Up and down, up and down. Along the hall and up the stairs, then stop at the bedroom door. Flo quickly turned her head, and fleetingly, she caught a glimpse of the dark haired man who looked almost like a tramp. He was dirty and unkempt and just as suddenly as he appeared he was gone. Flo shivered slightly. The room has gone so cold. Even in summer it's like an ice house in here. I suppose the new baby coming has started all these things up again, and it's that time of year. Something really terrible has happened in this house. I just know it. I wonder what it could have been? I just want to sit down and cry and cry and never stop. I feel so sad, and yet these feelings are not mine. I know they belong to someone else. I feel some poor woman has suffered in this house, and yet I never see her, only him all the time. I feel her tears but I can't see her. There was a knock at the front door. Flo opened it to a very white faced Joe Hobbs.

'Mr. Hobbs whatever is the matter? Do come in.'

'It's our Linda Mrs. Preston. She was out with the wife shopping, when she came over poorly. I'm afraid she's lost the baby.'

The poor man was on the point of breaking down.

'I am so sorry. So very sorry, she was looking forward to the happy event so much. Sit down and I'll pour you a stiff drink.'

His hand was trembling as he took the drink from Florence.

'I don't know how we're all going to get over this.'

'Sometimes these things are for the best. They say it's nature's way of rejecting a baby when something isn't right. She's young, I'm sure she'll be pregnant again soon and hopefully put this unhappiness behind her, especially when she's holding her new baby. Then all will be right with her world again.'

'I do hope so. I'll drink to that Mrs. Preston.'

Florence filled his glass again.

'Elspeth will be cross with me for getting you sozzled.'

'May I call you by your Christian name? You won't think it presumptuous of me, will you? It's Florence isn't it?'

'Of course you can. The family tend to call me Flo, the neighbours Florrie, but you can call me whichever you like.'

'I shall call you Florence . . . '

He began to slur his words slightly, as he held up his glass for another.

My goodness, he's getting tipsy. I'll have to call a taxi to take him home to Midanbury. He'll never make it under his own steam.

★ ★ ★

Four months later Linda found herself pregnant again. She was bouncing around, full of beans. I hope all will be well with her this time, prayed Florence. Her prayers were not to be answered. When Linda got to the twelfth week of her pregnancy she miscarried for the second time. Oh dear God not again. Is it this house? Should I tell them to leave and start afresh somewhere else? They would be so hurt. They wouldn't understand about the bad luck that seems to touch certain people connected with this house. They would both think I'm just a potty old lady. It is so close to the ambulance station for Ralph, and Linda loves the Common nearby. She can't wait to be pushing their baby in the pram, on the Common on fine sunny days.

When Florence voiced her fears about the house to Lewis a few days later, he told her not to be so silly. All these tragedies were just part of life and in all the years he had grown up in the house he had never once caught a glimpse of the ghost, or sensed anything supernatural.

★   ★   ★

Six months later, Linda announced she was pregnant for the third time.

'I'm sure we are going to be third time lucky. This time I feel everything will be alright. I just know it Mrs. Preston.'

'You're a very brave girl Linda. Not many

would keep trying like you. I do hope you get your baby this time, and all goes well with you. Have you thought of any names yet?'

'I have always liked Donald for a boy, but we can't make our minds up over a girl's name yet.'

★   ★   ★

When Linda reached the twelfth week of pregnancy everyone was on tenterhooks. Ralph wouldn't let her lift a cup when he was around. Florence insisted she had an afternoon nap every day, and Elspeth did all the shopping. The twelfth week of the pregnancy came and went without incident, much to everyone's relief. Florence became happier and more hopeful. The weeks turned into months. Linda was eight months pregnant and looking forward to the birth, when she went into labour prematurely.

Everyone was still feeling optimistic. Because after all lots of premature babies survive, thought Ralph trying to convince himself more than anyone else. Linda gave birth at 3 o'clock in the afternoon to a stillborn daughter. Florence wondered how long she could go on losing baby after baby. The poor girl was becoming so thin and frail, with lines of sorrow etched on her face.

★ ★ ★

When she was home from the hospital, she didn't mention any future births, or even mention other people's babies. Neither did anyone else. Florence thought perhaps she would not risk putting herself through any further pregnancies. She hoped not. It would be nice if she just got on with her life, enjoying holidays with her husband and parents. She's still very young, I hope it doesn't take her too long to get over her grief.

★ ★ ★

One afternoon when she was out shopping, Elspeth and Joe called in to see their daughter.

'I'm afraid she's not back from the shops yet. Do come in and wait. She didn't tell me this morning you were coming over. She must have forgotten.'

'No she didn't know we were coming. We just came on the off chance. But as we're here, we might as well have a little chat about things. Did you know our daughter was a diabetic?'

'No Elspeth I didn't. Do you think that's why she keeps losing all the babies?'

'I don't know I'm sure. She has always

408

been ashamed of being a diabetic, like it's her fault. Silly girl, people would understand. After all it's just an illness like any other.'

Elspeth was interrupted by the sound of a key in the front door.

'Hello Mum and Dad. I didn't know you were coming over today. You should have said. Then I wouldn't have gone out. Well now you're here, Ralph and I have come to a decision. We were going to tell you both together, but as Ralph is on late shift and won't be home till really late, I might as well tell you. We have decided not to try for any more babies.'

There was a deathly silence in the room, all eyes were on Linda, wondering what was coming next.

'We have decided to adopt instead. We shall give some unfortunate baby all the love it deserves. I hope you both approve of our decision. I know how much you both wanted a grandchild.'

'Of course we do. How could we not approve if it makes you happy.' Elspeth flung her arms around Linda, hugging her and choking back sobs at the same time. Even Florence dabbed a tear from the corner of her eye with her white embroidered handkerchief.

★   ★   ★

'Hallo Bridie. What's been going on up your end of the road? I heard there was a bit of a disturbance the other night.' Lewis greeted his sister-in-law.

'I was just telling Ellee. Mrs. Latimer went mad and tore all her clothes off, and ran down the road without a stitch on.'

'Now why do you think she would want to do that Bridie?'

'They say her husband drove her to it, with him carrying on, like he does with his fancy piece. Parading her right before her very eyes. He doesn't even try to hide it anymore. Do you know he wanted to move her in with them, but poor Dulcie wasn't having any of that. We heard this terrible screaming from over the road and then glass being smashed. Alan went outside to see what was going on and an alarm clock just missed his head. It came flying out of the window, as well as all their ornaments. Next came cups, saucers and plates. Someone called the police and an ambulance arrived at the same time and took her off to hospital. As soon as things had died down, who should come tripping down the road in her tight skirt and stiletto heels, but Margo Green the girlfriend. I heard her say 'Poor Claudie. It must have been terrible for you. I'll try and cheer you up darling'.' Bridie did a very good impersonation of her squeaky voice. Lewis and Ellee laughed loudly at Bridie's interpretation of events.

'How long has old Claud had this woman on the side then?'

'Years, he's been carrying on for years with different women, till he's finally driven her insane. Poor woman, she's had several nervous breakdowns and was being treated for depression by the doctor. Her daughter, Carol, couldn't wait to leave home and married the first man that asked her, and as for her brother Mervin, he's a teddy boy and hangs out with a real bad crowd. Alan has seen him hanging around the docks with them late at night. He can hardly walk his jeans are so tight. I don't know where he can buy a pair that tight. I didn't know the shops sold them like that.'

'He puts them on, then sits in a bath of cold water for half an hour till they shrink to his size,' offered Katey.

'How do you know that?' enquired Lewis.

'He told me. All the boys do it. He let me have a ride on his track bike on the Common the other day.'

'You keep away from him and his teddy boy friends. They sound a bad lot,' ordered Ellee.

'Yes listen to what your mother says, Katey. Alan said about three nights after he saw him, a young seaman was set upon by a gang of teddy boys and stabbed.'

'Did he die, Aunty Bridie?'

'Not straight away, he died later in hospital.'

'Was Mervin one of them?'

'We don't know. The police are questioning everyone in the docks, seaman and workers, to see if anyone can identify the gang.'

'Can Polly and me still go jiving down the pier?'

'No.' The answer came simultaneously from both Ellee and Bridie.

'Ohhhh . . . ' protested Katey. 'Can we still go to the school youth club 'Rock 'N' Roll' night? It's being held at the convent and run by the teachers and nuns.'

'Yes that should be alright.' Bridie nodded in agreement with Ellee.

★ ★ ★

Katey and Polly enjoyed the 'Rock 'N' Roll' night at the convent, even though a lot of the others girls found it very boring, not having any boys to dance with. It was strictly a female only evening. The two cousins had learnt a lot of Rock and Roll movements from the young teachers and some of the ballroom dances as well, like the waltz, foxtrot and tango. The evening came to an end at 10 o'clock sharp and as the two girls were walking home along The Avenue, they came face to face with a crowd of rowdy teddy boys.

'Hello girlies. Shall we walk you home?'

'No thank you. We're nearly there. We live just up the road,' lied a very frightened Katey.

'Look what we've got here boys, a posh one, lives in The Avenue.' He gripped her pony tail tightly and wound her long hair around his hand, pulling her towards him. He was so close to her she could smell the alcohol on his breath. He pulled a flick knife from his pocket and laid it across her throat.

'One word from you and you're dead.'

Katey kept absolutely still, fearing any moment her throat would be cut, and that would be the end of her. Suddenly two motorbikes screeched to a halt and two very large young men got off.

'Leave our girlfriends alone, or you'll have the rest of the gang to answer to.'

'Sorry Leo. We didn't know they were your girls. We didn't mean any harm. We were just having a bit of fun.'

'Right girls, get on the bikes, now.' Katey and Polly immediately obeyed, so grateful to have been rescued from the gang. Then the two motorcyclists sped off up The Avenue.

When they finally came to a halt at the top of Betts Lane, the girls thanked them for coming to their rescue, and said they didn't know what would have happened had they not turned up when they did.

'Nothing probably. That lot are all talk, but you never can tell. There were a few others in the group I'd not seen before. See you around sometime.'

Leo and Tony revved up their bikes and roared off, they were out of sight in seconds.

'Don't you think that Leo is really handsome, Katey? I really fancy him. I hope we see them again soon.'

'No I don't. He's not my type. He looks like Elvis Presley. I prefer blond boys, not dark.'

'So you thought he looked like Elvis as well. I think the other one, Tony, looks like Tommy Steele.'

'Come on hurry up, before we get in more trouble with our parents.'

23

'Wonderful news Mrs. Preston. We're going to adopt a baby boy. He's only a few weeks old so he'll be like our very own baby. We're going to call him Donald. We can collect him tomorrow. I can hardly wait till we get him home and we can be a proper family.'

'I'm so pleased for you both dear. At least when you adopt a baby, you can choose to have a boy or a girl.'

'I didn't mind which we had. I just told the adoption people, we'll have the first one which comes along, boy or girl, it didn't matter to us. We'll just love it anyway. He'll have everything we can possibly give him. When he's old enough, Ralph is planning to take him to 'The Dell' every Saturday afternoon to watch the football.'

Florence smiled at this.

'He'll grow up just like the rest of the men in the Lane, at the Dell on match days. Never a stroke of work being done in the home on a Saturday afternoon. You'll not catch one man at home around here between half past two and six o'clock on a Saturday. Lord knows where they go after the match.

They end up somewhere having a big conflab about the game, and God help us if the Saints lose. Long faces like you've never seen before.'

'Does Lewis go to the matches?'

'Yes, he doesn't miss a game. He's a big supporter of the Saints. He goes with his brother-in-law Alan from up the road, and sometimes they take their other brother-in-law Ronnie. Poor man, he lost his wife, Ellee's sister, in a tragic accident. He's never been the same since. It was some years ago now but he's never really recovered. Lewis and Alan try to cheer him up by taking him to football, and for a drink at The Elm Tree, but nothing seems to work. He still has that sad haunted look about him.'

'She must have meant a lot to him. Was she a sweet person like Ellee?'

'No she wasn't a bit like Ellee. She was a trouble maker, always stirring up trouble between her three sisters. I never liked her myself. She had the most terrible temper on her, but poor Ronnie just adored her. He could see no wrong in her. He's got a lovely singing voice, and when she used to give him some stick he would sing to her, 'You always hurt the one you love'. Perhaps we'll have a little get together and try to cheer him up. I'll get Lewis to invite him over one evening

416

and we'll have a good old sing song like we did in the old days.'

★ ★ ★

Lewis thought he would call on Ronnie Sunday morning, with the invite from his mother. He was usually in then, catching up on all his household chores after working at the bakery all week.

He rang the front door bell. There was no answer. He waited a few minutes then rang again. Still no reply. Perhaps he's in the garden hanging out his washing. The next door neighbour came out, and Lewis asked if he was in the back garden. The neighbour said he wasn't and he hadn't seen him all weekend. 'Maybe he has gone away for the weekend,' suggested the neighbour. Lewis knew this wasn't very likely. He looked through the letter box and the smell of gas was overpowering.

'Quick! Run down to the shops, and get them to call the police, and an ambulance. I think he may have done something stupid. Hurry!'

Lewis began trying to kick the front door in. Passers by began to gather, wondering what on earth was going on. Then one of them threw a brick through the front room

417

window. They tried to climb through, but the smell of gas was so strong they were coughing and choking, and decided they had better wait for the police to arrive. The police and ambulance bells could be heard in the distance, getting ever close by the minute. Someone put a hand on Lewis' shoulder.

'There is nothing anyone could have done mate. I think we were all too late. Best let the police take care of things now.'

The police confirmed they had found Ronnie in the back room, with all the gas taps turned full on. He had left a note.

★   ★   ★

An inquest was held and the Coroner recorded a verdict of suicide. The note he left read, 'I can't live another day without her. Sorry and good-bye, signed Ronnie Newman.'

★   ★   ★

Katey heard the roar of a motorbike engine racing up and down the road and went outside to investigate. At the same time Polly was in the front garden, wondering who it could be. Hoping against hope it would be Leo. She saw Katey down the road standing at the front gate. She waved and then started to walk down the road towards her. They met about half way between the two homes.

'Did you see who was on the motorbike, Katey?'

'No he'd just disappeared around the corner as I came out. I think he's riding around the block. I expect it's that Leo.'

'Do you think so? I hope it is.'

'Look, here he comes again. Yes that's him alright. Look at the big lion on the back of his jacket. Big jerk.'

'Don't be so horrible Katey.'

'Well I don't like him. He has such a high opinion of himself. Thinks he's the leader of the pack.'

'He is. He has his own motor cycle gang. You saw the other night how scared of him the teddy boys were.'

'Hi ya girls. Me and Tony thought we'd take you out one night.'

'Well you thought wrong.'

'Katey,' said a very shocked Polly. 'Thanks I'd like to go out with you.'

'What about her?'

'I'm not a her. My name is Katey and I have a boyfriend, so I'm not interested.' Katey tossed her head in the air and her pony tail began to swing as she walked off down the road.

'She's a bit stuck up aint she? Where did you meet her?'

'Oh she's alright really, she's my cousin.'

'Right then. I'll pick you up on the corner at eight o'clock tomorrow night. I want to get together as many of Southampton motorcyclists as I can. We'll do a big burn up around the town and then we'll get in a bit of jiving, either at the pier or the hop. I guess we'll have to find another bird for Tony, now Miss Snooty Knickers has turned him down?'

'Yes, I have another friend Sheila. I'm sure she'd love to come along. Katey's boyfriend Philip has a motorbike. Can I ask them to come along as well? She really is quite nice when you get to know her.'

'I s'pose so. If you're sure it's not beneath her to be in such common company. They're both welcome. What's the boyfriend like? Is he like her?'

'Yes a bit.' Polly tried to suppress a giggle.

'We can expect a fun evening then, with them two in tow.'

★   ★   ★

Katey thought it sounded like fun. As long as she was with Philip it would be alright. Philip was unsure about Leo's gang but if Katey really wanted to go, then they would tag along.

The next evening about twenty five motorcyclists met on the Common. The noise was deafening as they simultaneously revved their engines. Each bike had a girl on the back. Some of the girls were wearing their 'Rock 'N' Roll' skirts, ready for the jive session later. Others were wearing jeans. The one thing they all had in common were their heavily made up faces, except for Katey, who only wore lipstick.

'Polly you've gone a bit overboard with the makeup. That panstick has made your face look really orange, and you've far too much blue eye shadow on.'

'Oh don't be so square Katey. You sound just like Mum.'

'I'm surprised she let you out looking like that.'

'She didn't, I had to get made up at Sheila's house. Her mum doesn't care what she does. She's always drinking down The Elm Tree. She hasn't got a dad, just lots of uncles, usually brought home from the pub by her mum.'

Leo gave the signal to be off, and everyone followed him up The Avenue to the outskirts of Southampton. The bikes gathered speed.

As they headed for the open countryside they were reaching speeds of 70 mph, then 80, 85. Philip thought, he's going for the ton. This is where we bail out. I'm not doing a ton on this bike.

'What's the matter?' asked Katey. 'Why have we pulled over? Is there something wrong with the bike?'

'No nothing. I'm not risking our lives to keep up with that big head. He's planning to do a ton. Well he can get stuffed, and count me out of his little game.'

'Polly said all the gang call him the 'Ton Up Kid', because he's done 100 mph so many times on his bike. He's fearless.'

'Stupid more like,' snapped Philip.

As they stood talking in the lay-by, the bikers were all coming back down the road towards them. As they rode past they all yelled 'chicken'. Polly was hanging on to Leo for dear life, and enjoying every minute of it. They had reached the Common then they turned the bikes around, and were racing up The Avenue for a second time.

'I'm taking you home, Katey. We'll do something less dangerous, like watching T.V. with your parents.'

'How exciting,' moaned Katey sarcastically.

'Don't tell me you still want to stay with that mob. The ones on less powerful bikes will get nabbed by the police, if they don't kill themselves first. Someone is bound to phone them and report all the racing up and down The Avenue.'

'Yes you're right. We don't need that sort of trouble. Anyway I can't stand that Leo, I don't know what Polly sees in him. He's so vain. He's always looking at himself in his bike mirror, and combing his hair. He tries to look like Elvis.'

'So you don't prefer him to me then?'

'Definitely not.'

'I was afraid you would find me dull compared to that lot, and you would want to join their gang.'

'No I don't. I don't like any of them, and they don't like me. Polly said they think I'm stuck up and call me Miss Snooty Knickers.'

'Do they. I'll fill that Leo in one of these days.'

'No don't bother, he's not worth it. He doesn't like me because I've got a mind of my own and won't agree with everything he says, like the other girls do.'

★ ★ ★

Several months had passed, Polly was still Leo's girl and Sheila was still going out with Tony. Polly was quite proud to be the leader of the pack's girl. She enjoyed all the respect her position commanded from the other teenagers, and being the envy of the other girls, who would gladly change places with her any time. She could not describe the thrill she felt, being on the back of the lead motorcycle when they all took to the road. She only felt a slight pang of regret that Katey was not with her. It was the first time in the whole of their lives that they were not doing things together. When they were young they were inseparable. Now they seemed to be going their separate ways.

'Where is your cousin these days Polly? Why doesn't she come out with us?' asked Sheila.

'She's busy with her job being a secretary. She goes to night school 3 evenings a week, studying English, shorthand and typing. Can you imagine it? Giving up three evenings a week to go back to school again, she must be mad, when she could be out with us having a good time. Still it's her loss.'

'I couldn't stand to do that. I hated every minute of school when I was there, and couldn't wait to leave,' answered Sheila, who was not very academically inclined and had often been bottom of the class. 'Is she really stuck up or does she just look that way?'

'Yes, no, not really.'

'Make your mind up Polly. You don't sound very sure to me. Which is it?' They both giggled.

★ ★ ★

'Grandma, do you like my engagement ring?'

'Oh Katey it's beautiful, three diamonds in a star setting. It suits your hand. How old are you now dear?'

'Seventeen and a half. We got engaged on Mum and Dad's wedding anniversary. I think they were both quite pleased.'

'I was married young, at eighteen you know. When your granddad asked for my hand I said yes straight away before he could change his mind. He was so handsome and I felt very proud to take his name and be Mrs. Preston.'

'As if he would Grandma, I've seen photos of you both when you were young. You were very beautiful, you made a good looking couple.'

'You know how to make my day and cheer up an old lady.'

They were both laughing when Linda came in looking quite ill.

'Linda whatever is the matter? You look terrible. Sit down. Katey, get her a glass of water, you can move quicker than me.'

'I haven't felt well for quite a while. I must go and see the doctor. At first I thought it was my diabetes playing up, but there are other symptoms. Different to the usual ones. I'll go and see him this evening. If I can get an appointment.'

'Would you like me to call him in?'

'No, I'll be alright. I just need to rest for now.'

'Katey will pop along to the surgery and make you an appointment for this evening.'

★ ★ ★

As Katey was about to leave reception, the door to the doctor's room opened and out stepped a very red faced tearful Sheila.

'Hello Sheila, what are you doing here?'

Sheila went even redder when she saw Katey. As they walked outside she could contain herself no longer, and burst into tears.

'What's the matter Sheila? Is it your mother? Let's sit on the wall, and you can tell me all about it.'

'It's not my mother, she's alright, it's me,' Sheila said between gulps and tears. 'I'm pregnant Katey, what am I going to do?'

'Is Tony the father?'

'Yes of course he is,' snapped Sheila.

'I'm sorry, I didn't mean to sound rude. I haven't seen Polly for so long, I'm not up to date on all the news. You could all have new boyfriends for all I know.' She put a comforting arm around Sheila. 'Does Tony know?'

'No. I didn't want to say anything until I was absolutely sure, and now I am. The doctor has just confirmed I'm three months pregnant.'

'I'm sure Tony will stand by you. He seems decent enough.'

'I thought you didn't like him?'

'No, it's Leo I don't like. Tony is alright as a friend. His only fault is he's too much under Leo's influence.'

'What will my mum say? I don't know how I'm going to tell her.'

'Will she care?' As soon as the words were out Katey could have bitten her tongue off. 'Sheila I'm sorry that sounded really cruel. I didn't mean it to sound that way. What I meant was, she's quite open minded, not old fashioned or anything, and she doesn't care what the neighbours think. I'm sure she'll stand by you. Now dry those tears, give your nose a good blow, then go and tell Mum first, and Tony later. Let me know how you get on. I'll be your shoulder to cry on. I already have one wet shoulder from your tears. You might as well wet the other one, but next time they'll be tears of joy.'

Sheila felt much better after talking to Katey and braced herself to give her mother the news that she was about to become a grandmother. She won't like that bit of it, mused Sheila. She always pretends she's years younger than she is, especially to men. When she got home her mother was dolling herself up for an evening out with her latest conquest.

'Mum I've got something to tell you.'

'Not now Sheila, I'm late. My gentleman friend will be here any minute, to take me out.'

'But Mum it's important. I'm pregnant!' Sheila was determined not to be brushed aside. She was not expecting the response she got from her mother.

'What! You silly little bitch. You didn't have to follow in my footsteps. I could have made something of myself if it wasn't for you. You ruined my life and now you're going down the same road. I hope that Tony Stokes is man enough to face up to his responsibilities. If not, you'll just have to get rid of it. I can't have a kid around here. It would just get in the way. I have my own life to lead now, I'm going to make up for lost time. All the years I wasted bringing you up. Now it's time for me to have some fun. Which I intend to do.' She glanced out of the front room window. 'Here's Raymond, my date, I'm off. Just you get it sorted by the time I get back tonight my girl.'

She opened the front door. Her tone changed completely. 'Raymond, lover. Don't you look the smart one tonight. Where are you taking me? Somewhere nice I hope.'

'Aggie precious. Don't I always take you somewhere nice, tonight we're going to the dogs. A little flutter on the hounds, then drinkies with some friends, and who knows what else.'

Aggie let out a hard laugh. Sheila wanted to be sick. How could two grown ups talk to one another like that, it's beyond me. One thing is for sure though, she doesn't give a damn about me and never has done. Tony will look after me, he really cares about me, I know he does. She thought she had better do something about her face. Her tears had caused her black mascara to run down her face. When she looked in the mirror she was quite shocked at the sight staring back at her. A deathly white face with black streaks and bright red smudged lips.

★ ★ ★

429

By the time she met Tony she was quite composed. She'd had a few hours to get used to the idea. She wondered how he would take the news. Better than her mother she hoped. After she told Tony the news his face was ashen and he could not speak for a few minutes.

'What are we going to do? I can't afford to marry you. I'm still an apprentice.'

Leo came over, poking his nose in as usual wanting to know what was wrong.

'Tony boy. What's the matter? You look like you've seen a ghost. Come on, you can tell Leo all your troubles old mate.'

He put an arm around Tony's shoulder and led him away, leaving Sheila completely on her own. Polly rushed over to the tearful Sheila.

'What's going on Sheila?'

Sheila told her she was pregnant and Katey was wrong in thinking Tony would stand by her.

'Katey, what's she got to do with it? You mean you told her before me, and I'm your best friend. How could you, Sheila?'

'I couldn't help it. I bumped into her coming out of the doctors.'

'Don't tell me she's pregnant too.'

'No silly. Her gran's lodger, Linda, was taken ill and she was making an appointment for her. She saw how upset I was and came over to me. She's really quite sweet when you get to know her. Not at all how Leo makes out she is.'

Polly said nothing, she just glared at Sheila. She would not listen to a word said against Leo.

★　★　★

'What am I going to do Leo? My parents will go mad.'

'Ditch her boy and pretty damn quick. Who's to say the baby is yours anyway? Look at her mother. A right old tart. You know what they say. Like mother, like daughter. You know that chick Sandra has had a crush on you for months. Now's your chance to make all her dreams come true. Take her to the gig on Saturday at Bournemouth instead of Sheila. You have to show these dames who's boss.'

★　★　★

By Saturday it was clear to Sheila that Tony had finished with her. He didn't even have the decency to tell her. He was kissing and cuddling Sandra, right under her nose. She was so looking forward to the gig at

Bournemouth and now she couldn't go. His new girlfriend would be there, in her place. Riding behind Leo's bike in position number two. It was too much to bear.

★ ★ ★

On the Saturday evening Aggie sent Sheila to post some letters, at the same moment Leo and Tony were pulling away from Polly's house. Sheila cursed her mother for sending her out at that precise moment. These letters aren't important. They could have waited. She just wanted me out of the way so she could have a snog with Raymond before they go out. Leo and Polly looked straight ahead as they rode passed her, pretending they hadn't seen her. Tony could not look her in the face and just looked down at the road, but Sandra who was riding pillion, was laughing at her and made a rude gesture as they went by. Sheila ran down the road, tears streaming down her face. She tripped over a piece of pavement slab that was sticking up and went sprawling. She lay half on the pavement and half in the road. Blood was spurting from her knee. Katey and a man had just come out of the paper shop. They both ran forward to help Sheila out of the road before something worse happened. They carried her to the safety of the pavement, and someone in one of the houses rushed out to see if an ambulance was needed.

'No I don't think so. I know her, I'll look after her now, thank you,' replied Katey.

'You always seem to be coming to my rescue lately.'

'I've just been in the paper shop to get the Football Echo for Dad, and saw you trip as I was coming out. Why were you in such a hurry?'

Sheila explained why she was running and how upset she was that the gang had all ignored her, even Polly and Sandra had been laughing at her.

'That Sandra is a right little cow. She should team up with Leo, not Tony. They're two of a kind, and as for Polly, well I'm surprised at her. Still, she ignores me most of the time. She's under the spell of Leo and is to be pitied. Perhaps one day she'll come to her senses and see through him. In the meantime we'll just have to wait for her to come back to us again.'

'Katey you're really kind you know. When I think of all the nasty things Leo used to say about you. It makes my blood boil.'

'Never mind him. He doesn't worry me. You know what they say 'sticks and stones may break my bones',' they finished off the rhyme together both laughing, 'but words will never hurt me.'

'You're the only person I can talk to in the whole world. I always feel much better after talking to you. Mum couldn't care less about me, and says I must get rid of the baby.'

'Do you want to?'

'I don't know what to do. I want to keep it but I won't be able to afford it.'

'Now I want to ask you a favour Sheila.'

'Yes of course anything.'

'Careful, you don't know what I'm going to say yet. Will you be my bridesmaid? I'm getting married shortly. I'll ask Polly as well but I don't expect she'll agree unless the wild thing can come as well. I can't bear the thought of Leo at my wedding. I just detest him so much.'

'But what about the baby, I'll be so fat?'

'It's not till next year. You'll have had him by then, and he can come as well.'

'How do you know, it's a him?'

'I just know it. Will you agree, please? We can have some fun choosing materials for the dresses.'

'Oh yes thank you very much Katey.' Sheila started to cry. Not being shown such kindness in a long time.

'That was supposed to make you happy. Not start you crying all over again. If you don't stop you'll have me crying as well.'

Both girls hugged one another.

'I must go, Dad will wonder what's happened to his paper, and Philip will be here soon. Don't worry any more about the baby, something will get sorted out in the end. I'll probably see you tomorrow, bye.'

★ ★ ★

Katey was not expecting her words to come true so soon. A few days later Sheila had a miscarriage. As soon as Katey found out, she and Philip went to see Sheila immediately, with flowers and chocolates. They knew there would be no sympathy from her mother and they were right.

'Best thing that could have happened. Now you're free again. You have your life back.'

After hearing those words, Sheila felt she would rise up and strike her mother. It was a good job she felt so weak or she might just have done it.

24

Florence noticed that Linda was becoming increasingly clumsy. She seemed to be bumping into things all the time.

'Is anything the matter dear? You seem to be colliding with a lot of things lately. You can tell me you know. If you're not feeling well, or anything is troubling you. It's best not to keep these things bottled up. Get it all off your chest. That's my motto, and I firmly believe it really does help.'

'No, I'm alright. Just getting a bit clumsy lately, that's all, really.'

Florence was not happy about Linda's state of health. Now little Donald was toddling around he was becoming a right little handful and she was finding it increasingly difficult to cope.

Until finally, one day her mother Mrs. Hobbs called on Florence when Linda was out. She explained that Linda was suffering from kidney trouble and she was steadily losing her sight.

'Ah that explains a lot of the things that have been happening lately. I didn't think the bumping into furniture was due to clumsiness.'

'I'm afraid Mrs. Preston, Linda is going to have to live with us. She's not going to be able to carry on much longer like this. She'll be very sorry to leave you. She's been most happy here. I hope you won't be too upset.'

'I shall miss the three of them, but you must do the right thing for your daughter. They were the best lodgers I've ever had over the years. Believe me, I've had some terrible rogues under this roof. People that have robbed me, but your daughter, her husband and little Donald were like family to me.'

'Will you be alright on your own Mrs. Preston?'

'Of course, I'm not on my own. My son and family are next door and Katey is getting married on Saturday. That's something I'm looking forward to very much. She's marrying such a nice young man.'

'Have they anywhere to live yet?'

'They are having a bungalow built, outside of Southampton, but it won't be ready for 4 or 5 months, so they'll be living next door till then.'

★ ★ ★

Sheila had met a nice young man, who came into the store where she worked on a regular basis. She would often be moved around from department to department. He would wander around the store until he found her and then end up buying a lot of things he really didn't want just so he could speak to her. Eventually he plucked up courage to ask her for a date. She said yes without hesitation. He was really nice and polite. Not like the usual brash crowd she was used to hanging around with. After they had been going out for 6 months he popped the question. As he came from an orphanage and had no family, the pair decided on a quiet Registry Office wedding. The first available date was two weeks after Katey's wedding. They would just be back from their honeymoon in time to go to Sheila and Rod's wedding.

★ ★ ★

Katey was delighted that Sheila had at last had some good luck in finding someone who genuinely cared about her. She was really looking forward to the day. Having just had her own, she was still in a wedding mood. That is until the day actually arrived. She woke up feeling terrible, and not wanting to go to the wedding at all, but knew she must go. She couldn't let Sheila down. I don't understand why I feel so depressed. I must try and snap out of it, before anyone notices. I love weddings. What is the matter with me? I don't understand.

⋆ ⋆ ⋆

Philip and Katey were giving Ellee a lift to the shops, on the way to the Registry Office. Lewis was at work. He usually worked Saturday morning and finished at mid day.

'I'll just pop next door and see if your grandma needs anything from the shops. I expect she will, being the weekend.'

Florence heard the car doors slam and the trio drive off. The sun is quite bright this morning, although it's still a bit nippy for April. I think I'll leave the curtains shut a bit longer, it does dazzle my eyes so, when I'm trying to read my paper. Florence thought she heard a movement in the room and for an instant she thought she saw a man standing in the doorway.

'Who's there?' she called out. There was no answer. She stood up to investigate and suddenly felt quite dizzy. The room seemed to be revolving around her faster and faster, until she passed out and fell across the large four bar electric fire which was on full blast at the time. When she came around she was still lying across the fire. She was in terrible pain but could not move. She called out for help. Would anyone hear her? They were all out.

★   ★   ★

Lewis, having just come in from work, was hanging his coat up in the hall when through the wall he thought he heard a faint call.

'Ellee, Ellee, please help me.' Yes there it was again. It's Mum. He rushed next door. The front door was left open which was the usual practice of Florence. He ran straight down the hall to the back room and flung open the door. At first he could not see her through the gloom and the thick black smoke, then his eyes became accustomed to the darkness, and he saw her lying across the electric fire. He pulled her off it. Her clothes were on fire and so were some of the items in the room. He tried to smother the flames on her clothes with his bare hands, burning his finger tips. Her body felt hard, like a piece of black leather, and through all this she was still conscious. He stamped out the flames on the carpet and rushed to the front door to summon help. Betts Lane was usually busy on a Saturday morning with tradesmen delivering, and people going shopping.

He could not believe his eyes. There was no one in sight this lunch time, except for Polly who was knocking their door, looking for Katey, not knowing she was at a wedding.

'Polly quick, get some help,' shouted Lewis. She was gone like a shot when she saw what had happened. Ellee had just arrived back from shopping, and joined Lewis in trying to make Florence comfortable and stamping out the still smouldering carpet, she too burning her fingers in the process. The ambulance, fire brigade and police were soon on the scene. Florence was rushed to Odstock hospital at Salisbury, which specialises in burns cases.

The police notified Christopher of his mother's accident and Lewis collected Katey and Philip from the wedding, on route to the hospital. They all sat silently awaiting the doctor who was with Florence, to come and speak to them. Katey was white faced with shock and couldn't speak, not even to ask any further details of what had happened. She sat very still thinking, this was why I didn't want to go to the wedding. It was like a warning, I should have stayed home. Perhaps I could have saved Grandma.

★　★　★

The doctor appeared in the doorway. 'I am very sorry to have to tell you, Mrs. Preston has third degree burns to eighty percent of her body. There is nothing more we can do except make her comfortable. She is asking for Ellee. Were you the lady that travelled in the ambulance with her?' Looking towards Ellee.

'Can we all go in and see her?' asked Chris.

'Yes of course but only two at a time.'

Lewis and Ellee went in first. She looked straight at Ellee and asked 'Who is that man at the end of the bed? He keeps coming and looking at me, then going away again. He looks very like my Fred. Is it my Fred? No it can't be can it? He died long ago, didn't he? He looks so like him. Look, there he is again looking at me but not speaking. Can you see him Ellee?'

Ellee turned and looked at the foot of the bed. No one was there.

'It's just one of the doctors, coming to check that you're alright.'

Katey was watching all this from the doorway. Tears streaming down her face.

★   ★   ★

Florence lived until the following Wednesday and then slipped quietly away. Katey was inconsolable, the events of the past few days kept going over and over in her mind. The one thought she could not get out of her mind, and could not voice to anyone else, was that the house had finally got Grandma in the end. She was a very strong person, but it finally got her when she was old and weak, and could fight it no longer.

★ ★ ★

Who would the house claim next?

THE END

We do hope that you have enjoyed reading this large print book.

Did you know that all of our titles are available for purchase?

We publish a wide range of high quality large print books including:
Romances, Mysteries, Classics General Fiction Non Fiction and Westerns

Special interest titles available in large print are:
The Little Oxford Dictionary Music Book Song Book Hymn Book Service Book

Also available from us courtesy of Oxford University Press:
Young Readers' Dictionary (large print edition) Young Readers' Thesaurus (large print edition)

For further information or a free brochure, please contact us at:
Ulverscroft Large Print Books Ltd., The Green, Bradgate Road, Anstey, Leicester, LE7 7FU, England. Tel: (00 44) **0116 236 4325 Fax:** (00 44) **0116 234 0205**

Other titles in the
Ulverscroft Large Print Series:

FIREBALL

Bob Langley

Twenty-seven years ago: the rogue shoot-down of a Soviet spacecraft on a supersecret mission. Now: the SUCHKO 17 suddenly comes back to life three thousand feet beneath the Antarctic ice cap — with terrifying implications for the entire world. The discovery triggers a dark conspiracy that reaches from the depths of the sea to the edge of space — on a satellite with nuclear capabilities. One man and one woman must find the elusive mastermind of a plot with sinister roots in the American military elite, and bring the world back from the edge . . .

STANDING IN THE SHADOWS

Michelle Spring

Laura Principal is repelled but fascinated as she investigates the case of an eleven-year-old boy who has murdered his foster mother. It is not the sort of crime one would expect in Cambridge. The child, Daryll, has confessed to the brutal killing; now his elder brother wants to find out what has turned him into a ruthless killer. Laura confronts an investigation which is increasingly tainted with violence. And that's not all. Someone with an interest in the foster mother's murder is standing in the shadows, watching her every move . . .

NORMANDY SUMMER/ LOVE'S CHARADE

Joy St. Clair

NORMANDY SUMMER — Three cousins, Helen, Tally and Rosie, joined the First Aid Nursing Yeomanry. Helen had driven ambulances through The Blitz, but it was the Summer of 1944 that would change their lives irrevocably.

LOVE'S CHARADE — A broken down car, a mix-up of addresses and soon Kimberley found she was stand-in fianceé for a man she hardly knew. What chance had the pair of them of surviving this masquerade?

THE WESTON WOMEN

Grace Thompson

Wales, 1950s: At the head of the wealthy Weston family are Arfon and Gladys, owners of a once-successful wallpaper and paint store. It had always been Gladys's dream to form a dynasty. Her twin daughters, however, had no interest, and her grandson Jack had little ambition. And so, it is on her twin granddaughters, Joan and Megan, that Gladys pins her hopes. But unbeknown to her, they are considered rather outrageous — and one of them is secretly dating Viv Lewis, who works for the Westons but is not allowed to mix with the family socially. However, it is on him they will depend to help save the business.